Beach House Romance

by

CORA SETON

More by Cora Seton

Beach House Vacation

Beach House Wedding

For my husband, Lennard.
I love you.

CHAPTER 1

EMMA MILLER'S STOMACH lurched when she spotted the fat, legal-size envelope. She knew exactly how much bad news one of those could contain. It was rolled up to fit in the tiny post office box she'd rented when she'd moved out of her fiancé's apartment three months ago.

With a sigh, she pulled it out, along with a couple of advertising flyers, and went to sit on one of the cement benches in front of the plain brick building.

For weeks, she'd opened her mailbox to find notices for overdue utility bills, overdrawn bank accounts and late credit card payments, but Emma had handled that mess. First, she'd shut down her meal-kit delivery business, Food to You Fast. Then she'd sold her possessions one by one on the local online buy-and-sell page.

Now she was sleeping in an acquaintance's living room, paying her a nominal rent, working two jobs and scraping together the deposit for a new apartment. She figured she could do it by the end of next month if she wasn't picky about where she decided to live—and if Denise would allow her to couch surf that long. She'd probably overstayed her welcome by a mile already.

Setting the flyers aside, she let the early March sunshine warm her. It was cool by northern Florida standards but warm by anyone else's, and she had twenty minutes before she started her second shift of the day. Most mornings she woke up at four and got to work by five to prep for the breakfast rush at Millie's Diner, a popular local spot with a menu that surpassed any expectations its name inspired. She got off at two, did her errands and made it to the Beachside Grill at three thirty for a shift that ended long past eleven. She should have been bone tired by the time she went to bed, but sleep often evaded her for hours, which made the days that much longer.

How had everything gone so wrong?

Emma tore open the envelope and pulled out a stack of pages, refusing to let the past drag her under when she had hours to go before she could rest. On top was a typed letter, under it some kind of legal document. Her breath hitched when she spotted her grandmother's name. Nana Angela had been dead for almost a decade. Why would there be paperwork concerning her now?

She returned to the letter and started reading from the beginning.

Dear Emma,

I know this will come as a surprise, but I'm writing today to inform you that your grandmother, Angela Nelson, has left you a bequest.

Emma lowered the pages and stared sightlessly at a woman pushing a stroller past on the sidewalk.

A bequest. Now?

Emma remembered a day nearly ten years ago when an envelope just like this one was delivered to the little brown house where she lived with her father and sister. She and Ashley had come home from high school to find their father in the kitchen for once, eating fried eggs on toast. Normally he didn't come in from his workshop out back until far into the evening, and they'd long since stopped asking questions about what he did out there.

As soon as they'd entered the room, he'd picked up the envelope and waved it at them. "She's done it. The old witch up and died!"

"Who died?" Ashley had looked confused, and Emma knew why. They'd lost their mother young. Ever since, they'd been alone, the two of them orbiting an increasingly cold and silent father. Who else was there to lose?

"Your grandmother." He'd thrown the letter on the table. "She's gone. Says here she left us a bequest. You know how rich she was."

Nana Angela gone? The thought had left Emma

breathless, even if she hadn't seen or spoken to her grandmother in years at that point.

"You think she left us everything?" Ashley had reached for the letter, but her father snatched it back, folded it and stuck it in his back pocket.

"Of course she did. Who else would she leave it to? I've got to fill in some paperwork and send it back. Might as well take care of that now."

He'd grabbed a beer from the refrigerator and headed out to the workshop, where the lights blazed for hours, long after he'd driven to the post office and returned again. Emma had seen those lights from her bedroom window later that night. As usual, she'd lain in bed counting the days until she could put this ugly house—and her father's moods—behind her for good, but though she would turn eighteen in a month, it would be several years before she could make that happen. First she'd needed to get through culinary school. Next she'd helped Ashley get her associate's degree. Then they'd left—together.

The next few weeks she saw more of her father than she had during the previous six months. It became a ritual every afternoon for all three of them to check the mail and for her dad to speculate on how big the inheritance might be when it finally came. He had a lot of plans for the money. "We'll get out of this dump into a real house again, like the one we had before," he'd said. "Maybe you two can go to some fancy college, just like your mom."

His eyes had shifted away when he said that, and Ashley had exchanged a look with Emma. Their father rarely spoke about their mother, and he'd always said college was a waste of time. Emma and Ashley had long ago agreed they wouldn't mention their plans for higher education to him. Their local community college was only a ten-minute bus ride away, and they were confident he'd never notice they were attending it. He didn't pay attention to details about their lives.

One morning Emma woke to find her father at the breakfast table, something that hadn't happened in years.

"I have a good feeling we're going to get some news today," he'd told them as they moved around the kitchen getting ready for school. "The minute you get that inheritance, we'll find us a house. I've been watching the listings, and I'm going to call a realtor this morning."

It wasn't until she and Ashley had left to walk to the bus stop that Ashley spoke up.

"He said 'the minute we get *our* inheritance.'"

"What?" Emma had been digging in her purse for her bus pass, not really paying attention.

"*Our* inheritance. Yours and mine. Nana Angela left *us* the money, not him."

When Emma had looked up, anger blazed in Ashley's eyes. "He's already spending our money in his mind. Buying a house with it." When Emma didn't answer, Ashley had raised her voice. "You know what's going to happen. He'll lose it all, the way he always does!"

Shifting on the hard cement bench in front of the post office, Emma had swallowed, the memories ashes in her throat. She'd defended her father that day, although she wasn't sure why. Ashley was right; for years he'd lost every cent that passed through his hands.

In the end, their disagreement hadn't mattered. A package arrived in the mail that afternoon, just as their father had predicted, but instead of a financial bequest, it contained two dolls that had belonged to their mother when she was young. There was a note that went with them, written in Nana Angela's beautiful penmanship.

"Your mother dreamed of you two long before she had you. She loved these dolls as a little girl. She named the blonde Emma, the brunette Ashley. It's as if she willed you into life. I hope these will remind you of her love—and of mine—when I'm gone."

When her father had understood that was the extent of the legacy Angela left them, he'd thrown the dolls into the trash, got in the car and left. He hadn't come home again until the following day, at which point he'd locked himself in his workshop.

After that, he barely came into the house. The workshop had its own rudimentary bathroom. He'd slept on an air mattress—or not at all, Emma suspected. They had no idea what he ate or how he spent his hours out there. Soon it became clear he'd stopped paying the bills. Emma and her sister had shouldered them, working harder, scrimping more than they ever had before.

Emma had fished the dolls out of the trash, but Ashley didn't want hers, so Emma had gently packed them away in a box and stored it under her bed. Ashley never discussed the bequest or Angela again. "We're on our own" was all she'd said when Emma tried to bring it up. "We've always been on our own, and we always will be. We stick to the plan, and we get out of here as soon as possible."

Which was exactly what they'd done—even if Emma had deviated from the script and lost everything all over again. Her business was gone. So was all the money she'd invested in it.

She sighed and tried reading the letter again.

Dear Emma,

I know this will come as a surprise, but I'm writing today to inform you that your grandmother, Angela Nelson, has left you a bequest.

I was a close friend of your grandmother for fifty years, and I'm the executor of her estate. I was the one who shipped the dolls to you and your sister, at her behest when she passed, and I'm the one who has overseen the trust she created for you ever since.

The time has come for you to receive the contents of the trust. I hope you remember Brightview, the bed-and-breakfast that was your grandmother's home throughout her life, and the Cliff Garden, which the women of your family have tended for over a hundred years. Now they belong to you and your sister, as laid out in the paperwork I've included.

I hope the two of you come to Seahaven soon to take possession of this wonderful inheritance your grandmother has passed to you. Brightview and the Cliff Garden are true landmarks of our town. Angela spoke of you almost every day before she passed. I feel like I know you already and hope we become better acquainted in the future.

Yours,
Colette Rainer

Emma sat back, her hands trembling. This was the inheritance her father thought she and Ashley would receive a decade ago. Why had Angela withheld it for so long? Why open the trust now?

Before she realized what she was doing, she pulled out her phone and called Ashley.

Pick up, she willed her. She never knew if Ashley would these days. Her sister hadn't been impressed when she'd started Food to You Fast, and she certainly wasn't impressed now that it had failed.

"What?"

When Ashley's voice came on the line, Emma's pulse leaped. "You won't believe what came in the mail today. Nana Angela left us Brightview and the Cliff Garden!"

There was a long pause before Ashley repeated, "Us?"

"Yes, us. It says so right here. I'm sure you'll get a letter about it, too. The executor of Nana's will wrote me. We're supposed to go to Seahaven to claim it."

She wouldn't have to stay with Denise after all. She had a house—a bed-and-breakfast—in California. A place to live and an income all at once.

"Go there? Why not just list it?"

"List it? What do you mean?"

"Put it up for sale," Ashley spelled out as if she were a little child. Somehow she always did that these days—made Emma feel small even if she was the one who was two years older.

"You can't be serious."

There was another long pause and when she spoke again, Ashley's voice had a thread of steel in it. "You're the one who can't be serious. You have as much debt as I do. Probably more, with that business venture of yours." Ashley could never force herself to say the words *Food to You Fast* out loud. "We'll sell the property and pay off those debts. For once in our lives we'll have financial security."

All Emma's excitement deflated. Ashley was right, of course. It was the sensible thing to do. Sell Brightview. Get out from under her old debts, buy a smaller house that fit her needs. Save the rest for retirement.

"Whatever we decide, we need to do it together—in person." That was a reasonable request, wasn't it? There'd be paperwork to sign, a realtor to hire. Someone would have to sort through Angela's belongings if there were any still left in the house.

All the while, every fiber of her being rebelled against the thought. She didn't want cash—she wanted what Brightview promised. A life. A home—a real one. A place to start over.

"Whatever. Do what you want. I'm too busy to waste my time like that." Ashley's voice grew distant, as if she was turning away from the phone already.

"Ashley, come on. This is Brightview we're talking about. We have to go see it again. Look, I have to give two weeks' notice at my jobs and tie up some loose ends, but I'll wrap things up here as soon as I can and head straight to Seahaven. I'll let you know as soon as I get there. It'll be three weeks. Four, tops. You can drive down to meet me." Ashley was based in San Francisco now.

Another pause. Was her sister really going to refuse?

When Emma couldn't stand it anymore, she added, "I haven't seen you in six months. Why are you being like this?" She hated the whine in her voice. Knew Ashley hated it, too. Her sister had ditched her and their father years ago, done with them both, and rarely came back, which hurt more than Emma could say. The last time she'd seen Ashley had been at their father's funeral six months ago. She'd thought Ashley might stay awhile. Help with the disposal of his things. Ashley hadn't. She'd made some lame excuse about work and left the following day. Emma had been the one to put their father's affairs in order.

Now she was the one begging her sister to give her a few days of her time. How had it come to this? Once they'd depended on each other. She knew she'd made mistakes, but she wasn't a bag of trash to be left at the curb. Jordan had treated her that way. Their father had, too.

She'd never thought Ashley would do that.

"Fine. I'll drive to Seahaven. We'll have dinner and talk—but that's all, Emma."

Ashley hung up.

NOAH HUDSON KNEW something big had happened the moment his friend and cofounder of Maxwell Tech, Mark Maxwell, entered his office. He was a burly man with a shock of dark hair and tortoiseshell glasses. Usually calm and quick to crack a joke, today he was vibrating with some repressed emotion.

"I just got the call," Mark said.

"What call?"

"*The* call." Mark laughed, but there was an edge to it Noah hadn't heard before. In fact, he hadn't seen Mark this wired since that day at Stanford when he'd announced he was starting a business and needed Noah's help. "The one where a giant corporation offers us millions of dollars to buy us out."

Noah sat back. "You're kidding me."

"I wouldn't lie about this."

He wouldn't. This was the moment they'd both been working toward since their junior year of college. Noah had lost track of all the nights and weekends he'd spent in this little room. His office's window overlooked a car park. Its carpet was ratty, his desk made up of a conglomeration of folding tables. A battered file cabinet stood in one corner. Every other surface was piled with equipment and paperwork.

"How many millions?"

"Lots of millions." Mark named a number that gave Noah vertigo. "It's not a done deal. There are details to hammer out, and of course we need to leak what we've been offered just in case someone else wants to bid them up. We need to consult our lawyer and make a counter-offer. Think you can hang in there for a little longer?"

He grinned, knowing Noah wasn't going anywhere. Noah had sacrificed his twenties to the business, and he'd continue to work hard until he got his payday.

He'd begun to think it would never come.

"Get in my office," Mark demanded. "Let's go through the proposal line by line, see if there are any gotchas."

Noah glanced out the window, and Mark groaned. "For god's sake, don't tell me you were about to leave for Seahaven."

"It's Friday." He'd come in around sunrise so he could leave early enough to miss the gridlock that froze the peninsula in the afternoon. "I was hoping to do some surfing."

"Soon enough you can surf all you want," Mark pointed out.

Noah supposed that was true.

Another thought struck him. Andrew. Would he finally be able to set things right with his brother?

He hoped so. Without thinking about it, he tapped a browser tab he'd opened earlier to bring it to the front of his computer screen.

Mark moved to his side. "Seahaven Realty. Man, you work fast—thirty seconds ago you didn't even know about the buyout."

"I like to keep my eye on the listings. There's hardly ever anything for sale over there."

"There's plenty for sale." Mark pointed to the column of homes on the screen. "Just not empty beachfront lots." He knew all about Noah's aspirations.

"Just not empty beachfront lots." Noah nodded and refreshed the page out of habit. It was set up to filter the properties according to his preferences.

"There's one," Mark said. "It's got a house, but it's a tear down. Maybe that's your place. You can build whatever you want."

Whatever his architect brother *Andrew* wanted was more to the point. Noah owed him that much—the opportunity to build a masterpiece. "Can't go after it until we close the deal." He stood up. "Show me that offer."

Two hours later, Noah knew they wouldn't bother playing hard to get. The deal was more than they'd ever dreamed they'd earn from selling their company, and the terms were fair. Mark could stay on as CEO. Norringers, the company fielding the offer, had made it clear there was a place for Noah, too, if he wanted it, but no golden handcuffs to keep him tied to a job he was long since ready to leave.

"Go surf," Mark finally told him when they were done. "But let's celebrate tomorrow."

"You got it."

Noah appreciated that Mark wasn't trying to change his mind about sticking with the company long-term. He appreciated the experience he'd gained while working with his friend, but he'd never set out to be a desk jockey, and he'd clocked more than a decade here getting Maxwell Tech off the ground.

Time for a change. Time to pursue his dream.

Norringers had made it clear they wanted a quick turnaround on the deal. It was a matter of weeks, not months, until he could make his move. Back in his office, he dialed the number for Seahaven Realty. He couldn't make an offer quite yet, but he could drive down tonight, crash at the short-term rental he'd already booked for himself and in the morning see the property Mark had pointed out earlier.

"Troy Mallard," a voice answered.

"I'm interested in your listing at 534 Cliff Street," Noah began.

"It's sold."

Just like that, his daydreams for the property evaporated.

"Sold? I'm looking at the listing." Noah hit the refresh button. The listing reappeared with a "Pending" stamp on it.

"Sold this morning."

"I didn't even see it yesterday," Noah protested. He'd checked the site several times. It was his favorite form of procrastination.

"Listed this morning, sold two hours later."

Noah bit back a curse.

"Look, you aren't the only one looking for a building lot on Cliff Street," Troy said. "But if you want, you can give me your number. Sometimes I get a heads-up about a sale before it even goes live. I know everyone in the business—I've lived here all my life."

"I lived there, too. When I was a kid." He didn't mention his family had moved to Seattle when he was ten.

"A local. If that's the case, you better believe I'll keep you at the top of my list. I'll call you first thing if something comes up. What's your name?"

Noah gave him his information, but he knew he wouldn't sit back and wait for any phone calls. The minute the sale of Maxwell Tech went through and he had his payday, he'd spend twenty-four hours a day online until he found himself the right property. It was time to settle things with Andrew and finally get on with his life.

EMMA WAVED GOODBYE to the driver of the Dodge Caravan as it pulled out of Brightview's driveway, then took out the key labeled "front door" her grandmother's solicitor had sent her. For the fee of a hundred dollars plus a huge container of cookies she'd baked to share, she'd scored a seat in the back row of a minivan full of students who'd traveled to Florida on vacation and were now returning home to Sacramento. The trip had been grueling. Over the course of three days, they'd all chatted, sung along to the playlist one of the students had created, slept and gazed in silence at the scenery passing by—or at their phones—as they drove straight across the country with minimal stops for gas and bathroom breaks.

Exhausted, craving a shower and sick to death of fast food, she stood in Brightview's crushed gravel parking area and faced the door to a house she vaguely remembered from her last visit when she was eight. The house was still the same weathered, indeterminate color. To her right was a shed where Nana Angela had kept a bicycle, tools and other odds and ends. Her grandmother had called this the back of the house and the side facing the ocean the front. That had confused her as a child, but it made sense to her now.

This end of the beach house wasn't much to look at, but memories still crowded her mind, glimpses of sunshine and a grandmother with long white hair and the biggest smile Emma had ever seen.

She understood why the place—and her grandmother—had made such an impression on her. Compared to the tiny bungalow where she'd spent her earliest years, Brightview seemed palatial. Studying it now, she amended her opinion of it. It was a big house for sure. A mansion? Not even close.

She let herself in, pocketed the key, shut the door behind her and breathed in the scent of the place, alien and familiar at the same time. She remembered standing on a footstool to help her grandmother bake cookies. Afternoons at the beach, wading in the surf and finding seashells. Exploring every inch of the adjoining Cliff Garden, too restless to settle to weeding, even though Ashley took to it like a spider to spinning webs, her tiny hands flicking in and out of the plants, rarely making a mistake.

"You're a natural," Nana Angela had told Ashley. "Someday you'll inherit the garden and make it sing."

Her prophesy had come true, Emma thought. They'd inherited the house and garden. Would Ashley really force her to sell them? Could she force her? Or did they both have to agree?

Emma refused to even think about it. Ashley had

loved it here as a child, and as soon as she came to visit, she'd fall in love with it all over again, even if they weren't as close as they once were. Emma figured it would be the perfect opportunity to repair the rift between them. She would volunteer to run the bed-and-breakfast on her own but split the profits with Ashley fifty-fifty after all the expenses were paid. That way they could both pay down their debts. It would take a solid plan to convince Ashley it was possible, but Emma had learned a lot about business plans in the last few years, far more than she'd known when she'd started Food to You Fast in her early twenties.

Lost in thought, she made her way down the hall. Just inside the door was a mudroom and then a set of stairs to her left, a bedroom and powder room to her right. The hall opened to a large expanse at the ocean end of the house. To the right was the kitchen, separated from the rest of the space on two sides by a wide counter. Beyond it was a large dining room table. To the left, a huge sectional made the most of the view.

There was no television on this floor. Who needed one with the Pacific Ocean arrayed in all its glory in the distance? Sliding glass doors made up the far wall of the house, opening to a spacious deck complete with tables, chairs, a covered area for days that were too sunny or rainy, and a huge barbecue.

Beyond the deck lay a patch of grass. Flowers and shrubs bordered the lawn, and a white picket fence separated the property from its neighbor to the right and protected the unwary from the edge of the bluffs, which fell straight down to a strip of beach far below. She could hear the ocean crashing against the shore with comforting regularity.

Emma knew from her hasty research that March could be unpleasantly rainy in Seahaven, but the weather gods must have decided to give her a break, because today the sky was an unrelenting blue. Her fears fell away one by one. She'd been afraid Brightview would be haunted by memories of her mother, Audra, but surprisingly she felt few traces of her here. Was that because her mother had spent so much time lying on a rattan couch on the deck on that last visit? As a grown-up, Emma understood her mother must have been sick even then. As an eight-year-old, she'd been baffled by the way her vivacious mother was sliding into a disquieting lethargy.

Nana Angela, on the other hand, was exactly what a grandmother should be. Kind, patient, full of natural wisdom and animal lore. She was always pointing out a bird's nest or naming a flower or finding traces of field mice. Emma loved to ramble through the Cliff Garden and beyond with her, especially their field trips to the redwood forests in the hills nearby.

She'd never experienced a summer like that one before or since.

Emma took a stabilizing breath and turned to the

west, where Brightview's lawns segued into the winding pathways and curving flower beds of the Cliff Garden.

Gorgeous as ever.

Even this early in the year, drifts of small yellow flowers edged the picket fence near the street, pretty from this distance, but probably an indication that the garden needed tending, since they looked more like weeds than an intentional planting. There were other splashes of color, too. The benches placed here and there were almost all occupied. Nana Angela had always made the garden open to everyone in the neighborhood. Brightview's picket fence ran all the way around the Cliff Garden, with a sweet little gate placed near the street for passersby to enter through.

Time to loiter in the garden later, Emma decided firmly, even though it called to her now. She needed to take stock of the house and make a plan for the bed-and-breakfast before Ashley could shoot her down.

As she stepped back inside, she reminded herself that even though selling Brightview could be a quick fix for both her and her sister, keeping it and maximizing the business could provide stability for them long term.

Could she convince Ashley of that?

She made a quick circuit of the house. Although the kitchen appliances were certainly dated, they'd been well-tended and were perfectly adequate for now. The dining room and living room furnishings were well-worn but not overly shabby. A new tablecloth or two and maybe some fresh pillows and throws could brighten up the place.

Brightview's second floor didn't have many memories for Emma. These were the guest rooms—the ones Nana Angela rented to beachgoers who wanted a little more tending than they'd get in a vacation rental. Nana Angela treated her guests like royalty. She always served a sumptuous spread in the mornings and provided drinks and snacks throughout the day. The rooms were tidy, Angela always present so that the accommodations felt safe.

Ashley was the one who'd followed Angela from guest room to guest room helping strip the beds and gather the towels to be washed the summer they'd spent here. That kind of chore hadn't appealed to Emma back then. She'd preferred to escape outside, acting out the adventures she imagined among the winding paths of the garden. When it was time to cook meals, however, she appeared in the kitchen the moment she heard the clank of a spoon against a bowl. Ashley would settle with her collection of stuffed animals in the living room and tend them quietly while Emma chattered at her grandmother as if she was hosting a cooking show.

Emma's reminiscences evaporated the moment she reached the top of the next flight of stairs, where a bedroom was built into the eaves of the house on the third floor. This was the room she'd shared with Ashley. Nothing had changed in the intervening years, from the pink tulips on the comforter that covered the wide bed they'd slept in to the matching curtains that framed the set of French doors that led to the balcony. There was the bookshelf stuffed with field guides and craft manuals. The same spyglass sat on a battered desk pushed into a corner. Every inch of the room flooded her with memories. She'd loved the way the sun slanted in the windows on summer mornings. The way she could slip out onto the balcony when Ashley was sleeping to watch the moon track across the sky at night.

That had been a summer of both bliss and worry. She'd never felt so safe before. Never so loved and heard—and understood. Still, worry about her mother's indolence—and the absence of her father—had underlined it all like the sour note of milk that had just gone off.

Something had been wrong among all that rightness. She simply hadn't known then what it was.

The sliding glass door stuck when she first tried to open it, but it finally released with a metallic squeal. Emma stepped outside, forgetting everything else but the sight and smell of the sea. Up here a light breeze teased tendrils of her hair. Sunlight twinkled on the waves. Nothing could be wrong on a day like this, she decided. She let worries about the past slide away.

She owned Brightview.

She owned this place.

She looked several hundred yards to her right, where

the beach below the bluffs spread out wide. It was dotted with sunbathers, a flock of surfers in its waves.

Her memories hadn't failed her after all. This was paradise.

She vowed right then and there she'd never leave.

She could run a bed-and-breakfast. She was a fabulous cook, and cleaning up after guests couldn't be more difficult than running a start-up food delivery service. Colette, whom Emma had emailed several times since receiving the envelope, had managed the bed-and-breakfast in the years since Nana Angela's passing, although she'd hired a service to do the day-to-day work. That meant there must be a booking service in place and systems for getting everything done.

A tinkle of sound from the direction of the Cliff Garden sent a shiver tracing down Emma's spine. Were those the same wind chimes that had hung from a stunted apple tree the last time she was here? If she remembered correctly, they'd chimed only infrequently, when the wind came from an unusual direction. "The grandmothers are here," Nana Angela used to say. "Everyone look sharp. What are they trying to tell us?" Emma and Ashley would freeze, their gazes raking the garden and the ocean beyond for something unusual. Sometimes they spotted an eagle flying, once an owl, and once a friend of Angela's had come through the gate just then bearing a basket of special treats. There was the time a garter snake had slithered by their feet, and once a pod of whales had been spouting far offshore. Emma still remembered the thrill she'd felt when Nana Angela pointed them out.

Was Nana Angela with the other grandmothers now? It was a comforting thought. A line of women had tended Brightview and the Cliff Garden for the past hundred years, and surely Nana Angela deserved to take her place among them—if only in Emma's imagination.

When a phone rang downstairs, she sucked in a surprised breath, then laughed at the shock it had given her. She hurried down the two flights to the kitchen, where she lifted the receiver of an old-fashioned landline.

"Hello?"

There was a pause and then a man's voice. "Is this Brightview? The bed-and-breakfast?"

"Uh… yes. Yes, it is." Emma scrambled to find a notepad and pencil, sure this was bound to be information about an unpaid utility bill or something similar. Colette had promised to have everything ready for her visit, but you never knew.

"I'm looking for accommodations, and I wondered if you have a room available. I saw your sign the last time I was in the area and copied your number from it, but I couldn't find your website. Are you open? I'll be back in Seahaven a week from today."

"Um…" Emma panicked. What should she do? On the one hand, she was far from ready to host any guests, and she really should consult Ashley before making any commitments. After all, Ashley wanted to sell Brightview…

A ripple of chimes lilted through the air again, reminding Emma of her heritage. Brightview wasn't just a house—it was a legacy, and she wouldn't be the one to break the chain of women in her family who had cared for it for so long.

This man could be the first of many paying customers. Didn't she and Ashley owe it to Angela and the other grandmothers to try? After all, this was a beautiful house in a fabulous location in one of the best small beach towns California had to offer. The bed-and-breakfast had sustained Angela throughout her life. When Emma tallied up the pros and cons of the venture, there were lots of pros.

But then there always were when she wanted something. That's what Ashley would say.

"I didn't catch that," the man on the other end of the line said. "Do you have a room?"

"I… yes," Emma said. "I definitely have a room." That was true, wasn't it? There were five rooms on the second floor plus the bedroom down here on the first to rent. If she took her old bedroom at the top of the stairs on the third floor and rented out another bedroom, that would still leave plenty for Ashley to choose from when she came to stay.

"Awesome. I'll need it for six months."

Emma felt her mouth drop open. Six months? No

one stayed at a bed-and-breakfast that long.

"I know it's unusual, but Brightview is in the exact location I want to be. You're probably all booked up…"

"No," Emma sputtered. "Not at all. I mean—" She pulled herself together. "I think I can make that work." She thought fast. People usually visited bed-and-breakfasts in couples or groups. If she booked one of the second-story rooms for a full six months, that might hamper her ability to rent the rest of them to larger, lucrative parties. "If you don't mind a ground-floor room," she added. "It's at the back of the house, but it does have an en suite bathroom."

She waited for him to protest. Who wanted a bedroom at the back of a beach house?

"Sounds perfect," he said. "I'll be gone all day anyway, and I don't need a view while I sleep."

"If you give me your information, I'll send you links to the paperwork you need to fill in. Once that's done, I'll need a deposit." She had no idea how any of that worked, but Colette was supposed to stop by soon, and Emma was sure she'd help her get it sorted out. Emma knew she was playing with fire taking a booking before she spoke to Ashley, but she didn't care. She couldn't bear to give up Brightview now that she was here.

"Sounds perfect. My name is Noah Hudson." He gave her a phone number and email address. He had a deep, rich voice. Emma pictured a man in his early forties. Distinguished, with a touch of gray at his temples.

"You'll hear from me soon, Mr. Hudson," she told him when he was done.

"Thanks."

Emma hung up, excitement growing inside her. She owned a bed-and-breakfast on the California coast. She had her first paying customer. In no time, she'd turn it into a booming business and earn enough to pay off all their debts. Ashley would forgive her. She'd be able to hold her head up high.

But you don't have any money to spruce up the place, or buy food to serve for breakfast, or put soap and shampoo in the bathrooms, or pay for a hundred other things you might need before Noah Hudson's arrival. Emma heard Ashley's voice play in her head even though her sister was miles away.

"I'll figure it out," she said out loud. Meanwhile, she'd whip up a business plan, make her pitch to Ashley, prove to her they could make a go of it. Ashley would visit and fall back in love with the Cliff Garden. They'd patch things up—

And be a real family again.

Coming to a decision, she backtracked to the entryway, picked up her suitcases and brought them up to her new bedroom. Downstairs again, she took stock of the cabinets in the kitchen and the pantry shelves. There were a lot of canned goods. Some dried beans and pasta. Cases of juice and sparkling water that weren't past their sell-by date—and several bottles of wine. The refrigerator was empty, but she wouldn't starve.

She could do this.

The wind chimes rippled again, and happiness filled her. She was on the right track.

Finally.

NOAH POCKETED HIS phone and breathed a sigh of relief. It was strange for a business not to have a presence on the internet these days, but he was glad he'd taken the chance on calling the number on Brightview's discreet sign. Probably a bed-and-breakfast like that one had so many repeat customers they didn't need to advertise. Or maybe the website was simply down for maintenance. It didn't matter now that he'd secured his room.

He'd spent the last few hours playing with his neighbor's dog, Winston, in a nearby park while his real estate agent hosted an open house at his condo. She'd assured him afterward he'd probably have an offer in hand by tomorrow, if not sooner.

"Maybe more than one," she'd said as she walked out the door.

He'd already begun to move his things into storage in anticipation of selling the place. He'd listed his condo the day after Maxwell Tech received Norringers' offer, determined to take a concrete step toward the new life he'd craved for so long. He could live out of his backpack and a duffel bag until his new home in

Seahaven was built. He didn't care how long it took.

It was still hard to believe he was wealthy beyond his wildest dreams. That his twelve-year slog of desk work was over. That Troy Mallard, the Seahaven realtor, had called him a week ago to inform him about a new property about to go on the market.

"I've got three days to sell this sucker before I have to list it on the MLS," Troy said. "You want it, you tell me today."

"I want it," Noah said.

"You gotta see it first." The realtor sighed. "People always say they want properties sight unseen, but when we put in the offer and they take the time to actually spec out the place, they change their minds, and that's a real mess, believe me."

"Fine. I'm heading there now." Noah, who'd been working late, tying up loose ends, hopped in his Range Rover and drove to Seahaven. By the time he made it to the property, it was fully dark, and he could barely see it clearly, but he didn't care. As he let himself in through the white picket gate and stumbled around what looked like a bunch of flower beds, all he knew was the lot was spacious and the view would be astounding in the daylight.

Exactly what he needed to balance the books with his brother.

"I'm here," he said into his phone when Troy picked up. "And I still want it. I'm coming to your office right now. Let's get this done."

His full-price offer was accepted the following day, to his relief. They'd set escrow for June first. He would have preferred a shorter one, but he needed to give Andrew time to fly in, scope out the property and affirm there was no reason he couldn't build an award-winning home there. The seller accepted his terms, and the deal was done.

For over ten years he'd sat at a desk. Now in one month, he'd closed two life-changing deals. All his dreams were coming true.

When his phone buzzed, he answered it. "Noah Hudson."

"Noah, I was right!"

It was Felicity Bronson, the realtor handling the sale of his condo.

"We got a bite?"

"We got three bites," she crowed. "I'm coming over," she added. "Let's strike while the iron is hot."

"Definitely," Noah said. "Can't wait to hear what you've got for me."

He hung up, contentment filling him. He'd sold his company. He'd bought an oceanfront lot. He was about to sell his condo.

He was on a roll.

When his phone buzzed again, he saw it was his neighbor Roy Simmons on the line.

"Hi, Roy." He would miss the old man when he was

gone. Roy had been a judge before he retired nearly thirty years ago. He read voraciously but meticulously and took time to think before answering the most pedestrian question, but when he did speak, he usually had something interesting to say.

Noah found him soothing after scrambling to keep up with the needs of Maxwell Tech.

"Hi, Noah. I meant to ask when you were here if you could give Winston a run again tomorrow morning before work. My hip isn't feeling any better tonight."

"I'm sorry to hear that, but of course I'll take Winston out. It'll be early, though."

"I'll be up." Roy gave a laugh as dry as fall leaves shuffling together. "Don't sleep much these days."

Noah had been keeping him abreast of all the changes in his life, and he wondered what Roy would do when he was gone. He had caregivers coming in most days to help with chores and physical therapy, but who would help with Winston?

A problem for another day, Noah decided. He'd broach the topic tomorrow when he came back from the park.

"See you in the morning," he said.

Maybe he'd get a dog of his own when his house in Seahaven was built.

CHAPTER 2

WHEN EMMA OPENED her door, a tall white-haired woman on the other side beamed at her.

"Emma Miller, I am so pleased to meet you!" Colette stepped forward and enveloped Emma in a warm hug. "That's from your grandmother. She made me promise to hug you every time we meet to make up for all the years she couldn't see you."

"Oh… thanks. Come in."

"I'll stay only a minute today. Ask me any questions you have about the house and tell me about any problems you've spotted. I'll come back another time for a longer visit. I'm sure you're exhausted after your trip."

She was less so after her tour of Brightview, Emma thought as she ushered the woman in, but she appreciated the sentiment.

"I brought you some food." Colette handed her the cloth bag she was carrying, following Emma into the house.

Emma led the way to the kitchen. "Thanks." She unpacked the bag as Colette took a seat at the counter.

Everything looked delicious. Fresh vegetables and fruit, a couple of casseroles and a pan of brownies.

"Like I said, I won't keep you. Do all the lights work? You found the towels and linens?"

"Yes, thank you." Everything appeared in working order so far. Colette must have disposed of her grandmother's clothing and personal possessions long ago. The house was nicely furnished, with plenty of books, artwork and knickknacks around to give it a homey feeling, but it was obvious the rooms were set up for guests now. "I couldn't find a website for the B and B, though. Is there one?" She bit her lip. She was putting the cart before the horse, wasn't she? She'd barely said hello to this woman.

A smile spread over Colette's face. "Then you're going to keep running it? Angela would be so pleased."

"I'm… considering it." Emma didn't want to explain that Ashley wanted to sell the place, but neither did she want to lie and pretend it was a sure thing she'd stay. Something about Colette demanded truthfulness.

"I brought Brightview's laptop and all the passwords," Colette said, pulling out a slim laptop and placing it on the kitchen counter. "As Angela's executor, I've been overseeing the bed-and-breakfast. I paid the bills and took a small salary. There is a website, but I've taken it down for the moment. I didn't want you to get bookings when you weren't ready for them."

"Thank you."

"Here's a manual for the business." Colette reached into her oversized handbag and pulled out a paisley-covered binder. When Emma opened it, she saw there was a section for everything. Website. Advertising. Reservations. Bookkeeping. And more. "You'll find everything you need in here. There is one thing, though."

"What's that?" Emma asked absently, still perusing the binder.

"Before I took down the site, a party of women booked the entire second floor for seven days, starting next week, and somehow I missed it. I was going to cancel the reservation, but if you're planning to stay open, maybe I shouldn't. They'll probably be the perfect first guests."

"Next week?" Emma's chest tightened. "I—I booked another guest."

Colette laughed. "You're a go-getter, just like your grandmother said. No moss growing under your feet! Sounds like you'll have a full house."

"I told him he'd have to take the first-floor bedroom."

"Your grandmother must have been watching over you," Colette said.

Emma hesitated. "I feel like you know so much about me, and I don't know anything about you."

"Give it time." Colette patted her hand. "I have questions, too, but not on your first day. Just know your grandmother loved you very much, and there was never a time she didn't pay attention to what was going on in your life, even if she wasn't able to be close to you."

"O-okay." Emma held the binder, not knowing what else to do. "Would you like a cup of tea?" she remembered to ask. "I'm sure there's some here somewhere."

"Second cabinet." Colette pointed. "No, I'll leave you to settle in and reacquaint yourself with the place. Call me anytime. My number is in the binder along with everything else you'll need. Let's get together for a good long chat soon, okay?"

"Okay." Emma trailed her to the door, where Colette gave her another hug.

"It really is wonderful to see you here in Brightview, where you belong." Colette moved to where she'd leaned a bicycle against the picket fence that enclosed the property. She gave a cheery wave before pushing off and cycling away.

Emma went back inside, her head spinning. She heated up one of Colette's casseroles, ate a helping from it gratefully, opened a bottle of wine she found in the pantry, poured a glass and went upstairs.

When she stepped onto the balcony, a light breeze made the evening chilly as the sun sank in the west. Soon she'd need to fetch a sweater if she was going to stay out here. March days in Seahaven could be hot sometimes, but the nights were cool.

It was sweet to be alone up here after the cramped quarters in the minivan during her cross-country trip.

She'd enjoyed meeting Colette, but she was content to be on her own tonight with the setting sun and her dreams.

"Hello!"

Emma nearly dropped her glass at the unexpected interruption. She half turned to her right to see a woman standing on the balcony of the house next door, waving at her enthusiastically. An excessively large three-story building with a wraparound deck and a distinctive blue-tiled roof, it was as close on its side to the picket fence dividing their properties as Brightview was. Which meant it wasn't far away at all.

"Hi," she called back when she regained her voice.

"Perfect night to watch the sunset, isn't it? I'm Ava. Ava Ingerson."

"It is. I'm Emma Miller. Nice to meet you." Emma studied her neighbor, who looked to be about the same age she was, or perhaps a year or two older. Her auburn hair was knotted in a twist on top of her head, and she looked like she'd been cleaning.

Ava leaned back and gestured in the other direction. "That's Penelope Rider."

Emma could just make out another young woman waving at them from the house next to Ava's.

"We're both new here, too. Come over. Bring your drink." It was more of a command than an invitation. Emma looked down at herself. She hadn't had time for a shower or a change of clothes yet. "Come on," Ava encouraged her. "We don't care what you look like.

Sundown drinks are a casual affair."

"Be right there," Emma called back. It was only smart to meet her new neighbors.

Ducking inside, she rummaged in one of her suitcases, found something approximating a clean outfit, ran a comb through her hair and redid her ponytail. She grabbed the bottle of wine she'd just opened and her glass, slid her feet into a pair of flip-flops and made her way next door.

Ava greeted her. "You dressed up," she said in mock-disapproval.

"First impressions and all that," Emma said.

"That's okay. Come in. Hi, Penelope," Ava added, looking over Emma's shoulder.

"Hi!" Penelope hurried up, the bangles at her wrists jangling. The olive tones of her skin hinted at a Mediterranean lineage. Where Ava had the lean, athletic build of a yoga instructor, Penelope was bigger-boned and curvy. She wore khaki green shorts and a cream T-shirt, and her thick, dark waves were held back with a rolled-up printed bandanna she wore like a headband.

"Hi," Emma said. "I'm Emma."

"Come upstairs." Ava beckoned them in. "I've got the deck all set up. We've been dying to know who was going to move into Brightview." She led the way through a small entryway to a staircase. Emma spotted hiking boots near the front door and a pair of binoculars on top of a couple of field guides on a small table. As they climbed, they passed a series of framed vintage national-park maps. "Tell us everything about yourself," Ava commanded.

"I inherited Brightview from my grandmother," Emma began as she followed, Penelope tagging along behind. "I'm going to continue running the bed-and-breakfast, like she did."

"You were able to keep her permit?" Ava asked.

Permit? "I… hope so," she said. Surely Colette would have mentioned if there was any issue with a permit. "I'm still sorting things out." She'd better go through the binder Colette had left. Tomorrow. She'd had all she could take today, and she hadn't even told Ashley she was going ahead with booking guests.

"That's wonderful," Ava said. "I inherited the Blue House from my aunt, and I met your grandmother a few times when I came to visit as a child. She was lovely." They reached the second-story landing, and Ava kept going.

"I've known your grandmother my whole life," Penelope piped up. "My uncle owned the place next door. Fisherman's Point." She pointed to the house where Emma had first seen her. "He used to run fishing tours and kept quarters for his clients to stay in. My family came to visit each year, and when I was older, I worked for him. I wonder if the three of us were ever here at the same time?"

"It's possible," Ava mused.

"I was here only once," Emma told them. "When I was eight."

Penelope nodded. "My uncle left the house to me when he passed away, but I'm going after a different customer base now. No fishermen." She sighed. "It hasn't been easy to make the shift. People keep calling, wanting me to take them on charters like my uncle did. I miss him, and I miss your grandmother, too, Emma. She was always so welcoming and ready to help. I can't tell you how many hours I've spent in the Cliff Garden—and on the Trouble Bench when I was a kid and she was around. You must miss Angela a lot."

"I do." The Trouble Bench. Had Angela kept up that tradition?

Had Colette?

Emma considered that as they reached the top floor. Ava let them into a room that spanned the length of the house. At the end closest to the street was a small kitchen and bathroom. The rest of the space was taken up by a sitting area and bed, neatly made up with a floral bedspread. There were books everywhere, and a collage of photos on one wall showed Ava hiking, camping, wading in rivers, poking around in tide pools and engaged in other outdoor activities with friends and family. Feathers, seashells, pinecones and rocks littered the flat surfaces. Ava led them out onto her balcony.

"Have a seat." She gestured to the chairs placed around a small café-style table. Emma sat down, placing her glass of wine and the bottle carefully in front of her, still thinking about Penelope's reference to a certain bench that overlooked the ocean.

The summer she'd spent here, it had been a game to Emma to spot them—the unhappy souls that turned up in the Cliff Garden, sat on the Trouble Bench and stared into waves far below.

It was the way they held their shoulders that told you when someone needed care, Nana Angela always said. Plenty of people came to look at the view, chat with a friend or rest their legs before walking home. The ones who needed tending sat alone, tense and unmoving. It was her duty to go to them, and she never failed.

Emma would shadow her while she gathered a slice of banana bread, a lemon poppy-seed muffin, a slice of pecan pie—whatever she had on hand. Nana Angela never used disposable plates when it came to missions of mercy. "That would imply impermanence, and that's not what people need in troubled times." She served her offerings on thick hand-fired dishes that had been given to her by a grateful friend. Sea-blue, glazed—each one as unique as the waves that marched across the bay. Angela would fold a cream-colored cloth napkin over the top, pour a glass of water and step calmly onto the deck, down to the yard, then along the central path through the garden beds to sit down and offer comfort. Emma had never seen that comfort refused.

She was in charge of Brightview now—along with its

kitchen. Did that make her responsible for the Trouble Bench, too?

Or was it Ashley's job? Her sister was the one who'd loved to tend the Cliff Garden.

What was it her grandmother used to say about it?

The Cliff Garden has healed a hundred hearts.

"Interesting, isn't it?" Ava broke into her thoughts when they were all comfortable. "We each lost a loved one this year and inherited a beach house. We could be sisters."

"I've always wanted a sister." Penelope sighed again. "It's always been just me and my mom—and Uncle Dan when I came here. Mom remarried three years ago and moved to Costa Rica. She's having a blast, but it's like we changed places. Now she's the kid having all the fun, and with Uncle Dan gone, I'm the one worrying about bills."

Emma thought of her strained relationship with Ashley. "I have a sister," she said slowly, "but I don't think you can have too many of them. I'd be happy to have some new ones." Hadn't she learned this past year not to put all her eggs in one basket? Besides, she was already warming to both of these women. Ava struck her as intelligent and adventurous. Penelope friendly and fun. She'd drifted away from her restaurant friends during her years with Jordan. Always worked too hard to have much time for friends, anyway. Maybe she could change that now.

"As long as we're wishing for people, I'll take a man,

too. Is there a Mr. Emma?" Penelope asked.

"No." Emma wondered what they could read in her face. This was a sore spot. She'd lost years of her life to her relationship with Jordan, only to have him walk away from her, straight into another woman's arms. She'd always thought she'd be married by now. Now she wondered if she ever would.

"Boyfriend?" Penelope pursued.

"Not that, either." After Jordan dumped her, she'd been too shell-shocked to look for a replacement. Denise had tried to convince her to try a dating app and had even set up an account for her. Emma had taken it down the very next day after receiving several messages that made her skin crawl. She took a sip of wine to cover her embarrassment.

"We don't have husbands or boyfriends, either," Penelope assured her. "What?" she asked when Ava gave her a little shove. "It's good to establish the basics right from the start. Sisters tell each other everything," she reminded them.

"I suppose you're right." Ava lifted her glass. "To sisters, by blood or other common bond."

Penelope lifted hers, too, "To the Cliff Street Sisters. Our love lives might be disasters, but at least we have this." She gestured to the ocean spread before them as the sun slid down to the west.

Emma could drink to that.

"WELL, THAT'S THAT. Time to hit the beach!" Noah Hudson shook Mark's hand. "Been a pleasure doing business with you."

"Wish you'd stay," Mark told him. "It's not going to be the same without you."

"How many millions can one man make?" Noah joked as he backed away. He'd been dreading this conversation. He wasn't good at smoothing an awkward goodbye. "Time to get back to what I do best."

"I know." Mark shoved his hands in his pockets, looking more like the freshman Noah had met at Stanford fourteen years ago than a man who'd just sold his start-up for many millions of dollars. "And I appreciate that you stuck it out this long." He shook his head. "I still can't believe we really did it."

Noah understood his disbelief. Most start-ups failed. They were the lucky ones.

And he'd never meant to come on this ride at all.

Mark had nagged, begged and mock-threatened to try to get him to help when he started Maxwell Tech in their dorm room at Stanford. Noah had been pursuing a dual degree in computer science and business, but the truth was he'd really been killing time. He'd promised his older brother he'd stick it out and get a bachelor's degree, because it was what their parents would have wanted, but he'd known since junior high what he wanted to do, and now he was finally going to pursue it full-time.

"We did it," he assured Mark. "I've got the bank account to prove it. So do you. Why don't you call it quits and come hang out at the beach? I'm going to have plenty of room in my brand-new house. Andrew keeps upping the bedroom count in the plans every time I talk to him." His brother had been over the moon ever since Noah had closed the deal on the beachfront lot in Seahaven. Noah had given him carte blanche to design any house he wanted. Noah would have the final say on the details, of course, but he had a debt to repay to his brother and knew Andrew meant to use the opportunity to secure an award—and hopefully coverage in some of the major architectural and home magazines. He was ready to take a big step forward in his career.

"This business has never been about money for me, and you know it."

That was true. Mark loved programming, loved creating things and pursuing ideas. Noah's job had been to help make the deals and handle the annoying parts, as Mark always described them. Turned out Noah excelled at that, but it wasn't his calling.

Photography was. Action photography, to be precise. He was happiest when he was in the water catching surfers glide through waves or wedged into cracks in a granite cliff face capturing the grit and determination of free climbers. He loved to be outside, pushing himself and his equipment to the limits. Desk work was fine now and then, but full-time office work for the last twelve years had left him itching to get out and do things.

Now he'd get his chance. He'd build a beautiful, modern home in Seahaven. Divide his time between the beach, the Sierra Nevadas a few hours away and trips anywhere else he felt like going.

What could be better?

"You ever hear from Caitlyn?" Mark asked, a little too casually.

Noah's good mood took a nosedive. "Nope." And he wasn't going to discuss her, either. Noah didn't care if Mark couldn't figure out why he'd ditched his cousin several months back. Noah wasn't going to tell him it was because she'd wanted to pursue other options. Several other options at the same time—while they were still together.

He wasn't down for that.

"You ever going to settle down?" Mark was married, and he'd made it clear he thought Noah should be by now, too.

"Hell, no." He was about to launch himself into the rest of his life. He would date, but he didn't need anything serious. Not yet.

Maybe not ever.

"You think Kristin and I should move to Seahaven, huh? How long is the commute from there? Twenty minutes? Thirty?"

As if he'd even consider it. Mark loved to be in the heart of Silicon Valley. Besides, he came with Noah to surf in Seahaven often enough to know the distance by heart.

"You know damn well it's a couple of hours either way with traffic. Worse on Fridays," Noah reminded him.

"Probably can't move in with you, then. Save me a guest room, though. I'll come visit when I can."

As Noah clasped his friend's hand, it sank in how infrequently he'd see Mark from now on. For one moment he wondered if he was making a mistake.

Mark shook his head, as if reading his mind. "Get out of here, Hudson. You know we'll end up talking all the time, even if we aren't in the same place."

Noah nodded. "See you soon." He took a last look at Maxwell Tech's new digs in the large complex Norringers had moved them into a week ago. "You did really good, you know. Thanks for everything. You changed my life."

"Couldn't have done it without you."

Noah left before the moment could get too heavy. Mark was right; they'd talk all the time. He would make a point of driving up this way a couple of times a month. Mark would make it down to see him when he could. It would be fine.

But as he walked out of the building toward his Range Rover, his steps felt unsteady somehow, like the coefficient of gravity had changed. Maxwell Tech had been his whole life since college. He didn't have a girl.

Wouldn't have Mark's constant company. His folks were long gone. His brother was based in Seattle.

As soon as he moved to Seahaven, he'd be alone.

His unsettled mood lasted until he got home, changed his clothes and went to gather Winston from his neighbor's place. All week he'd been giving Winston a good run before and after work, but his worry about Roy only increased as the days passed and his hip wasn't getting better.

"I had a replacement about twenty-five years back," Roy had confessed to him a few days ago. "Doctors are saying it's time to think about getting it redone. Hard to face at my age."

Today when he let himself into Roy's condo, Noah found his neighbor seated in his favorite russet-colored easy chair near the window, Winston at his feet. The golden retriever leaped to its feet, eager to go, and Noah grabbed his lead from the peg near the door.

"Need to talk to you when you get back," Roy told him. "Have a favor to ask you."

"Sure thing."

Roy didn't seem his usual cheerful self, and it was hard for Noah to give Winston the time he deserved playing and running before he took him home again.

"What's on your mind?" he asked when he did.

"Winston's future," Roy said succinctly. "I've been talking to my kids all week. Talking to my doctors, too. The writing is on the wall. I've had a good run at living independently, but it's time I had more help. There's an opening in Westside Care, a senior living complex I've had my eye on for a while. I can stay in one of their apartments while I'm able, then move into their assisted care units when I need them. I'll have more company. People around to help while I have my hip surgery. The only problem is Winston."

"Pets aren't allowed at Westside?" Noah wasn't surprised at the direction of the conversation. Roy had spoken about moving before.

"A dog as big as Winston doesn't fit their idea of a pet," Roy said ruefully. "He deserves a more active life, anyway. Somewhere to run and play. I'll miss him, but it's the right thing to do. Would you consider taking him? Sounds like you're about to have the kind of arrangement perfect for a dog like him."

Noah hesitated. He loved Winston and would gladly take him, but he was about to stay in a bed-and-breakfast for six months. He caught the look in Roy's eye and snapped his mouth shut before he could say that, however. Roy really loved Winston. Giving him to a stranger would be more than he could bear.

"Of course," he said. He'd figure it out, one way or another, he decided. "I'd love to have Winston, and I'll stop by to let you see him every time I'm in town."

A grateful smile broke across Roy's face. "Thank you." The roughness in the old man's voice let Noah know he'd done the right thing. "I'll look forward to those visits," he said honestly. "You've been a good neighbor and a good friend."

"I'll look forward to them, too," Noah told him truthfully.

As they sorted out the details, his sense of obligation turned into something closer to anticipation. Having Winston around would be a great first step in the transformation of his life from desk jockey to adrenaline junkie. Every outdoorsman needed a good dog.

"What do say, Winston? Are you going to like the beach?"

Winston barked, and both men laughed.

"I think that's a yes," Roy said.

"BYE, EMMA!" GINNI Chester called out as she shut the screen door behind her. She gave a whoop as she hurried after her friends, four women in their midtwenties who'd booked the second floor of the bed-and-breakfast for a week. With guidance from the binder Colette had handed her, Emma had gotten the hang of Brightview's booking system, sussed out how Colette—and Nana Angela before her—had advertised the B and B and started sketching out plans for how to improve both systems. As soon as she put the website back online, she got several more bookings. She'd called Ashley a few times, bracing herself for the confrontation she knew would come, but Ashley hadn't called back, and Emma wasn't eager to push the matter. She figured she could ramp up the business and then present her plans to her sister, with encouraging income figures in hand.

Emma thought wistfully of her guests striding down the short half block in their bikinis and wraps to the steps that led to the beach. She knew they'd come back sun-kissed, salty, tired and hopefully happy in a couple of hours and planned to enjoy the quiet until then—and catch up on a few tasks.

Colette had left the bed-and-breakfast clean and tidy, but Emma had delved into her nonexistent funds and maxed her credit cards to provide the rooms with new linens, bath towels and other up-to-date touches to spruce up the place a bit, convinced they hadn't been replaced since Nana Angela passed. She'd have to do more as she went along, but there was no money left, and one of the sections of the binder, labeled "repairs," had informed her she needed to replace the shingles on the roof before the rainy season started this fall. Possibly several windows, too.

As she loaded dishes into the fifteen-year-old dishwasher, Emma hoped it would keep running long enough for her to save up to replace it. The washer and dryer were equally old, and she was going to give them a run for their money doing all the sheets each time her guests left. With the dishes loaded and the counters wiped down, she whipped up a veggie platter and dip to have on hand when the women returned. Technically, she offered only breakfast, but Emma figured some extra special touches would lead to good reviews. She needed them. Looking over the accounts she'd found in the laptop Colette gave her, it seemed the business had slowed down these past few years. She saw the same names reappear in the bookings over and over again and wondered if Colette had decided to book reservations only for repeat customers. After all, she had to be in her eighties. Even if she used a service to prep for and clean up after each set of guests, it took time and energy to run a business, not that Colette seemed to lack either of these.

A familiar trace of guilt and sorrow eddied through her. She wished she'd reached out to reestablish a connection with Nana Angela when she was a teenager, no matter what her father said. It shamed her to realize that despite the wonderful summer she'd spent with her grandmother when she was young, she'd accepted all the accusations her father had leveled at Angela as fact over the years. Why had she taken his interpretation of her grandmother's actions at face value? He'd been so unreliable in so many ways. She should have thought for herself.

Ashley could be excused for going along with it; she was only six when they went to California. Emma had been eight. Old enough to understand Nana Angela's gentle soul. Plenty old enough to remember all the good things her grandmother had done when her father harped on her stinginess.

She'd realized in the last six months there were a lot of things about her father she hadn't thought to question before but now got under her skin. After their mother died, it was as if he'd purposefully cut them off from anyone who might look into their situation too closely. Every now and then, she thought about the long, lonely years during which she and Ashley had worked so hard to cover up the fact that he was barely caring for them at all.

Why had she thought that was normal?

No, it wasn't that she'd thought it was normal, Emma decided. It was that she'd had no idea what to do about it. No one to ask for help.

If she'd reached out to Nana Angela, would her grandmother have come?

It wasn't lost on Emma that her sister had moved as far as possible from Florida when she'd graduated from college. Emma had watched her create the normal life she'd always craved. Her outfits, probably gleaned from secondhand stores around San Francisco, looked impeccable in the photos she posted on her social media feeds. She had to be splurging on her hairstylist, but Emma had the feeling she scrimped and saved every last dollar she could, because it took her only a couple of years before she put a down payment on a tiny condo just outside the city and furnished it bit by bit.

As Emma moved around the bed-and-breakfast, she tried to shake the memories. The ups and downs of her childhood were too much to think about. Comparing Ashley's success to her own failures didn't help, either. She wanted peace and security—just like Ashley, she supposed.

When Jordan had first slipped into her life—and her business—she'd loved the companionship she found with him, something she'd missed since Ashley left, but soon he became yet another reason she never saw her sister. On her first visit home, Ashley disliked Jordan on sight.

She should have listened to her sister's intuition, Emma thought as she moved around the large, open living room, tidying things that were already tidy.

At least all that was in the past. Jordan was gone. Food to You Fast was gone. If she could keep booking Brightview's rooms, she'd be on her way to getting her debts under control and be able to help her sister.

What could Ashley hold against her then?

Emma straightened a photo she'd brought with her from Florida. It was taken the day her sister graduated from a tricycle to a two-wheeler. Sporting matching pink helmets, Emma straddled a purple bike, Ashley a turquoise one. Their hair had been done in matching braids. They wore jeans, matching pink sneakers and matching pink jackets. Emma remembered that day well. She'd cheered her sister on as her mother taught Ashley to ride her new bicycle. It must have been only months before her mom got sick, and the photo always reminded

Emma that she'd had a normal life once.

She was just about to head outside when a knock sounded at the door.

Was it her other guest, Noah Hudson? He said he'd arrive sometime in the late afternoon. The previous evening, at what had become their nightly get-together at sundown at Ava's house, Ava and Penelope had both cautioned her when she admitted she'd allowed a man to rent a room. "It's fine" was the way Penelope had put it. "Almost all my uncle's guests were men. Just make sure you've got a charged cell phone in your pocket at all times and a lock on your bedroom door."

"You've got to be careful," Ava added more worriedly. "My aunt always said most guests are great, but some… aren't. I try to mostly book women and couples."

Emma gave a final pat to one of the pillows and made her way to the back of the house to see. The man on the other side of the door didn't look like trouble, or at least not in the sense her new friends meant. He was about six feet tall, she estimated, with an athletic build and piercing blue eyes. In gray hiking pants and a black T-shirt that stretched over the muscles of his chest, he looked ready for action—and far younger than the venerable age Emma had assumed him to be. Emma hadn't mentioned to Ava and Penelope how long he was staying. They were right; she should be more cautious about who she allowed in her house.

"Hi." The man smiled, and Emma's breath caught. That grin was something, tugging at her insides in all the right places. She'd barely looked at a man since Jordan had dumped her, since the hurt was still too raw, but maybe she'd underestimated the rate of her healing. She was sure looking now.

"Hi." She recovered herself and ushered him in. "I'm Emma Miller. Welcome to Brightview. Let me take your bags."

Noah shook his head. "If you think I'm going to make a woman carry my bags to my room, you weren't raised in the kind of house I was."

She let herself smile at that. "Your room is right here, anyway." She gestured to the first door on the right. "You really don't mind it doesn't have an ocean view?"

"I don't mind at all." He flashed that grin again. Comfortable in his skin, she thought. Oh, to be so confident. All her gumption had disappeared with Jordan and her business.

"You won't get sick of it after a month or two?" Why on earth was she trying to run off a paying customer? Emma wasn't sure, except something about the man was getting under her skin, a tug of interest deep inside her she hadn't felt since… well, since she'd met Jordan.

This man wasn't anything like Jordan, though. He was obviously a doer, judging by the way he prowled around the bedroom, easily lifting two large suitcases onto the bed. Jordan was a man who liked to talk about doing things, brag about doing them and make a whole lot of promises he had no intention of keeping. If only she'd realized that before she got engaged to the man and made him a partner in her business.

"Nope," Noah said simply. "This is perfect." He gestured to the large closet, the one good thing about the room aside from its cozy charm. "I have a lot of gear I need to stow, and this will get the job done. You mentioned there was room in a storage shed outside for my bike and surfboards?"

"That's right."

"I'll keep my cameras in here. And…" His grin slipped a bit as he ran a hand through his hair. He ducked his head. Looked up again sheepishly. "There's something else."

Oh god, he'd brought a woman along, and now he was going to try to foist an extra guest on her—an extra guest who'd be in her house for six months. Should she bill him double? Refuse her? Emma told herself the panic rising inside her was purely to do with business and nothing at all to do with her disappointment that Noah was taken.

"It's Winston."

"Winston?"

"My dog," he explained.

"Dog? You didn't say anything about a dog."

"I acquired him recently. Real recently. Like… yesterday. He's a good dog, though. Come and see."

A dog that was going to stay for six months? Emma's thoughts spun. Would she have to warn other guests about him? Put it on the website? She'd designated Brightview as pet free…

She followed him outside to the Range Rover he'd parked in one of the spaces. Inside sat a very good dog.

Such a good dog.

Emma's heart melted instantly.

"Winston?" she heard herself say to the fluffy golden retriever sitting upright in the back seat. "Oh, my goodness. You are obviously a sweetheart."

The dog lifted its head at the praise. Rested its chin on the edge of the open window and cocked a doggy eyebrow at her.

"He can stay?" Relief was plain in Noah's voice. He opened the door, and Winston hopped down. Obviously an older dog but still active, he immediately sat by Noah's feet and waited to see what would happen next.

Emma crouched next to him and let him sniff her hand. When he licked it, she petted him, scratching behind his ears. When she found herself hugging the dog a minute later, she knew she was lost. She missed Buster, the retriever her family owned when she was little. He passed away the same year her mother did, which had broken her heart. A retriever made everything better, especially when it was a patient, older dog like Winston.

"He can stay—for now. If the other guests don't mind," she cautioned. Looking up, she saw that Noah's earlier grin had softened into something like appreciation as he looked down at her. It sent a zing of interest through her body that Emma quickly quelled.

"Fair enough. I'm willing to pay extra." Noah held out a hand. She took it, and he helped her to her feet.

Flustered by the sizzle of attraction that zipped through her at his touch, she boldly said, "I'm afraid I will have to charge you extra. I'll have to notify the other guests of his presence, and it might cause some people to choose different accommodations."

"You got it."

"How did you end up with him?"

Noah's smile faded. "He belonged to a man in my building who's moving into a retirement home in a few weeks. He's not allowed to bring a dog as big as Winston. I told him I'd take him and bring him to visit now and then."

"You're a good friend."

Noah shrugged. "Who could say no to a face like this? Come on, Winston. See your new home." Noah lugged another bag out of the Rover and shut the door.

The retriever obediently followed him inside. Emma trailed after them, marveling at the way the man seemed to take everything in stride. "Settle in, then come and have a snack," she told Noah.

"Be right there."

She continued to the kitchen, surveyed the veggie platter in the fridge and decided that wouldn't do for a hungry man. Instead, she brought out muffins she'd baked earlier and several kinds of juice, soda and sparkling water.

She was looking forward to his reappearance only because of Winston, she told herself, but when she heard the women returning from the beach before Noah joined her in the living room, her heart plummeted. Ten minutes later, Emma admitted defeat. Her female guests had surrounded Noah the moment he appeared, playing with Winston, laughing and flirting with his owner so outrageously that Emma felt embarrassed for them.

Noah seemed used to it, however. Probably enjoyed it.

She knew how men were. If she was smart, she'd nip her attraction to him in the bud right now.

Emma ushered her guests out onto the deck, where they could sit on the wicker furniture without worrying about getting it sandy, and busied herself passing out muffins on small plates, tucking a napkin into each guest's hand as she went. She set the veggie platter on the table.

"Does anyone mind about Winston's presence?" she asked when there was a brief break in the conversation, everyone savoring their first bites.

"Mind? He's a bonus!" Ginni said, and the others agreed.

"Emma, these muffins are amazing. We're supposed to go out to eat tonight, but I could stay here and eat nothing but these," one of the women said. Her name was Annie, a petite blonde who Emma thought probably barely ate at all usually. She was devouring her muffin with alacrity, though.

"They are wonderful," Kate said. She was more reserved than her friend, and this was the first time she'd talked to Emma. "Why don't you advertise your wonderful cooking on the website?"

"It's definitely a plus," Leslie said. A few years older than the others, Leslie was laid back, with a biting sense of humor Emma enjoyed.

"I guess I should," Emma said, biting back a sigh. She was a phenomenal cook, and the recipes she'd created for her meal-delivery service were top tier. The customers she garnered had praised her to the skies. Jordan was supposed to be in charge of building out the supply chain, cutting costs and expanding the reach of the business. To say he'd failed miserably was an understatement.

And then there was the pricey business coach she'd hired to guide them through the process, who instead had guided Jordan right out of her life and into her own bed.

Emma retreated before anyone could notice the change in her mood and returned several minutes later with a tray of drinks. As she passed them out, she felt

Noah's gaze lingering on her. She turned his way, and he lifted his eyebrows and gave a little shrug, as if to say he'd preferred when they were alone.

Heat rising in her cheeks, Emma ducked her head and handed another drink to one of the women. Was he really interested in her?

Or was she fooling herself again?

THERE WERE WOMEN everywhere. Eligible, flirty, easygoing women in string bikinis who would be gone in a matter of days, and he was going to fall for his landlady?

Not smart, Noah told himself. He'd been damn lucky to find accommodations in this location, and he'd signed a contract for six months. He couldn't roll into bed with Emma, roll back out and then pretend it never happened for the remainder of his stay.

Talk about awkward.

Emma didn't strike him as the kind to roll in and out of bed, anyway. He'd be much smarter to choose one of the women clustered around him, petting Winston, cracking silly jokes at each other's expense, mellow from their time in the sun and the snacks Emma had served.

When had his body ever followed orders from his brain, though? He wasn't smart when it came to dating or women, as much as he pretended to himself he was. Caitlyn's antics last fall had tripped him up more than he cared to admit. He'd been dumped by women before, and done a fair amount of dumping himself, but he'd never been played so thoroughly and carelessly. She'd laughed in his face when he'd called her on it.

"Grow up." Her sneer cut bone-deep. "Big boys know it's all a game." She'd left before he could come up with a stinging answer. The kicker was that he hadn't been in love with her. The longer they dated, the clearer it became they weren't compatible for anything serious. It was all fun and games, but still he'd thought they shared the same understanding of the rules. Monogamy while they were together. Fine to move on when they mutually decided to call it quits. When he found out she was sleeping with not one—but two other men, it felt like a sucker punch.

Thank god he made it a rule to be in charge of protection. Still, Noah found it hard to reclaim his former easygoing attitude toward women and dating, even after he'd verified he wouldn't pay a lasting price for Caitlyn's indiscretions. These days when he met an interesting woman, suspicions skewed his thoughts. What secrets was she hiding? What games did she mean to play?

Caitlyn had gotten in his head.

He found himself on his feet.

"Where are you going?" Annie complained. "You haven't even finished your drink."

"Gotta get out there." He pointed to the ocean, deciding on the spot not to wait a moment longer to hit the waves. A splash of cold water in his face would do him good. "Thanks for the food," he said to Emma as he made his way inside. He deposited his dishes by the sink. "Want me to take care of these?" he asked when he noticed she'd followed him.

"Of course not. I'll get them in the dishwasher in a moment. You're surfing?"

"You got it." His good mood returned. Emma's friendly face and upturned nose did things for him, and if he couldn't follow his desires, at least he could enjoy her company.

"What about Winston?" The dog had padded in after him.

"He knows what to do. Come on, Winston." The dog had proved to him many times he could be trusted to behave. He went to his room, shook off his bad memories as he gathered what he needed and, fifteen minutes later, was paddling into the surf. Out here he could forget everything, including Caitlyn.

Still, he was finding it hard to get Emma out of his mind.

He wasn't surprised to find the waves crowded. Noah shouted a greeting to a man he recognized from previous visits, Greg Nolan, and a moment later, Greg paddled over.

"You surfing or shooting today?" he called out as he approached.

"Surfing. Need to get a feel for the waves before I get back to taking photos." It felt like years since he'd been in the water with any regularity. The drive down from the peninsula took too long, and often he and Mark had worked through weekends and evenings. These last few years, they'd gotten so busy that sometimes months went by between his forays into the ocean.

"You know the rest of the Surf Dads?" Greg waved a hand at some of the nearest surfers.

Noah laughed. *Surf dads?* "No, can't say I do."

"A bunch of us who've known each other since middle school realized we were all juggling work and kids—still trying to catch some waves now and then. Our wives like surfing, too. We decided to make it easier on ourselves and gang up together to hire people to watch the kids while we get out here or do chores at home. Now the dads are out here three times a week, and the moms take their turns on opposite days. Sundays are a free-for-all. The kids get to hang out on the beach together, and we know they're safe. Come on, I'll introduce you to some of the guys."

Noah figured he met an even dozen dads during the next two hours. He made sure to mention his photography, and it cheered him up considerably to find that a couple of them already knew who he was.

"You took that shot of Harley Anderson two years ago, right?" one of them asked.

"That's right." He'd gotten into *SurfWorld Magazine* with that photo.

He caught a few waves, too. He might be rusty, but it

was like riding a bike. You didn't forget how to surf. The splash of the water and the warmth of the sun on his face reminded him that all his hard work had been worthwhile.

This was his time to pursue his real passions, and he meant to make the most of it.

CHAPTER 3

EMMA WAS UP with the dawn the following morning, but when she stepped outside to savor the quiet, Ava was already leaning against the railing of her balcony next door. She waved, and Emma waved back, cheered to see a friendly face after a somewhat anxious night with a house full of guests.

"I've got something for you if you're up for it," Ava called softly. "Can I come over for a minute?"

"Sure—if you're really quiet. I've got someone in the downstairs bedroom."

"Will do!"

Emma threw on a robe and went downstairs to meet her friend, opening the door as carefully as she could and ushering Ava in, hoping they weren't waking Noah. She beckoned Ava to follow her upstairs where they could talk.

"What's that?" she asked when they'd made it to her third-floor bedroom and she'd shut the door behind them, gesturing to the bag Ava was carrying.

"A clothesline. A very special clothesline." Ava took

out the old-fashioned line-and-pulley system Emma had seen only on television shows and held it up. "I've got one rigged between my house and Penelope's. I thought you might like one, too."

"For hanging clothes?" Emma wasn't sure she wanted her guests to see her unmentionables strung up between the houses.

"For sending each other bottles of wine, mostly." Ava pulled out a sturdy cloth bag. "Once you attach this to the rope and get the pulley system set up, you can send it back and forth between our houses easy as pie."

"I love it." Emma saw the possibilities immediately and was thrilled to have the kind of neighbor who would think of such a thing.

"We won't wake your guests up by installing it now. I'll come back later and do it."

"I'll send you some muffins tomorrow morning when it's up and running," Emma promised.

"My evil plot is working." Ava grinned. "I'll figure out something to send you back. Is everything else going okay? How's that guy you've got staying here. Is he creepy?"

"Not at all," Emma assured her. "He's the opposite of creepy."

"Interesting. That could hold its own challenges, though," Ava said. "I'd better get back. I'm supposed to meet Penelope. See you later."

"I'll walk you out. Thanks." Impulsively, Emma gave

Ava a hug. Ava returned it warmly. They tiptoed downstairs again, Emma feeling like she was a teenager as she let Ava out the door.

In the kitchen, she got to work, pulling out eggs, sausages, fruit, juice and more to set up the buffet she would offer her guests when they woke up. She set up the waffle iron and whipped together the batter, making sure it would be extra fluffy.

When a text came through on her phone, she smiled to see it was from Penelope.

Heard you're installing a clothesline delivery system! Want to join Ava and me for our dawn walk tomorrow?

Love to, Emma texted back.

Meet us in the Cliff Garden—that's where we start from. See you tonight at sundown for drinks. If you're busy, at least come upstairs and wave to us.

Will do, Emma promised her.

The pad of doggy footsteps warned her she wouldn't be alone long. Emma crouched down when Winston appeared.

"Is your dad up already?" she asked him, giving the retriever some love. The door to the back bedroom had been closed a minute ago. Noah must have gotten up at least long enough to let Winston out.

Noah didn't appear, so Emma washed her hands and got back to work as Winston kept going toward the sliding door she'd opened to the deck. He went outside and lay down, yawning broadly.

No one else in the house seemed to be awake. Emma surveyed the room. Brightview was already cozy when she'd moved in, but now it was fresh and welcoming. The buffet breakfast was spread enticingly on the counter that separated kitchen from the rest of the room. Outside, she'd spread the large picnic table with a turquoise-and-white-checked cloth that set off Angela's blue dishes perfectly. She'd decorated the table with a fresh bouquet of flowers in a lovely vase, a basket of linen napkins, and ceramic mugs holding knives, spoons and forks.

The day was lovely. The food she'd serve was impeccable. She was good at all of this. An accomplished businesswoman. Which made it hard to accept she'd lost Food to You Fast over problems she should have been able to solve. Jordan's constant need for supervision and his way of cutting corners had tripped her up, along with the mountain of debt she carried through no fault of her own.

Which led her to thinking about her dad again.

When her phone buzzed, she grabbed it gratefully, barely registering it was her sister calling before she accepted it.

"Finally," Emma said. "I've been calling you for days."

A pause. "I've been busy."

"Well, it's so good to hear your voice. I thought you'd come down to stay with me before now. You have to see Brightview again. It's so beautiful. And the garden—it's just like I remember."

"Emma—"

Emma knew if she didn't confess to Ashley what she'd done, she'd lose her nerve. "I have something to tell you. It's about Brightview."

"Emma," Ashley said again. "Let me go first."

"It really is beautiful here, and it's in such a good location. I'd forgotten the view."

"Emma, I need to tell you—"

"I'm staying. Here at Brightview. I've already booked guests into the bed-and-breakfast. In fact, the whole place is booked right now, and one of my guests is staying for six months! But I'll make space for you anytime, and I'll split all the profits with you, even if I'm doing the work. If you want, you can quit your job and come live here, too. It would be like when we were kids." Emma broke off, running out of breath. Her heart was beating hard as she waited for her sister's reaction.

"Like when we were kids?" Ashley repeated. "You're—staying? Are you kidding me? What do you mean you've already got guests? I thought we agreed to sell."

Emma sucked in a breath. "I—"

"What about paying off our debts? What about starting fresh?"

"I can do this. I know I can make Brightview a going concern. It supported Nana Angela all her life." Emma faltered. "Ashley, you have to visit."

The line went dead. Emma pulled the phone away from her ear and checked, but it was clear her sister had hung up. Remorse swooped through her. She'd done this all wrong. She'd let her excitement carry her away. Why hadn't she slowed down, written up a proposal and a business plan and then sent it to Ashley? Her sister liked everything done right. She'd want to see all the information before she made a decision. She didn't make leaps from one idea to another the way Emma did.

Was Ashley going to shut her down?

"Morning."

Emma clapped a hand to her chest when Noah walked in. Winston gave a little woof of greeting from the deck but didn't get up.

"Morning," she managed to return, willing her pulse to return to normal.

"Everything all right?"

"Yes." She swallowed, set the phone down and got back to work. No matter what revenge Ashley might be planning, she needed to focus on her customers or it wouldn't matter what happened next. When she had a spare moment, she'd create that business plan and send it to Ashley. Maybe after she read it, her sister would have a change of heart. "Would you like a couple of waffles?" She willed her voice to sound calm, unsure if she was succeeding. If Noah noticed anything, he didn't pry.

"Absolutely." He walked to the sliding doors and

looked outside. "Beautiful day."

"Yes, it is," she said absently. Her hands were doing the required tasks to serve him his meal, but her mind was elsewhere. She'd hoped to repair her relationship with Ashley. Had she damaged it even further?

Who else could she talk to about the business? Ava and Penelope? Could they help her come up with a good plan?

Noah came back, plucked a homemade doughnut from a basket and took a bite. Closing his eyes, he moaned, an interesting sound that caught her attention. "Did you make this? If so, you are an amazing cook."

"I did and I am." The words came out more sharply than she'd intended, and she shut her mouth with a snap. She had to get a grip. She wasn't angry at Noah.

He opened his eyes again and looked at her curiously. "You sure nothing's wrong?"

"Everyone loves my cooking. I'm great at customer service, too." It was her superpower, which made what had happened with Food to You Fast that much harder to bear.

"And that's a problem?"

"I lost my business." Damn. She hadn't meant to tell him that. "A few months ago," she went on, pouring the waffle batter onto the iron and closing it. "I made some mistakes, the first being my choice of business partner."

"The right partner can make a business. The wrong one can doom it," he agreed.

He seemed interested in the topic. Did a surf bum know anything about business? Maybe he did, the way he was throwing money around booking a room for six months. "My company was a failure," she said baldly. "I lost everything."

His brows went up, and he made a show of looking slowly around the lovely room they stood in. "You did a pretty spectacular job of losing everything. Looks like you failed your way right into a dream. You own this place, right?"

She nodded. "You know what? You're right." When the waffle iron beeped, she opened it, fished out the waffles and put them on a plate, which she handed to Noah. "I'm really lucky. If I was smart, I'd forget all about the past."

NOAH WANTED TO ask more questions, but his phone buzzed in his pocket. Assuming her other guests would be down for their breakfasts soon, he set his plate on the counter, walked outside to the deck and answered the call.

It was his brother, Andrew.

"Morning."

"Morning." Andrew sounded chipper. "I just emailed you the first set of plans. Can't wait to hear what you think about them."

"Can't wait to look. I'm away from my laptop right now."

"Come on, Noah—I've been working night and day on these."

"You haven't even seen the site yet." He was thinking about those waffles he'd left inside. They looked delicious.

"I worked from the map you sent me. Open the plans on your phone. You'll be able to get the idea."

Noah did so. The plans were tiny on the small screen, but he could see immediately his brother had designed an impressive house.

An impressively *large* house.

"It's huge," he said, lifting the phone to his ear again.

"Five thousand square feet spread over three levels. It's going to be stunning."

"I'm sure it is." What the hell was he going to do with five thousand square feet? He was single, for god's sake.

"Six bedrooms, a great room, a games room that will leave you speechless, a theater." Andrew was off and running, ticking over all the details. Noah tried to follow along, consulting the plans now and then, keeping notes in his mind of problems to address later. "Temperature controlled storage for five hundred bottles of wine," Andrew said, "and wait until you get a load of the deck. It features an entire outdoor kitchen, complete with a pizza oven. And don't forget the infinity pool."

Noah wasn't much of a wine drinker. Give him a craft beer any day of the week. And a pizza oven? He could run a barbecue, but other than that, he wasn't much of a cook.

"Noah?" Emma called from inside the kitchen. "Your waffles are getting cold. Want me to make you a new batch?"

"That's not necessary." He moved inside and juggled his phone while he helped himself to butter, syrup and raspberry sauce. The breakfast spread was lavish, and soon his plate was overflowing with eggs, sausages and sliced fruit, too.

"Who's that?" his brother asked.

"My landlady. Emma." He sent a smile her way and moved back outside just as the women flooded into the kitchen, oohing and aahing over the beautiful spread of food.

"Who are all those people?" Andrew demanded. "I hear voices."

"The other guests here at the B and B I told you about."

"Sounds like you're surrounded by women. Maybe I should come down there. I'm sure as hell not having any luck in Seattle."

"Anytime."

Andrew grunted. "Look over those plans. Send me a list of adjustments to make, although I think you're going to be hard-pressed to find anything I haven't put in this house already."

"That's for sure." Noah caught himself. He'd given

Andrew the go-ahead to design any house he wanted.

There was a silence on the other end. "You're not backing out on me, are you?"

"Absolutely not. Design the house you think is going to get the awards," Noah told him. He hung up, pocketed his phone and sat at the picnic table to eat.

By the time the women joined him, he was nearly done, but he couldn't stop thinking about the list of features his brother had included in his beach house. Who was going to use them?

Who was going to clean the thing, for that matter? Would he have to hire someone to come in? The thought made him cringe. He was trying to simplify his life. Cut back on responsibilities. Working at Maxwell Tech had kept him on a short leash. He didn't want any obligations hampering him from following his dreams now.

"Be right back," he told them as they settled in around him.

"Hurry up," Annie said. "We already miss you."

He waved her off, wondering again why he wasn't pursuing something being so obviously offered to him.

No time, he told himself. He needed to focus on getting his house built.

He grabbed his tablet from his room, went back outside and pulled up the plans on a larger screen.

"What's that?" Ginni asked. She leaned in to look over his shoulder.

"It's a house. What do you think?"

"It's amazing," she said a minute later after she'd scrolled through the plans. "That's a house fit for royalty."

"Let me see," Annie said, eager to join in. Ginni handed her the tablet, and everyone took their turn exclaiming over the designs. "Did you design this?" she asked Noah.

He shook his head, noting Emma was moving past to pick up empty plates and replenish juice and tea. "My brother did. What do you think?" He held out the tablet toward Emma when it was returned to him. She set down the teapot and took it.

A minute later, she whistled. "That's a heck of a house."

Annie was surveying him shrewdly. "Can *you* afford a house like that?"

Whoops. He didn't want to invite that kind of attention. "They're just plans," he said, evading her question. "And I'm off to the beach. What are you ladies up to?"

"We're going to the beach this morning, too. We'll do some shopping later on," Annie told him. "See you down there."

"See you." He whistled for Winston and eagerly escaped inside. Somehow, Emma had slipped in ahead of him and was scraping a stack of plates she'd gathered. She looked up when she saw him, but her gaze slid past him to the window at the side of the house.

"Oh, no," she said.

Noah turned to see what was wrong. There was a clear view from here of the lot next door. His lot. Pathways twisted among garden beds. A bench faced the ocean. An older woman sat there, her back to them, shoulders rigid. She was probably staring at the waves, but something told Noah she wasn't seeing them.

That was a woman in pain.

Emma sprang into action, fetching a blue plate from the cupboard, slipping a muffin and a couple of slices of fruit onto it, adding a knife, fork and cloth napkin, then filling a glass with water.

"Can you get the door?" she asked him.

"Sure." Noah hurried ahead of her down the hall, opened the door and followed her outside. Emma stepped sure-footedly across the gravel parking area to the street, and he moved ahead of her again to get the gate that led into the garden. He wondered why she hadn't simply gone out through the sliding glass doors, across the deck and yard to the garden. Probably hadn't wanted her other guests to notice what she was doing, he decided.

"How on earth did Nana manage this on her own?" she asked under her breath but moved away down the path before he could ask her what she meant.

Noah hung back when it was clear she would join the woman on the bench, but he didn't leave. Instead, he busied himself pacing the paths slowly, pretending to examine a bush or flower now and then while Emma began a conversation with her. He caught only a few words here and there, but he gathered the stranger had lost her husband recently and was finding it difficult to know what her purpose was now. She didn't have children.

Emma sat on the bench with her hands clasped in her lap, her gaze darting here and there, although she was listening carefully. Noah didn't think she knew this woman, and it seemed to him she was struggling to find the words to answer her.

Should he try to help?

When the stranger stopped talking, the silence between the two women stretched out uncomfortably long until a light breeze picked up, setting chimes hanging from a nearby tree tinkling. A chill traced over Noah's neck, although he couldn't say why. Emma, who'd cocked her head at the sound of the chimes, straightened. "What would your husband say, do you think, if he were here?"

The woman tapped her chin with one finger. "He would tell me to get off my bottom and be helpful at the garden."

"Which garden?" Emma asked. "This one?"

"No, the one near our house—the Giving Garden. It's open to everyone but especially those who don't have homes of their own. I used to teach people to grow some of their own food. Some of my students even went on to get jobs at nurseries and nearby farms. When Arthur got ill, I stopped volunteering."

"That sounds like a lovely program." Emma looked around as if considering the possibilities.

"No, dear, you can't replicate the program here in the Cliff Garden." The woman patted her arm. "This place has another purpose, and it's served it admirably today. I feel better already. Thank you, Angela."

"Emma," Emma corrected her, frowning and leaning closer in concern.

"Of course." The woman chuckled. "Don't worry, I'm not losing my memory. It was only a slip of the tongue. I've been thinking about your grandmother ever since you sat down. You are Angela's granddaughter, aren't you? I heard a rumor you'd finally come to stay at Brightview."

"I am."

"Well, I'm glad to see you following in her footsteps. Colette Rainer has done an admirable job keeping up the place, but the garden isn't the same without a resident wise woman to offer advice and comfort."

"Oh, I'm not very wise," Emma hurried to assure her.

The woman patted her again. "Wise enough. You'll do fine." She stood up.

"Don't forget your muffin." Emma offered her the plate.

"Thank you. I'll return your dishes tomorrow."

"No hurry."

When she had taken the plate and gone, Emma rose to her feet slowly. Noah came to meet her, and together they turned toward Brightview.

"I thought you were going surfing," she said.

"I wanted to make sure everything was okay. How did you know that woman wanted to talk?"

"That's the Trouble Bench," Emma said. "It's been there for a hundred years. There's always been someone at Brightview keeping watch."

"Trouble Bench, huh?" This time they followed a path straight to Brightview's deck rather than going around to the street. A bench that had been there for a hundred years? That was a lot of history.

"That's right." Emma seemed to relax the closer she got to her house. Had she been afraid she wouldn't know how to help? He thought she'd done a good job. She nodded to the women still gathered at the picnic table and entered Brightview through the sliding glass doors. "I'm so glad I moved here. This place is so special."

"You've got a terrific house," he agreed, following her to the kitchen.

"Seems like you're going to have a terrific house, too," she said as she began to shift dishes to the sink. "Where are you going to build that mansion you showed me earlier?" Her teasing tone caught him off-guard, and he must have shown his surprise because she laughed. "You don't strike me as the kind of guy who moons over house plans for fun."

He nodded ruefully. "You're right. It is going to be my house."

"Are you building it in town?"

Noah's heart sank as he thought about the Trouble Bench and the beautiful garden surrounding it. When he'd purchased the lot, he'd hardly even noticed the garden since he'd been in such a hurry to make sure he didn't lose it to someone else. Now he wondered how he could have missed how carefully it had been tended. He remembered how dark it had been when he'd arrived to scope out the place. How little time he'd spent there before calling the real estate agent and preparing an offer. He'd always thought of a lot as something empty waiting to be claimed and built on, but Emma loved the Cliff Garden. Apparently, many other people did, too.

"Noah?" Emma prompted. "Are you building your house in town?"

"I'm… building it next door."

EMMA STOPPED IN the middle of the room and faced Noah. She was still buzzing from her first successful encounter with the Trouble Bench, but his words cut right through the glow of pride she felt. She couldn't have heard him right. "Next door where?" Ava lived in the blue house next door. On the other side of the Cliff Garden stood an enormous residence she remembered from when she was a child. Was he going to tear it down?

"You have to understand, I bought the lot before I knew you. I didn't even notice the garden. My realtor got the heads-up about the land and sent the information straight to me. I'd made it clear this was the area where I wanted to build…." He trailed off. "Emma?"

Was her mouth hanging open? She thought it might be. Emma pulled herself together, fear making her voice shake. He couldn't mean…

"Are you talking about the Cliff Garden? You can't build anything there. I own that land!"

Noah pulled back. "You can't own it. I mean… I bought it, Emma. It was listed a week and a half ago. The sale is still in escrow, but when it clears, it's mine."

"Who on earth did you buy it from?" She didn't understand any of this. He had to have made a mistake. There was no way he could buy a lot that wasn't for sale, unless….

She remembered what Ashley had said earlier. "There's something I need to tell you." But how could Ashley sell a property they owned together? How could she sell the garden without selling Brightview, too? They were part and parcel—weren't they?

"I own the Cliff Garden," she asserted. "Someone scammed you."

"I don't think so." Noah pulled out his phone. "I never met the owner, but I have her name right here. It's on the documents." He searched a minute longer.

"Ashley Miller." Noah looked up. "Miller. That's your last name, right? Emma Miller? Are you—?

"Ashley's my sister," she said automatically, "but she can't sell you the Cliff Garden. We own this property jointly, Brightview and the garden. It's all one and the same."

Noah looked down at his phone again, then at the Cliff Garden. "If that's true, I'm in a real mess. Are you sure you've got that right?"

He didn't sound particularly perturbed, and Emma's horror grew as she realized she might be the one who was wrong. Colette's letter had said she and Ashley inherited Brightview and the Cliff Garden. Emma assumed she meant they'd inherited both together.

Had she misunderstood?

Ashley always took her to task for skimming important documents.

"There's been a mistake." But she sounded unsure to her own ears.

"No mistake on my end." Noah was still watching her closely. "I worked with a realtor. Did everything by the book. Believe me, I had no idea the property meant anything to anyone. It was listed as a building lot, and I paid more than full price for it. Didn't want to lose out to someone else—it's hard to find one of those in Seahaven."

Tears pricked Emma's eyes. She fumbled to pull out her phone, but there was no text message from Ashley she'd somehow missed. No unopened email. Her sister had never said a word about listing the lot for sale.

"Emma—I'm sorry you didn't know," Noah said.

When he reached for her, she batted away his hand, afraid the tears that pricked at her eyes might spill over.

"There's been a mistake," she repeated. "I need to make a call. I'll figure this out."

"There hasn't been a mistake," he reiterated as she fumbled with her phone again. "That's why I booked a room here for six months. So I can keep an eye on the build."

She wasn't a violent woman, so the impulse to push Noah across the room and out the door took her by surprise.

"It'll be a high-end house. You saw the plans," he rushed on. "I promise I'll do everything I can to be a good neighbor."

Emma couldn't stop herself. She shoved her phone back in her pocket and grabbed his arm.

"Emma?" Noah allowed her to drag him down the short hall and out the door. "Where are we going?"

She kept walking without a word.

NOAH KNEW IF he dug in his heels, there was no way Emma could budge him. He was helpless against her distress, however. She pulled him outside through the main door, no doubt wanting to avoid the other guests, who were still lounging on the deck. Tears slid silently down her cheeks as she retraced their earlier steps, bringing him out to the street and back to the little gate in the white picket fence that led to the Cliff Garden—the same style of picket fence that edged the entire property—house and garden alike—he realized now. Once through the gate, she waved a hand at the winding pathways and raised beds.

Now that he wasn't blinded by thoughts of the house he'd build here, or curiosity about Emma's visit to the Trouble Bench, he could see the care and thought that had gone into planning the extensive garden. He noticed more benches placed just so to take in the spectacular views. The whimsical touches—a fairy house here, painted bird houses there, a tiny "library" next to a bench of its own. As early as it was in the season, flowers were blooming, and the air was filled with their scents mixed with that of the sea.

There were other people in the garden, too. A couple bent over a butterfly perched on a flower. A mother and two children sat reading a book they'd found in the library. A young man played guitar softly on one of the benches tucked into a corner. Had he been blind to them before? Or too busy watching Emma?

"My grandmother inherited that house and this garden from her mother," she said, jabbing a finger first at Brightview and then down at the dirt on which they stood. "Both are over a hundred years old. She tended this land her entire life, exactly the way her mother and grandmother and great-grandmother did. This is a special place. A magical place. Everyone in this neighborhood knew Angela, and they knew they could come here and find peace, no matter what was wrong in their lives."

He could accept that. It was peaceful here with a bird trilling on a bush nearby, the soft ocean breeze playing around them.

"She was special. She always knew what to say. People would come here crying, and she'd have them planting bulbs or pulling weeds, talking through their troubles, finding solutions they didn't even know were possible. You know what everyone says about this garden? They say it's healed a hundred broken hearts."

Every word was a dagger, accusing him of something he hadn't known he'd done. "It's a great garden," he said helplessly.

"If you can see that, then you know you can't destroy it," she cried. "Let me buy it back from you. I'll pay full price, I swear. You can buy another lot."

"There are no more lots. Not for sale. I tried to buy something else, and it was gone before I could make an offer. That's why I jumped on this one so fast."

"Then build somewhere else!" Emma held her hands out wide. "You can't ruin the Cliff Garden!"

Noah didn't know what to say. He couldn't explain what he owed to Andrew, and he wasn't sure he should have to. The land had been for sale. He'd bought it. He'd done nothing wrong.

But her distress tugged at him. He wasn't blind; he could see this place was special. He had a soft spot for his grandparents' farm in Ohio. It was hard when property passed out of a family's hands.

Emma stared at him, her eyes growing wider when it was clear he didn't mean to answer.

"I've—got guests to tend to." She strode away quickly. It didn't take a genius to realize her tears were falling fast now. Two women just entering the garden stopped and questioned her worriedly, but she passed them by without answering. They both watched Emma rush to the back door of Brightview and disappear inside.

"That poor young lady. If the garden couldn't comfort her, it must be bad," the first woman said. She looked around her. "I swear this place has saved my sanity more than once."

"Me, too." They wandered past him, deep in conversation.

Noah sat down on the closest bench, all his anticipation for this venture gone. He doubted Emma had the money to buy back the land, even if he wanted to sell it, which he didn't. Who knew when another lot like this would come up again?

Was there somewhere else he could find a building lot that would meet Andrew's needs? Up in the mountains, maybe? Homes up there could be dramatic, placed among redwood groves or in clearings in the forest, but they couldn't hold a candle to an oceanfront build, and he didn't even want to consider another town like Santa Cruz or Carmel. Seahaven was his place. Always had been. He might not have lived here since he was a kid, but it was his go-to surf and escape spot the entire time he worked at Maxwell Tech. Besides, oceanfront property was scarce everywhere.

Noah shook his head. He couldn't back down now.

Which meant he'd better kiss goodbye any idea of a relationship with Emma—even a friendly one.

Even if he didn't want to.

CHAPTER 4

THANK GOD HER guests had made themselves scarce for the afternoon, Emma thought several hours later as she gave the deck a final pass with a broom and surveyed the lawn, which would need a trim soon. When Ashley hadn't returned her repeated phone calls and texts asking for an explanation, she'd given up, run loads of laundry, returned fresh towels to the guest rooms, done some prep work for tomorrow's breakfast and driven to the grocery store and bank.

All the while her thoughts spun with disbelief and her stomach ached with the coming loss. The Cliff Garden—gone.

Angela's legacy destroyed.

Emma knew she had to stop it, but she didn't know how. Should she leak the information to the local paper? Post on the "locals only" social media sites? Go knocking door to door up and down the streets? Neighbors would be up in arms if they knew.

She wasn't sure it was smart to go after Noah so directly, though. Especially before she talked to Ashley.

She pulled out her phone and tried her sister again.

"What?" Ashley snapped when she picked up.

"You know what." She forced herself to speak more calmly. Ashley could easily hang up again. "How could you sell the Cliff Garden? How could you even list property we own jointly?"

"We don't own it jointly." Ashley confirmed the worst of her fears. "You got Brightview. I got the Cliff Garden. I get to do whatever I want with it."

"Then why were you acting like you could force me to sell Brightview?" So much for keeping calm. Emma could hear the stridency in her voice and knew Ashley would react to it.

"I shouldn't have to force you. You should see it's the right thing to do! No more debts—ever. Isn't that the most important thing?"

"I can make a go of the bed-and-breakfast and then pay my debts. I know I can."

Ashley made a noise like she'd stepped in something noxious. "You always know you can do something, and then it turns out you can't. Just like Dad."

"Stop saying that. I'm nothing like him!"

She could almost hear Ashley counting to ten. "You sure about that?"

Emma was glad no one was present to see the flush creeping up her neck into her cheeks. Her sister always knew how to hit her where it hurt. Her entrepreneurship was something she was proud of. She'd never been reckless—

"Food to You Fast wasn't exactly a breakout success, was it? You scraped by for years and then lost it all. What makes you so sure you'd do better with a bed-and-breakfast? Why can't you see that it's safer to work for someone else? Let them take all the risk while you reap all the benefits."

The thought of losing Brightview, going to work in someone else's kitchen, made Emma shrink inside. She'd worked in restaurants for years before breaking out on her own, and she'd hated most of it. She needed latitude to try ideas—

"I'm not going to bail you out when you fail again," Ashley went on when she didn't answer. "I'm done cleaning up other people's messes."

"You've never bailed me out. I've never asked you to. Who paid the bills while you finished community college? Did I ever ask you to reimburse me? Of course not. And when Food to You Fast went south, I never asked you for help. I paid those debts."

"But you still owe a bundle, just like I do."

She had no answer to that. Of course she did. That wasn't her fault. It wasn't Ashley's fault, either.

"Brightview is a home and business all in one. What could be better than that?" She remembered the reason for her call. "But if you sell the Cliff Garden, you're diminishing the value of my property. The garden is partly on my lot. Besides, you loved that garden, Ashley.

Why would you sell it?"

"I loved it when I was six, before I knew what the world was really about. I'm buying a partnership in the company I work for. It's going to cost… a lot, but once I do, I'm golden. I'll have a job for the rest of my life. I'll be the youngest partner they've ever had," she added with pride. "And I'm going to pay off my condo in full. There will still be a little left over for a good start on my retirement accounts."

There it was, Emma thought, the trifecta of her sister's aspirations. Steady job, paid-for house, retirement funded.

"What about the Cliff Garden? Don't you remember working with Nana Angela? Tending the flower beds? All the games we played there?"

"I remember that Nana Angela ditched us," Ashley said doggedly. "Where was she when we needed help?"

"She was here, tending her house and garden, building something of value to leave to us."

Ashley scoffed at that. "She didn't allow us to inherit it for ten years! Who does that kind of thing? We needed help a decade ago."

Over a hundred hearts healed.

She didn't realize she'd said the phrase out loud until Ashley said, "Oh, give me a break." There was a little hitch in her voice, though, one only Emma would notice.

Over a hundred hearts healed. That's what everyone said about the Cliff Garden, and Ashley had said the phrase more than anyone else the summer they'd spent there. It made the grown-ups laugh, but Emma knew why her sister had clung to the sentiment.

Their hearts had been breaking. Their mother, the center of their family, had been fading in a way she and Ashley couldn't understand. Looking back, she pieced it together that her mother was diagnosed and went through chemo that spring but hadn't bounced back afterward. They'd come to California so Nana Angela could care for all three of them.

"Gardens don't save hearts," Ashley said. "They certainly don't save lives."

"Nothing could have saved Mom," Emma said softly.

"I know that," Ashley snapped, "but Nana Angela could have saved us afterward. We lost our house. We lost everything—twice!"

"That wasn't Angela's fault, and it wasn't her job to save us. Dad should have done that."

"Dad wasn't capable of doing that."

Maybe not. What did it matter now, anyway? She missed both her parents, and she missed Ashley, too—the girl she used to be. The bright, loving, creative girl who'd been her constant companion.

Her mother's death had begun her sister's transformation. Her father's betrayal had made it so much worse.

But it was her own choice of entrepreneurship over a safe career that turned Ashley into the brittle stranger she'd become.

"Grow up," Ashley said. "Sell Brightview. Pay your debts. Buy a condo. Get a job. Start fresh." And she hung up.

"I GUESS I can't blame you for liking it here," Mark said the following day. He and Noah had met at the beach near Brightview for an early morning surf session. Now they paddled back to shore and sat on the beach, their surfboards planted in the sand nearby. Winston sat beside Noah. He'd stood sentry on land patiently while they'd played in the waves, then wagged his tail happily at the men's return. They'd seen Greg and a few of the other Surf Dads, and Noah had received an invitation to join them for one of their potlucks in a couple of weeks.

"I don't have any kids," he'd protested.

"We'll give you a grace period. Just get working on it," Greg joked.

Noah figured he'd go and pass out some business cards, if nothing else. He appreciated the locals reaching out to him. Surfers could be territorial, but this group seemed far more mature than some he'd come across over the years.

"Glad you could come down today," he told Mark, linking his arms around his knees as he stared out at the waves pounding the shore.

"Sounded like you needed some moral support."

"Guess I do." He heaved a sigh. Normally after a

session in the waves, he was calm, able to take a long view on things. Pleasantly tired in his body and peaceful in his mind.

Not today. His thoughts were going round and round, tangling with each other. Emma had been avoiding him since their conversation the previous day, and he'd finally texted Mark to see if his friend could get away for the morning. He'd been a little surprised Mark was willing to drop everything and come.

"I thought everything would be easier here," Noah went on. "I was wrong." This situation with Emma was becoming more complicated than any mess he'd sorted out for Maxwell Tech.

A couple of girls in bikinis walked by. Mark watched them go, then adjusted the wedding band on his finger. "Problems at the building site?" he guessed.

"You could put it that way." Noah caught him up on the situation.

"So your landlady's sister sold the adjoining lot, and your landlady is upset. So what? There's nothing she can do about it. You bought it fair and square. Are you afraid she's going to go after you in some way?"

Mark was missing the most important part of the equation, which wasn't surprising. Noah hadn't explained that thoughts of his landlady were keeping him up at night, trying to figure out how to get closer to her.

Something in his expression must have given him away because Mark groaned. "No. Tell me you aren't hot for this woman. How old is she?"

"Late twenties?" Noah guessed.

Mark straightened. "And she owns an oceanside B and B here? She must be loaded."

Noah shook his head. "Barely holding on, as far as I can tell."

"Then she won't be able to take any legal action against you, not that she has any grounds. Leave her alone, man—are you trying to screw yourself?"

"I could buy another lot somewhere else." He should never have gotten out of the water. Everything was simple out on the waves.

"Build your house," Mark told him. "On the lot you already bought and paid for. Remember how hard it was to find that one? Who knows when something else will come up for sale at the beach? This woman, whoever she is, will get over it. Trust me."

Noah didn't think so.

"Show me Andrew's plans for the place. I'll bet it's amazing. It'll bring up the property value of your landlady's place, too. That ought to simmer her down."

Noah found his phone and pulled up the plans. He handed it to his friend. Mark was quiet as he went through them, zooming in and out to see the details, a furrow forming in his brow as he went.

"That's a big house," he said quietly, handing the phone back. "How does it sit on the lot?" He stood up. "Show me."

Noah got up and led the way to Brightview, where they dropped off their surfboards in Emma's shed, peeled off their wetsuits and took turns rinsing off in the outdoor shower. Dressed again, they approached the Cliff Garden. It was full of visitors today. Mark's eyebrows rose as he took in the various ways people were enjoying it. He kept quiet until they entered the gate and Noah pulled up the plans again. They took turns reading off the dimensions and pacing them out, trying not to draw attention to themselves. When they were done, Mark shook his head.

"This house is going to block a big section of your girl's view, not just ruin her grandmother's garden."

"Yep."

They surveyed the flower beds grimly. "From the looks of things, everyone in the neighborhood is going to hate you, too." Mark waved a hand to encompass all the other people in the garden.

"Yep."

"Doesn't mean you can't go ahead. It's your land." He didn't sound as confident as he had on the beach, though.

"I know." Noah couldn't help but turn to survey Brightview. Emma's other guests were back from their morning outing, talking and laughing. A minute later Emma appeared with a tray of drinks.

"That her?"

"Yes, it is."

Mark was silent a moment. When Noah turned, he found his friend studying him.

"You really like her." It was a statement, not a question.

Was it that obvious? He was doing his best to keep his impulses under control. "Emma? Yeah—I like her," he said.

"Like a summer fling kind of thing?" Mark asked hopefully.

Noah couldn't answer that. Emma wasn't someone you had a fling with, he knew that instinctively, and yet he still wanted her. Last night, tucked into his bedroom at the back of the house, he'd found himself imagining what it was going to be like living together for six months. Waking up and having breakfast with Emma. Talking to her about his day when he came home from the beach or some other adventure. Hanging out on the deck with her. Sharing meals. Chores.

He hadn't lived with a woman since his parents died, despite several serious relationships. He was anticipating the experience—even if she was mad as hell at him now.

His overactive imagination had supplied him with images of what it might be like, and he wondered if she might ever feel as attracted to him as he was to her—if she ever got over what he was doing to her grandmother's garden.

Would they sleep together?

Last night his mind had returned again and again to

that question until he'd needed to take care of things if he was ever going to fall asleep, but once his more carnal instincts were fulfilled and he'd dozed off, different images filled his head.

Creating a home with Emma. Going on a trip. Celebrating an anniversary.

Starting a family.

He'd woken this morning with the confused feeling something had been decided, even though he wasn't sure what. Why was his brain thinking about settling down so soon after the lesson he'd learned with Caitlyn? Noah had no idea. He could only suppose it was his age. He'd slain the dragon of career success. The obvious next step was marriage and children, even if it had never seemed obvious before.

He was supposed to be a free spirit now.

"Then you've got to make Andrew scale back this behemoth, for a start," Mark said as if Noah had replied. "That's your only hope."

Noah knew he was right… but he was afraid it wouldn't be enough.

"Come on—I'll take you to lunch," he told Mark.

EMMA PUT DOWN the binoculars and checked to see that none of the women on the deck had noticed what she was doing. She'd heard the outdoor shower running fifteen minutes ago and looked out to see Noah and his friend head for the Cliff Garden.

She'd snagged Angela's old binoculars off a nearby shelf and watched the two men progress down one of the garden's paths, stopping to chat. Since then she'd moved back and forth from the living room to the deck, keeping the women plied with snacks and then sneaking back inside to get a glimpse of the men. When Noah pulled out his phone and his friend started pacing straight lines, she knew instantly what they were doing—measuring out the dimensions of the house he intended to build.

He had a lot of nerve.

Both men looked toward her suddenly, and she guiltily set the binoculars down with a thump on the nearest window ledge. She hurried to the kitchen and grabbed a tray of drinks, hoping they hadn't been able to see her clearly enough through the window to know she'd been spying on them.

She spent the next few minutes chatting on the deck with the women, firmly establishing the "fact" in their minds that she'd been with them, not inside acting like a peeping Tom.

When Noah joined them there with his friend a few minutes later, her pulse leaped, and not only from surprise. The breadth of the man's shoulders and the way he moved did something to her insides—made her fluttery and on alert, despite her anger with him.

Judging by the smiles on the other women's faces, she wasn't the only one he affected.

"Noah," Annie cried, patting the seat next to her. "Join us."

"Just wanted to introduce my friend Mark Maxwell," Noah said smoothly. "We're heading out to eat in a minute."

Emma stood, and Mark came to shake her hand. His grip was warm and firm, and she had the feeling he was assessing her. Feeling slightly self-conscious, she gestured to the empty chairs nearby. "Please, have a seat."

"We've got to keep moving," Noah said firmly. "Mark has to get back to work."

"Give me a minute inside," Mark said to him.

"Bathroom's down the hall," Emma offered.

He waved his thanks and disappeared into the house.

"Do you have to go?" Annie whined at Noah.

Noah nodded. "Be back in a few hours." As he turned, Emma quickly gathered a few empty dishes and followed him inside.

"Have you thought about my offer?" she asked, catching up to him.

"Offer?"

"To buy back the Cliff Garden. I'll call the bank today to make an appointment to get a loan. I have the B and B to use as collateral."

"Look, I know you love that garden, but—"

"But what? Winner takes all? Is that what you're going to say? I can get the money," she repeated.

"Emma."

"Ashley made a mistake. She never should have listed it."

"Sounds like it was her decision to make," he said softly. True sympathy shone in his eyes, shaking her to the core. If he'd been mean about it, she could have railed against him. His kindness made her feel she'd already lost.

"Noah? You ready?" Mark asked from down the hall.

"Yes." He hesitated. Was it her imagination, or did he want to invite her to eat with them?

She took a step back. She wasn't falling for that trick. He'd ply her with food and drink and persuade her he had every right to ruin the Cliff Garden.

He was wrong. That garden was there long before either of them were born, and it would outlast them by a long shot.

She just had to figure out a way to save it.

A HALF HOUR later, washing fish tacos down with glasses of a local craft beer at Seahaven Brewery, Mark sat back in his booth seat.

"You're going to have to go through with it. You bought the lot, you told your brother he could design you a house. It's a shame you didn't realize earlier what that garden meant to the people around here. You'd better give something back to the community—donate to a local cause or something."

"This isn't what I wanted." Noah took a drink. "This is supposed to be my time to have fun. I'm supposed to hang out on the beach, throw parties, take photos, get a cover or two of my own, maybe. Not get into a battle with my next-door neighbor."

Mark stretched. Pulled out his phone and checked the time. "I really need to get on the road if I'm going to get anything done today." He considered Noah. "What if you invite Andrew for a visit? Introduce him to Emma. Show him the garden and explain the situation. Tell him he needs to get creative and preserve Emma's view, at least. And help redesign the boundary between the two properties so she isn't left with a mess."

It would be a compromise, Noah supposed. "I guess."

When their waiter dropped the bill on the table, Mark grabbed it. "I got this."

Outside, they stood by their vehicles. Mark had brought his car so he didn't have to backtrack to Brightview before getting on the highway.

"There's another way to skin this cat," he said.

"What's that?"

"Make Emma fall in love with you."

"You think she'll forgive me for obliterating her grandmother's garden if I'm dating her?" The idea was intriguing but not very realistic.

"You could dangle the possibility you'd like her to move into your brand-new beachside mansion someday."

Noah couldn't picture Emma in the stark, modern house his brother had designed.

"If we get together and then break up, it'll be worse than if we never were together at all, in the circumstances."

"You don't have to worry about that," Mark told him. "If you manage to make her like you, you won't break up."

"How the hell do you figure that?"

"The way you looked at her when you introduced me earlier. It was the look of a man who's identified his target and locked his sights on her. I've got five older brothers, remember? I saw each of them go through this before they got married. Then I did it myself."

"I just met Emma," Noah protested. "I haven't made any long-term decisions."

"Yes, you have. You just don't know it yet."

CHAPTER 5

THE KITCHEN SINK had a leaky faucet.

Emma had ignored its infrequent drips for a couple of weeks, but it had picked up speed in the past forty-eight hours, and she supposed it wasn't smart to ignore it much longer. Should she call a plumber or tackle it herself? Jordan used to handle this kind of thing. He was good at repairs, even if he'd been lousy at business.

She was almost grateful when the landline rang and prevented her from having to decide.

"It's me again," a familiar voice said.

"Colette?"

"Got it on your first try! Mind if I stop by? I'll bring food."

"That would be wonderful." She could finally ask some of the questions she'd been dying to have answered. She wasn't sure she had the heart to tell Colette about the Cliff Garden, though.

"Be there in a jiffy."

Emma spent the intervening time getting a load of

her clothes in the washing machine and looking over her finances in preparation for calling the bank. Sooner than she might have expected, Colette arrived, holding up a paper bag triumphantly.

"I got us curry from Spice Time, the best Indian food in town."

"Just what I was craving." Emma fetched two bowls and helped divvy up the meal, then led the way to the deck to eat.

"How are you settling in?" Colette asked. "The place looks wonderful."

"Thank you. So far it's a dream. My first guests are doing well. Mostly," she added.

"Hmm, trouble in paradise?" Colette took a bite of her curry. "Oh, this is as delicious as always."

Emma tried hers. "It is good," she agreed. "It's just…" She still wasn't ready to tell Colette that Ashley had sold the Cliff Garden. She didn't want to prejudice the older woman against her sister. "It's… one of the guests," she went on. "A man."

"Sounds interesting. What about him?"

"I kind of like him." Maybe that would divert Colette from the true problem.

"Is that so bad?"

"I don't think we have compatible views of the future." She definitely didn't agree with him ruining the Cliff Garden.

"That could be a problem." Colette thought it over.

"But maybe right now you should take it one day at a time. Things often have a way of working themselves out, don't you think?"

"Maybe." Emma thought about Ashley, how her sister never seemed to see anything from her point of view these days.

"You don't sound convinced."

"Sometimes two people are so different they can't even understand each other, let alone come to any kind of consensus. Especially when the other person is determined to tell you you're wrong no matter what you do."

Colette put her fork down and lifted a napkin to dab at her mouth. "Are we still talking about you and your mystery man, or someone you've known a little longer. Like… your whole life?"

Whoops. How had they gotten back to her problems with Ashley? She'd meant to talk about Noah. "You're good at this," she told Colette.

"I've had a lot of practice. I live with my daughter and granddaughter." Colette took a sip from her glass of water.

"Sometimes I don't see eye to eye with my sister." This was venturing on dangerous territory, and Emma wasn't sure how far she wanted to go with the topic, so she hurried on, bringing up a new thread. "Speaking of relatives, I can't help wondering what happened between my grandmother and my dad after Mom died. They didn't seem to see eye to eye, either." Maybe it was unfair to ask given that she'd met Colette only recently, but it was the kind of burning question it was hard to put off very long when you were in the vicinity of someone who could answer it.

"Angela tried. She really did." Colette picked up her fork again and poked her curry absently with it. "Your father was a stubborn man. And maybe"—she flicked a look up at Emma—"not an entirely well one?"

"You mean, was he depressed? Almost certainly so. I understand that now," Emma admitted. "When I was young, I didn't even question his behavior." When she grew older, she decided his grief over their mother's death must have been the root of all his problems. Ashley, on the other hand, figured once he'd realized he could get away with neglecting his responsibilities, he just kept going.

"I'm not sure depression encompasses everything that went on." Colette took another bite. Chewed and swallowed. "I don't want to speak ill of the dead."

Emma appreciated that, but she wanted answers, and Ashley never wanted to talk about their past. "Dad got a little… weird… after Mom's death. Reclusive, I guess you could say. He hid in his office or workshop all the time, depending on where we lived. We hardly saw him."

"Was he working?"

Was it Emma's imagination, or did she ask the question a little too nonchalantly? "Kind of. He was always on his computer, as far as I could tell. Ashley and I weren't allowed in there. I think… I think he was day trading and didn't want us barging in when he was in the middle of a transaction."

"Ah" was all Colette said.

A light breeze brushed her cheek. Emma concentrated on her food, but when a minute went by and Colette didn't guide the topic onto safer ground, she found herself saying, "He wasn't very good at it."

Colette gave her a sympathetic smile. "I don't think too many people are."

"Was that what Nana Angela and Dad fought about?"

"It went deeper than that." Colette set down her fork. "But it did start with the gambling problem Angela thought your dad had. She saw evidence of it right from the start, even though your mother tried to hide it, and when she spoke up, your dad made it clear she wasn't welcome at your house anymore. Angela didn't see much of you when you were young until that last summer when your mother had no choice but to bring you to Seahaven."

"Because she was sick," Emma filled in.

"That's right. I think she was making up for lost time, in a way. She and your grandmother had a summer together, at least, but Angela was devastated when you all returned to Florida and your mom passed away that fall. I think she lost her sense of perspective. She was mourning and very worried about you and Ashley. She went too far, I guess you could say."

"What did she do?" Emma was consumed with curiosity. She'd judged her grandmother as a child did a grown-up—all-knowing and all-powerful. Grown-ups didn't make mistakes.

"She asked for custody of you girls." Colette let her words sink in. "She thought your father couldn't handle raising you alone. She confronted him right after your mom's funeral. Told him it was what Audra would have wanted. She said she could devote herself to you girls in a way he couldn't. I think in the end, she lost her temper." Colette shook her head. "Your grandmother was a saint in so many ways, but she was also human. She told me later she knew it was unfair to blame Audra's illness on him, but she always felt he didn't take good enough care of your mother. Needless to say, your father said no."

Emma tried to picture the conversation. Her dad was a proud man—and a very, very stubborn one.

"She never came back," she said.

"He wouldn't let her," Colette told her. "He was furious. Maybe rightly so. Angela came home with her tail between her legs. We talked about the situation for weeks, hashing out every possible action to take next, but in the end she decided the only thing she could do was wait. Someday he'd change his mind or need help and then she'd have her chance."

The picnic table's rough wooden planks were warm where Emma's hands rested on them. She wasn't even pretending to eat anymore, too caught up in the story of her past. A chill traced down her spine as something she'd never understood suddenly made sense. "Is that what happened when I was eleven? She took her chance?"

"That's right." Colette turned away and studied the ocean. "Angela got an email, but not from your dad. From an old friend of your mother's who'd moved away from Florida but came back to visit her family and stopped by to check on you."

"I don't remember that." Emma was sure a visit like that would stand out—no one came to their place in those days.

"You wouldn't. She went to your old house first, found out it had been sold and managed to track you down to your new address. You have to understand, Angela hadn't received any communication from your dad in ages—she didn't know you'd moved, so this was the first she was hearing about it."

Emma remembered the ugly little rental house they'd moved to when she was ten and Ashley eight, a squat blue home that had left Emma aching for the tidy bungalow where she'd grown up. "I'm sure it didn't make a very good impression on her."

"It didn't," Colette confirmed. "There didn't seem to be anyone home, so she parked on the street and waited—until she ran out of time and couldn't wait anymore. Just as she was leaving, the two of you came around the corner. She wrote that you were both skinny as rails, but even so, your clothes were too small, and Ashley's were too big. Neither of you looked entirely clean. You were both wearing braids, but it was clear they'd been done by a child. You walked right by and into the house. Not a grown-up in sight. She couldn't stay and investigate further because she had a plane to catch, but she told Angela someone had to do something."

Emma found she couldn't look up from her plate, and her throat was thick with the memories. After her mother died, she'd tried to take her place when it became clear no one else would. Her father slept all day. When he was up, he stared at his computer screen. He never answered the door. Rarely went out until their need for groceries was desperate. She was the one who tidied up the house, made mac and cheese for Ashley, did the wash when she remembered, but she wasn't very good at it, and her father never listened when she told him she was growing out of her things. Ashley always complained her braids weren't straight, but Emma didn't have the dexterity to do them any better. Ashley was the one who'd eventually learned to be good at things like that.

"Angela thought long and hard about what to do," Colette said. "She wanted to swoop in and take you away, of course, but she knew your father would fight her tooth and nail, so she tried another tactic."

Emma nodded. For the first time, events were becoming clear. "She gave him the money to buy the peach house."

Colette smiled. "Is that what you called it?"

"It was the obvious name," Emma said, trying to return her smile but not sure if she succeeded. She didn't know Nana Angela had done that. She and Ashley assumed their father had made the money himself.

"Angela hoped her gift would turn things around for you and your father," Colette said. "She meant for you to have a safe home and enough money to pay the bills for years."

Emma couldn't prevent the sound that escaped from her throat.

Colette reached over and patted her hand. "Angela's second mistake," she said softly, "was giving it to him all at once."

Emma remembered the joy she'd felt when she'd first set eyes on the peach house—and the utter horror of the day they lost it.

Colette gave her hand a squeeze and let go. "Angela never forgave herself for what happened."

"She still didn't come."

"She thought your father would invite her to stay after she helped him, but the invitation never came," Colette said softly. "She'd try to call and find your phone number had changed. She'd write emails and send cards but never hear back. As soon as the money was in his hands, your father went right back to threatening her if she came near you. It was a mess. She consulted a lawyer, of course, but he pointed out that you were living high on the hog in your new house now, and it would be hard to call you neglected."

He was right. Around the time they moved into the peach house, her father had finally purchased them new clothes, as well as their first phones and laptops. Ashley discovered all the video tutorials online about hairstyles, makeup, clothing and homemaking, and they'd quickly increased their skills. Their father's office was right off the dining room. If anyone had come to check on them, he would have been home—gambling all their money away on day trading. When he finally couldn't pay the bills anymore, they'd moved a third time to the shabbiest house of all. That's where they'd lived until she left home.

"She did call CPS several years later," Colette went on. "After your father ran out of cash and called to ask for more."

"And when they came, they found two perfectly happy teenage girls in a small and ramshackle but tidy home, who explained all the ways their perfect father doted on them," Emma said in a monotone. By then, she and Ashley were old enough to know about foster care—and know they wanted no part of it. As bad as things were at home, they weren't that bad. When a woman showed up asking questions, they'd joined forces to run her off.

"That's right." Colette sighed. "I think Angela gave up then. You were fifteen, Ashley thirteen. It was clear you were conscientious about raising your sister, and both of you were intelligent. Your father was keeping a roof over your head, even if it wasn't a very nice one. She decided to wait three more years and contact you when you were eighteen to establish a relationship separate from your father's influence. Unfortunately, her health was failing."

"And she died," Emma finished.

"And she died," Colette echoed. "Your grandmother loved you your whole life, Emma, and she would have been there if she could. She was so sorry not to get to know you better."

"I'm sorry, too." Emma swallowed past the lump in her throat. She'd missed Nana Angela all this time. Had always wondered why she was so loving the summer they'd spent with her and so absent ever since.

"Let's leave it at that for today," Colette said. "I hope that in running Brightview you'll get a sense of the woman your grandmother was."

"I think I am already," Emma said. She packed up the remains of the food and cleared the table while Colette gathered her purse.

"I hope we can meet again soon," Colette told her on her way out the door. "As friends."

"Of course." But as she closed the door, her head was spinning with everything she'd just learned. Her grandmother hadn't abandoned them after all. Through those lonely, hard years, there had been an adult who wanted to care for them.

And her father had prevented it.

Anger, sure and fierce, swept through her. She could have grown up at Brightview instead of in the cheerless, lonely houses her father found for them. She could have known what it was like to have someone around who could see her—love her—

No use whining about the past, she told herself sternly, shutting down that train of thought. It was done, and nothing could change it. She was healthy and safe. She had a home and a business.

The drip of the kitchen faucet caught her attention again, and she focused on it gratefully. That was what she needed to worry about, not the mistakes her father made in the past.

She called two plumbers, asked for quotes and decided she'd better try to fix it herself before she booked an appointment. Three do-it-yourself videos and one trip to the hardware store later, she was about to dive in when Noah returned from lunch.

"What's going on?" he asked when he spotted her crouched near the sink, peering into the cabinets beneath it to try to identify the water shutoff.

"Leaky faucet. It's under control. Go about your

business."

"I don't have any business today." He came to crouch next to her. "Have you fixed a faucet before?"

"Lots of them," she lied. Noah's proximity was making her nervous about her ability to pull off this task. He had capable hands. A calm sense to him that he knew what he was doing, while she was making it up as she went along. He pointed to a handle.

"That's the shutoff for the water."

"I just said I know what I'm doing."

He studied her, and she couldn't help looking back. Up close, his lashes were dark and thick, framing eyes that pierced straight through her. He had to know she was lying. What would he do about it?

"I was raised a bit old-fashioned," he said conversationally. "Which means when a woman's doing a dirty job, I'm going to take it over whether she likes it or not. It's not a dig at your capabilities or an attempt to impinge on your independence. It's more like a chance to show off. Can you live with that?"

He nudged her out of the way, looked over the tools she'd gathered, frowned and picked up one of the parts she'd bought from the hardware store. "This isn't right. Come on, let's return it and get the one we need."

"I can do this myself." This was the man who was going to destroy Nana Angela's garden. She couldn't let him repair her faucet.

"I know you can. I just want to do it with you." He

stood up and held out a hand. "Come on."

With a gusty sigh, Emma took his hand and allowed him to help her up. "I'm trying to hate you, you know."

"Believe me, I know." He looked around. Located the bag and receipt from the hardware store on the counter and put the offending part back in it. "You can tell me how much you loathe me on the drive."

NOAH WAS PLEASED with how many opportunities he found to connect with Emma on their short trip to the store. He took her hand whenever he could get away with it. Guided her through the aisles until they found the part they needed, then to the till, where they negotiated the exchange. He regaled her with stories of his youth and how his father had taken every opportunity he could to teach his sons practical skills.

"He must be very proud of you," Emma said when they were riding home.

"Well, maybe," Noah said. "He passed away when I was a teenager. Both my parents did. There was a car accident."

She was silent a minute, and he hoped she didn't think he was fishing for sympathy.

"My mom passed away when I was young, too," she finally said. "I still miss her—a lot."

"Miss my folks, too."

They didn't talk for the rest of the ride. Once they were back in the kitchen, Noah was desperate to lighten the mood. He didn't want her to think he wallowed around in old memories all the time. He set the bag on the counter and stripped off his shirt.

"What are you doing?" Emma gaped at him. Noah suppressed a smile as he flexed a muscle or two. All that desk work over the past decade had left him aching with restlessness each night, so he'd had one of those fancy all-in-one gyms installed in his condo and used it for hours every night. He'd sold it before coming to Seahaven. Who needed the gym when you had the great outdoors?

"I'm preparing to work hard. Wouldn't want my shirt to get in the way of excellence."

Emma snorted. "No, we wouldn't want that, would we?"

He got to work, feeling her gaze on him, and he hoped she was thinking of other times when she might see him shirtless. Using the power of suggestion this way might be unfair, but he decided he was going to use every trick in the book to get Emma's attention.

Mark was right. He'd set his sights on her, and he meant to accomplish his objective.

When he stood up fifteen minutes later, job finished, he was gratified to catch Emma's gaze lingering on his biceps. He moved closer, bent in and reached past her to grab a glass from the cupboard.

"Thirsty?" he asked.

"Uh… oh… no. Thanks."

He'd managed to fluster her. Had she thought he was coming in for a kiss? God knew he wanted one. "Someday," he told her.

"Someday, what?"

"I'm going to kiss you. But not yet."

She blinked. "Who said I want to kiss you?"

Oh, she wanted him to kiss her, that was plain, but she was also furious at him—with good reason, and he needed to take things one step at a time. It wasn't enough for Emma to be interested in him or even attracted to him.

She needed to want him.

And he was willing to wait.

"I HOPE YOUR appointment goes well," Penelope said early the next morning when she, Ava and Emma returned from their walk and reached the stairs that led from the beach up to the road at the top of the bluffs. "You coming up?" she added when Emma lingered in the sand.

"I need a few more minutes before I face my guests," Emma told the other two. "Go on. I'm going to sit and watch the waves until it's time to make breakfast."

"Good luck today." Ava touched her arm before they left.

"Thanks." Emma needed all the luck she could get. She wasn't at all sure her finances left her in a position to get a loan big enough to buy the Cliff Garden, but she had to try.

Heading toward the water, she spotted a familiar dog sitting sentry on the beach, nose toward the sea where a group of surfers were plying the waves. Winston's fur gleamed in the bright sunshine, his eyes glued to the action in the water, every line of his body tense with anticipation of Noah's return.

She could sympathize.

She should be angry at the man, and she was, but every time he walked into her frame of vision, her body betrayed her, yearning for the one person who should be off limits.

Clothed or in board shorts, he was something to behold. Yesterday when he'd stripped off his shirt at her sink, his muscles stretching and flexing in the most captivating way, she'd been hard-pressed not to reach out and run a hand over his skin.

Then he'd come so close she'd thought he was about to make a move, but all he'd done was fetch a water glass. She'd burned with embarrassment when he told her he wasn't going to kiss her yet.

Someday.

He was so aggravating.

And hot.

It wasn't just his appearance that caught her attention, though, and he wasn't aggravating all the time. Sometimes he was so… sweet. It drove her wild. He had a way of listening when she spoke, as if she was the only one who mattered in the world. Whenever he looked at her, his gaze left her breathless. She couldn't figure out how he'd taken over fixing the faucet yesterday. One minute she was in charge of the job. The next minute, he was. And yet she hadn't minded.

Not really.

When was the last time a man had actually helped her with anything?

If he hadn't bought her grandmother's garden, she could have fallen for—

No, she told herself sternly. Under no circumstances could she fall for Noah. She was off men completely from now on. She needed to focus on her own future.

Still, she found herself moving to Winston's side and dropping down on the sand beside him. It had been a good idea to join Ava and Penelope on their sunrise walk this morning. "Sunrise and sunset," Penelope had intoned, chiding her for missing their sunset balcony ritual last night. She'd been too flummoxed from her conversations with Noah to even remember it. "If you honor the start and end of the day, it'll honor you."

Nana Angela used to say things like that, Emma thought as she petted Winston's fur absently. From what she'd seen the summer she spent here, Angela lived her life by the rise and set of the sun, the change of the seasons and the turn of the tide. She always knew the phase of the moon and what the next day's weather would be. She practically lived in the Cliff Garden, tending it morning, noon and night, so Emma supposed it was only natural.

Guilt washed through her at the thought of how little she was tending it. She'd met Ava and Penelope there this morning and been glad to see it wasn't in bad shape. All the tools were accessible in a little shed at one side of the lot, and she had a feeling people from the neighborhood were pitching in, weeding a little, watering here and there. She was more grateful than she could say.

Winston gave her bare shoulder a lick, then turned back to the ocean. Emma followed his gaze. There were at least thirty people on surfboards, most of them men but a fair number of women among them, too. It took her a long time to pick out Noah, but when she did, she nearly laughed. It shouldn't have been hard, because he was the only one sitting on his surfboard, legs dangling to either side, snapping photos of everyone else.

The swells were decent today, but nothing to write home about, so his photos probably wouldn't end up in a magazine, but maybe he had other reasons to take them. Emma knew almost nothing about how a sports photographer picked their shots.

She also didn't know how one could afford to build an oceanfront house. Emma pulled out her phone, realizing she should have done an internet search on him long ago.

There were a lot of Noah Hudsons, but her Noah—

or rather the one staying in her bed-and-breakfast—featured prominently in the results, and soon she realized why.

Noah was in tech? She scanned the waves again. Found him paddling farther from shore. According to her search engine, he'd helped take a company from start-up to success story, and when he and his partner—the same man who'd visited him yesterday, she realized—sold it recently, he'd cashed out.

For a lot of money, from the looks of it.

She couldn't picture Noah working at a desk for a decade or more. Not when every move he made hinted at coiled strength and barely restrained energy. Poor guy.

Emma snorted. Poor guy? Hardly. He was the kind of newly minted millionaire who snatched grandmothers' gardens out from under unsuspecting people like her.

As she read, she had to admit he'd earned his reward. It sounded like he'd put in a lot of work to create the success he was now celebrating. She read an interview about his plans to leave the company.

"I've loved building Maxwell Tech," Noah was quoted as saying, "but sports photography is my real passion. I'm lucky enough that I get to pursue it full time now."

He was a man pursuing his dream.

While she was on the verge of losing hers—twice over.

Emma ducked her head when she remembered telling him about Food to You Fast going under. At the time he'd sounded like he understood. She supposed he probably did understand the difficulty of getting a business up and running.

He'd never experienced failure, though.

She wished she'd kept her mouth shut.

"Hello!"

Emma let out an involuntary yelp. She'd been so busy reading about Noah, she hadn't noticed him paddling toward her.

She shoved her phone in her pocket, flustered.

"I was just keeping Winston company," she called back.

"Fantastic morning." He got off his board when the water was waist deep and splashed into shore. "Do you know how to surf?" He set his board on the sand nearby and came closer, his skin glistening with droplets of water, his hair slicked back.

"No, I never learned."

"I'd be happy to show you anytime."

"I don't think so." But Emma was itching to try. She'd always been at home in the water.

"Think about it. The offer stands, and we'd have a good time together." When he bent down to give Winston a good scratch behind the ears, Emma pictured Noah's hands on her bare skin as he guided her to stand on a board. Longing suffused her, catching her off guard, and Noah, glancing up, must have caught something of it on her face. He smiled a slow, pleased grin that left her swallowing in a suddenly dry throat.

"You have the best dog," she scrambled to say, hoping she wasn't flushing too badly. Why was she flirting with him? She should be giving him the cold shoulder at the very least until he agreed to sell her the Cliff Garden.

She thought of the articles she'd read online, especially the one in which his business partner admitted he'd strong-armed Noah into being part of the company. "Noah would rather be mountain climbing," he'd said. Staying angry at him would be a hell of a lot easier if he wasn't so likable.

If she wasn't such an easy mark.

Her phone buzzed in her pocket, and she pulled it out, grateful for the interruption. It was too confusing being attracted to the person who was intent on gutting you. "It's Ashley," she told Noah. She lifted it to her ear. "Hello?"

"Emma?" Ashley's voice sounded strained. "Can you come get me?"

"Get you?" Emma met Noah's questioning gaze and shrugged. "Where are you?"

"At the hospital—don't freak out, I'm fine."

"What are you doing at the hospital if you're fine?" Emma scrambled to her knees.

"I… fainted yesterday. At work."

"Fainted? Are you pregnant?"

"No!" Ashley blew out an impatient breath. "How on earth would I be pregnant? I haven't been with a guy for months."

"You don't tell me anything about your personal life, so how would I know?" Emma stood up and started for the house, Noah and Winston trailing her.

"I must not have eaten a good enough breakfast or something. They can't find anything wrong."

"Are you sure?" Emma wasn't buying that. Ashley ate the same thing for breakfast every day. Had since she was a teenager.

"They kept me here overnight. Did a million tests. Now I'm free to go, but they said I shouldn't drive—and someone should keep an eye on me for a couple of days. I know it's a lot to ask, but I don't want anyone here to know what's happening."

Reaching the stairs up to the bluff, Emma stopped, gripped the railing with her free hand and closed her eyes.

I don't want anyone here to know.

How many times had they said that to each other when they were teenagers? How many years had they spent hiding the conditions in their home—and in their hearts—from everyone else?

Enough so it was ingrained in them both, she suspected. She was sure Ashley had plenty of friends who would love to help her, but she understood, too, why her sister wouldn't reach out to them. Did she keep them all at arm's length, the way Emma always did with her friends? Did she make sure to be chatty and fun at get-togethers but never available for the type of one-on-one situations where confidences were exchanged?

Enough wallowing in self-pity, Emma told herself. All that was changing. She was friends with Ava and Penelope now, and she didn't hold back from them—much. Besides, this was the perfect excuse to get Ashley to Brightview.

"I'm on my way. It's going to take me a while to get there, though."

"That's okay, I haven't been discharged yet, and you know how slow hospitals are. Text when you're near."

"I will. Then we'll swing by your place so you can pack a bag. You'll stay here as long as you'd like." They'd have to share her room for a few days until the rest of the guests left, but that was fine. They'd always done so growing up. "Are you sure you're okay?"

"Positive," Ashley said firmly, but something in her voice made Emma uncomfortable. Her sister was definitely not fine.

"I'll be there as soon as I can."

NOAH CAUGHT UP to Emma on the stairs to the bluffs, surfboard under his arm, Winston at his heels. "You're driving to San Francisco?" he asked, making sure not to sideswipe her with the board.

"Something's wrong with my sister. She fainted at work yesterday, and they kept her overnight at the hospital. She says she's fine, but I'm not buying it."

When they reached the top of the stairs, Noah reached out to touch her arm. "Let me drive."

"You? Why?"

"You'll eat up a ton of gas driving that big passenger van all the way there. My Range Rover is a lot more comfortable. Besides, I can help if your sister feels bad on the way home."

Emma looked like she'd protest, but instead she nodded. "I need to quickly set up breakfast for the other guests. I hope they won't mind that I'm not there to make the waffles…"

"They're grown women. One of them can manage a waffle maker," he assured her.

They hurried down the road, dodging passersby on the wide sidewalk that was thronged with walkers, skaters and bicyclists now that the sun was up. Cliff Street was designed for locals and visitors alike to enjoy the view as they got some exercise. At the B and B, Noah showered and dressed, and by the time he rejoined Emma, she had breakfast well in hand.

"Of course we can cook for ourselves," Kate was saying to Emma when he walked in. "Go, get your sister. We'll be fine."

"Help yourselves to anything you find in the fridge and cupboards," Emma told her, grabbing her purse and sunglasses.

"We're going out for lunch, anyway," Annie said, "so we won't want to fill up too much this morning. See you this afternoon when we get back."

"We should be home by then," Noah said. Emma shot him a curious look, but he just shrugged. Brightview was his home for the next six months.

"Come on, Winston," he called. "Let's go."

It was a beautiful day for a drive. As they made their way up Highway 1, Noah wished Emma could enjoy it, but judging by the way she was clutching the door handle, she was far from comfortable.

"You don't know why your sister fainted?" he asked to break the silence after they'd driven for a while.

"No. She claims she's not pregnant." Emma gave a little smile. "She said the doctors ran a bunch of tests and couldn't find anything."

"Did you ever find out why she sold your grandmother's lot? It's strange she didn't tell you—or give you a chance to buy it first."

Emma blinked. "I forgot about the bank. I've got an appointment this afternoon." She pulled out her phone and checked the time. "I should still be able to make it."

"You have a loan appointment?" His fingers tightened on the steering wheel. If by some miracle she came up with the cash to make him an offer, what would he do then?

"That's right. Ashley sold the lot to you because she needs the cash to buy into a partnership at her firm. She says she'll have enough left over to pay off her condo and start a retirement fund, too."

"Sounds like a sensible plan."

"Sounds like a horrible plan. What use is life if you have to sell the things that matter the most?" Emma turned to look out the window, and he had the feeling she was blinking back tears.

He seemed to have that affect on her.

"Does she think the Cliff Garden matters the most?" he asked. "Sounds like she has other priorities."

Emma turned on him, tears shining in her eyes as he'd suspected. "She has other *fears*, you mean. She's acting from her worst impulses, and she's going to hate herself for it someday."

"What impulses are you acting from?" He didn't know why he was goading her, except he hoped there was some outcome in which he wasn't the bad guy. He liked this woman with her thick blond hair and accusing eyes.

"I'm acting from the best ones. I want to preserve what my forebears worked so hard to build—and what my sister loves, even though she's walking away from it. What's wrong with that?"

"Nothing," he had to admit. Should he tell her why it was so important to him to keep the property? Why he'd made the promise to his brother in the first place?

Then he'd have to explain what he did to owe Andrew so much.

And he didn't want to talk about that.

He reached over and turned on the radio, grateful for

the spill of music. Emma didn't protest. She watched the scenery slip by, while Noah settled into his own thoughts. When they finally reached San Francisco and pulled into the hospital's visitor parking lot, he was ready to stretch his legs. Emma texted Ashley that they'd arrived, and soon they were face to face in the hospital lobby.

"I shouldn't have made you come all this way," Ashley said. "I don't know why the doctors are making such a fuss. I feel fine. I should have called an Uber and gone home."

She looked worn and drawn, the corners of her mouth turned down. Noah saw Emma take notice. She drew back her shoulders as if mustering her forces to shore up her sister's depleted ones.

"It's no fuss at all. I've been hoping you'd come and visit, and this is the perfect opportunity."

"It's just... my friends are all so busy. They're like *me*, working night and day." She bit her lip. Noah wondered if she realized it had sounded like she was implying Emma didn't work at all.

Emma simply shook her head. "Of course they are. Besides, it's family you want around you when you're sick. Even if you're already feeling better," she added. "Let's get your things, grab something to eat and get out of here. The fresh air at the ocean will do you good."

"Hi, I'm Noah Hudson," Noah interjected when it became clear Emma had forgotten his presence.

Emma flushed. "Sorry, I should have introduced you…" She broke off at Ashley's openmouthed expression.

"Noah Hudson? The man who bought Nana's garden? Emma, how do you even know him?"

"He drove me here," Emma admitted ruefully. "He has a better car. We were talking when you called."

"You were… talking?"

"Noah is a paying guest at my bed-and-breakfast," Emma explained. "I didn't know he'd bought Nana's garden because you didn't bother to tell me it was for sale."

Ashley chewed on her lip. She looked like she had a lot to say but didn't want to say any of it in front of him. "You know, you can drop me off at my condo. I'll be fine there."

"No way," Emma told her. "The doctor said you need looking after, and we drove all the way up here in the middle of a workday. You're coming with us. Besides," she added, taking Ashley's arm and hustling her out the doors toward the parking lot, "you can't avoid me forever. You're my sister, even if you haven't been acting like one. You know I never would have let Noah book a room if I'd known who he was."

Noah sped up and led the way to his Range Rover, refusing to take any of this personally.

"I didn't tell you because I didn't want you to kick up one of your fusses," Ashley said. "The last thing I needed was your dramatics."

"I'm not dramatic!"

"Really?"

They arrived at the car. Noah opened the doors, ushering Emma into the front passenger seat, Ashley in the back, where he wordlessly handed her a pillow and blanket he'd stowed there just in case. Winston, moving over to make room for her, woofed softly.

"Make yourself comfortable," Noah said.

Once both women were strapped in and Ashley gave him her address, Emma started up again. "I'm dramatic when I care about what's happening, and I care about Nana's garden—and you. You're going to be miserable when it's gone."

"Emma, I was six when I loved that garden. It means nothing to me now. Let it go. Besides, it's too late to change what's done." Ashley thumped the pillow into the corner and leaned against it.

"No, it's not. I'm going to the bank this afternoon. I'm getting a loan, and I'm buying it back."

Ashley sat up again. "Buying it back?" She leaned forward and pinned Noah with a hard look. "You're willing to sell a lot you just bought?"

Was it Noah's imagination, or did she almost sound hopeful? He needed to nip this in the bud, he thought as he buckled his seat belt, but Emma looked so sure of herself he hated to burst her bubble. He doubted the bank was going to give her a loan anywhere near big enough for her to offer full price for the lot. She didn't have a job, and she had only just started running the bed-and-breakfast. Let them disappoint her.

He didn't want to.

"We'll see" was all he said. He turned on the engine, and music spilled from the speakers, drowning out both women.

Emma reached over to turn it down. Noah intercepted her, taking hold of her hand when she reached for it again. He held it until a flush crept up her cheeks. When he let it go, she folded her hands in her lap.

Noah turned down the music, but only a little. He met Ashley's gaze in the rearview mirror. She was assessing him, that frown back.

"Let's get your things," he told her.

CHAPTER 6

EMMA WAS EXHAUSTED by the time they got home, and the day was barely half-over. She was relieved the other guests had cleaned up after breakfast, put the food away and run the dishwasher. That was one less chore to do.

"You'll have to bunk with me," she told her sister. "The place is full for a few more nights. Then we'll move you into one of the upstairs rooms."

"I'll be gone by then," Ashley said grumpily.

"You don't have to share," Noah interjected. "Ashley can take my room. I'll sleep out on the deck. That couch with the blue cushions is big enough."

"I'm not going to make you sleep outside!" Emma was aghast. He was a paying customer. What would the other guests think?

"You're not making me; I'm requesting permission to do so. I like sleeping outside, and the weather is supposed to be dry and warm the next few days. Is there a place I can store my things?"

"Of course." This wasn't professional, but she didn't

have the strength to argue. "Ashley, what do you think?"

"Sounds good. Thank you," she said, but she didn't look him in the eyes. Emma wasn't sure where her animosity was coming from. Was she embarrassed to be taking his room? Chagrined that she'd have to live side by side with the man to whom she'd sold Nana's garden? Did she regret selling the land?

Or was she just being Ashley, still suspicious of outsiders until they proved themselves?

Fifteen minutes later Emma had stored Noah's things in the laundry room and left his bedding nicely folded there for the time being. Ashley helped her remake the room, even though Emma told her to rest.

"I don't need to rest. This is all so silly."

Emma tuned out her fussing. Ashley had never fainted before, as far as she knew. Something had to be wrong with her.

"I've got some chicken marinating. I was planning to barbecue, but maybe I should grab burgers instead?" Ashley had said she wasn't anemic, but there was no harm in erring on the side of caution.

"Chicken is fine," Ashley said.

"I can man the barbecue tonight." Noah stuck his head in the door of the room. "I'm a genius when it comes to grilling. You ladies go and sit on the deck and enjoy the afternoon. I'll take over and serve you a feast when it's dinnertime."

Emma checked her phone. "I've got to run if I'm

going to make it to the bank, and I want to change first. Ashley, you'll need to relax without me for a while."

A loud knock at the door at the back of the house brought her up short.

"Are you expecting someone?" Ashley asked.

Emma shook her head. Maybe Ginni and the others had forgotten the key code to get inside.

When she opened the door, however, a stranger stood on the front stoop. He was a tall, serious man with sandy brown hair.

"Hello?" she said uncertainly.

"Andrew! What are you doing here?" Noah asked.

WHEN ANDREW LUGGED an overnight bag in with him, Noah knew he was in trouble.

"I'm here for that visit I promised you. We have a lot to talk about, and I figured we might as well do that in person. I can crash here with you, right? That way we can get all the details sorted out in a day or two."

Noah checked to see Emma's reaction, but before he could say anything, his brother pushed right past him down the hall and into the living room. Noah followed, Emma right behind.

"Wow, look at that view. Yours will be even better, you know," Andrew tossed over his shoulder. He spotted Emma and thrust out his hand. "Andrew Hudson. You must be Emma. Noah mentioned you." She shook it uncertainly. Then Andrew noticed Ashley, who had trailed after them into the living room.

"Hello," Andrew said warmly. "I'm Andrew Hudson. Noah's brother. Do you live here, too, or are you a guest?"

"Just… visiting," she said slowly.

Noah could almost sense the cogs in Andrew's brain turning. He'd broken up with a long-term girlfriend earlier in the year, and he wasn't the kind of man who liked to be alone. Ashley was just his type. Pretty. Intelligent. A go-getter, from what Emma had said.

"Ashley is Emma's sister. She's down from San Francisco for a few days," he supplied. "She works at a forensic accounting firm there." Just as he'd expected, his brother's interest increased.

"Great. Glad you're here. When my brother gets boring, I'll have someone to talk to."

"Does your brother get boring often?" Ashley asked.

Was she… flirting with Andrew? Her fatigue seemed to have faded away. There was a little pink in her cheeks instead of that paleness.

"He's a regular snooze-fest."

"Hey," Noah protested. "I'm an extreme sports photographer. I'm definitely not a snooze-fest."

"Always talking about himself," Andrew said in a stage whisper to Ashley. "It's endless."

"Go fuck yourself." Noah had to laugh, though. Even Ashley was smiling now. "Hate to break it to you, dude. Ashley, here, stole my room, so you'll have to bunk out on the deck with me. I've got dibs on the couch with the blue cushions. You can have the swing."

Andrew looked outside. "No way I'm going to fit on that swing."

"Should have thought of that and called before you came."

"I have a blow-up mattress," Emma interceded. "Usually guests use it for kids, but we can set it up for you somewhere, Andrew, if you like."

Was Emma hoping they'd both take themselves off to a hotel? Noah wasn't sure, but he didn't want to leave.

"The blow-up mattress is fine for Andrew," he announced. "We'll deal with that later tonight." He moved to the kitchen and began to pull out ingredients for his signature barbecue sauce. While he was at it, he found some finger-food snacks and set them on the counter.

"What are you doing?" Emma asked him as Ashley went to move her belongings into Noah's old room and Andrew prowled around the bed-and-breakfast.

"I'm helping," Noah said. "I know, I know," he added, raising his hands in mock surrender. "Too little, too late. In my defense, I didn't imagine any of this happening when I came to Seahaven."

"Any of what?"

He waved a hand. "That Brightview would be so great. That the food would knock my socks off. That my brother would show up—and your sister. That I'd meet the girl of my—" He cut off, realizing what he'd just been about to say. "That I'd meet the woman whose grandmother tended the garden I'm about to destroy." He took Emma's hand. Rubbed his thumb over her palm, wanting to do so much more. "I don't want to hurt you, Emma."

She sucked in a breath, grabbed her phone. "I'm going to be late." She yanked her hand out of his, turned on her heel and hurried out the door.

"WE CAN CERTAINLY give you a loan," Regina Cho said, turning to face Emma across the wide expanse of her desk. "But I'm afraid we can't offer a mortgage in the amount you've requested." An attractive woman in her early thirties with a sweep of dark hair twisted into a knot at the nape of her neck, Regina had been perfectly friendly and helpful throughout her appointment, but Emma was starting to get frustrated. This wasn't the answer she wanted—or needed.

"How much can you extend?"

Regina named a number far short of what she needed to buy the Cliff Garden. She'd found the sale price online, so she knew the exact amount to ask for. In fact, she'd shown Regina the property she wanted to buy, so the woman knew all the details of the transaction she was trying to make.

"I don't understand. I own Brightview free and clear. It has to be worth more than a garden lot with no house on it."

Regina raised an eyebrow. "For one thing, with a beachfront property like the one we're talking about, the land makes up the bulk of the value. You could sell your house for more than the price of the Cliff Garden but not twice the value. That's not the only problem, though. You have no real income, and you have outstanding debt as well. Depending on the interest you're paying on those debts, you might be better off folding them into the amount still owing on Brightview's mortgage."

"Brightview's mortgage?" Emma repeated.

Regina turned her screen and showed Emma a number so large her mouth went dry.

"That's not possible." She swallowed the fear that rose in her throat. "I haven't been informed of any mortgage."

Regina pursed her lips, clicked through a few more pages and picked up her phone. Emma struggled with the feeling she might be sick, too shocked to listen in to the other woman's conversation. If Brightview had a mortgage, she was sunk. She could cover her expenses with the earnings from the bed-and-breakfast if bookings kept coming, but she'd never factored in a big monthly payment. When Regina hung up, Emma braced herself for unpleasant news.

"You're not the first person who signed paperwork without reading it carefully, Emma," Regina said kindly. "Several times during her tenure at Brightview, your grandmother took out a mortgage against the house. The most recent one was very substantial. She worked with another bank, so I don't know the details about why she needed all that money, but she wasn't very aggressive about paying it off."

Emma appreciated the explanation, but she was having a hard time taking in the implications of what Regina was telling her. Her father's death had hit her hard coming so close after Jordan's desertion and the failure of her business. She'd been so overwhelmed with gratitude when she learned about the inheritance, she'd signed everything her lawyer put in front of her. What else had she missed?

"Angela and her trustee always made her payments on time," Regina added, "but you're late on your first one. I explained to the loan officer at the other bank that you were unaware of the obligation, and they've agreed to a grace period. You should make an appointment with them immediately."

"So I can't buy the Cliff Garden?"

"I love the Cliff Garden," Regina said, softening. "I live about five blocks inland from you," she added with a smile. "I visit it about once a week. Angela was great—I still miss her."

"I do, too." Emma wasn't going to let herself cry, though, because she knew exactly why Angela had taken out that mortgage.

To save her granddaughters.

A chill shivered through her spine as Emma remembered the day they'd moved into the peach house. As soon as her dad had opened the door, she and Ashley had raced through it, shrieking with delight at the pastel bedrooms, one for each of them, the huge kitchen and dining room, the formal living room and the enormous family room with sliding glass doors that led out to a swimming pool.

"We're in," Ashley had crowed. "They'll love us now."

Emma knew exactly who she meant: all the girls at school who whispered about them currently. They didn't fit in with the other kids and were always too embarrassed to ask anyone over. Now she pictured pool parties. Treats served in the kitchen. Falling asleep to the soft whir of a full-house air conditioner instead of the loud hum of a fan on hot Florida nights.

They hadn't bothered packing their clothes or dishes or furniture. Their father had bought everything new. A week later they'd returned to school with their heads held high for the first time in years.

She'd never once asked herself how her father could suddenly afford such a house. They'd never understood exactly what he did on his computer. They'd simply accepted he'd done it right for once.

But he hadn't done it. Angela had.

And now Emma was going to have to pay it back.

"I'm sorry you're not in a position to buy the Cliff Garden," Regina said. "Honestly, I had no idea it sold."

"Neither did I, until it was too late." She explained Ashley's practical reasons for doing so, trying to keep her sadness and anger out of her voice.

"If there was more time, you might have been able to petition the town to buy the land for a park."

Emma nodded. Now that she knew the worst, she wanted to go home and lick her wounds—and revise her business plan. The thought of losing Brightview, too, was more than she could bear.

"The person I spoke to at the other bank said it looks like Angela had her mail sent to a PO box. Do you have the key?"

Emma thought of the big envelope Colette had left her. Was there a little key in there?

She thought so.

"You might want to check that box today," Regina said gently. "You might have missed something else important."

"I will."

"Emma," Regina said, standing up with her as the appointment ended. "I'm sorry about the circumstances, but I'm really glad I met you. Like I said, I loved your grandmother, and I'm glad to know you, too." She handed Emma her card. "Call me if you'd like to go for coffee sometime. We are neighbors, after all."

Emma's heart warmed at the kindness, despite everything else. "I'll do that."

"I'm always here to help. Let me know if you want to

consolidate those loans."

"Will do."

Emma drove home slowly, her thoughts tangled in her memories. When she was really little, her father had left the house every day to go to work at the electronics repair shop he owned in town. Her mother had worked as a hygienist at a dental clinic. Thinking back, Emma wondered if her father's business had been failing even before her mother's illness began. Who repaired anything these days when it was cheaper to buy a replacement instead?

Had her mother's income been the stabilizing force in their lives? Had it paid the bills on the little bungalow where they'd lived when she was young? All her best memories were set in its small but tidy living room and the bedroom she'd shared with Ashley. The rental they'd moved into after her mother's death was too ramshackle to feel cared for, and as big and new as the peach house was, it had never felt like a real home, either. The last rental they'd lived in—that brown box of a place—was the worst of the bunch.

Back at Brightview, it sounded like a party was going on out on the deck. Emma spotted Ashley sitting with Noah, Andrew and her other guests. She slipped up the stairs to her room without being seen and locked the door.

Only then did she allow her tears to fall. The garden was lost. That's all there was to it.

Angela was really gone.

A sob escaped Emma's throat as she sat on her bed, grabbed a pillow and held it to her face to stifle the sound. She didn't have time to cry. Wouldn't let this new failure knock her down. She simply had to keep swinging for the fences. What other choice did she have?

A knock at the door made her leap off the bed.

"Emma?"

It was Noah. Just what she didn't need.

"I'm busy." She hoped her voice didn't betray her anguish.

"Can you let me in?"

"No." No way would she let him see her like this. So… defeated. You never let anyone know when you were down. Chin up. Shoulders back. That's what Ashley would say. She scrubbed at her eyes.

"Emma. I've got something important to say."

With an exasperated huff, she gave up and crossed to the door. She opened it only a few inches, though.

"What?"

"Can I come in?" When she didn't answer, he added, "Please?"

He wasn't going to give her a break, was he? She wasn't sure she could afford to alienate a paying guest, either. His six-month lease might be the one thing standing between her and destitution. When she opened the door wordlessly, he entered, took her hand and led her to the bed. "Sit down a minute."

Emma wasn't sure why she was obeying him. Maybe because the touch of his hand sent shivers through her. He was so handsome up close like this, a hint of stubble on his strong jaw, his tan limbs contrasting with the white of his T-shirt.

"I made up my mind. I'm going to talk to Andrew at dinner tonight and ask him to scale back his plans for the house. I'll ask him to leave some of the garden." His gaze searched hers.

She could only stare back wordlessly. Some of the garden? Didn't he see it was a living whole—something organic created out of the property over generations?

"Give me a chance," he pleaded. "Let me see what Andrew and I can do." He lifted a hand to brush her cheek. Emma hadn't realized she was still crying. She couldn't seem to stop. "Emma," he said.

And then he kissed her.

The kiss was just a brush of his mouth over hers at first, but when she didn't pull away—couldn't pull away—it deepened into something more searching and powerful. She forgot everything else when his hand tangled in her hair, and she leaned into him, not protesting when he gathered her nearer.

Here was the comfort she'd been craving. Noah's strength, his broad shoulders were a welcome shelter from the storm. She'd always thought she'd face life with a partner—

No.

She was half in his lap when she pulled away breathless and flushed with heat.

What was she doing? This man was her enemy—

And she'd tried life with a partner before.

"Uh-uh," she said, but Noah caught her hands in his.

"Yes," he said firmly. "Emma, I'm not going to let this property stuff get in the way of knowing you better. Trust me, okay? There's a way to solve this." He stood up, pulling her up with him. "I'm off to dinner with Andrew. I'll talk to him. We'll figure something out—a compromise."

She watched him go. A compromise?

There was no compromise when it came to Nana Angela's legacy.

A moment later Ashley appeared in the doorway. "What was that all about?"

Emma, still standing in the center of the room, beckoned her in. "I don't know," she said truthfully.

"How'd your appointment go?"

Emma's temper flared. Ashley was the one who'd sold the Cliff Garden to begin with. Why wasn't she offering to buy it back?

"It was only a preliminary meeting," she evaded. She didn't know why Ashley even cared. She'd been in such a hurry to get rid of the garden she hadn't even warned Emma what she was going to do. Hadn't given her a chance to keep the property in the family. They'd been given an opportunity to stitch the generations back together, and Ashley had tossed it to the winds.

She thought her sister would pursue the topic. Usually Ashley worried and poked at a subject until it was in tatters, but instead she asked, "What do you think of Andrew?"

"Noah's brother?" Emma swallowed her surprise. "I—He's okay, I guess."

"You don't like him?" Ashley took a seat on the bed and began to pick at Emma's comforter absently. "He seems interesting. He's educated. Well-traveled. Has a good job."

He's the architect who's designing the house that's going to obliterate our grandmother's garden, Emma wanted to say but didn't.

"I've barely spoken to him," she managed instead. Was Ashley lonely, too? Her sister seemed to avoid commitments. She dated from time to time, but she'd never moved in with a boyfriend.

"You're too busy having one-on-ones with Noah."

"He had something he wanted to tell me." She thought of their kiss and felt the heat rise in her cheeks.

Ashley cocked her head. "I just bet he did."

"EMMA!" NOAH CALLED softly when he spotted her entering the Cliff Garden the following morning. He'd already been there a half hour walking the paths, even though the sun was only just now threatening to clear the horizon. Last night she'd been in her room by the time he got home, and he hadn't had a chance to talk to her.

"What are you doing here?" Emma approached him uncertainly. Dressed in jeans that hugged her curves, a mint green T-shirt and a white hoodie, she looked ready to greet the day despite the early hour.

"Wanted to get a fresh look at the property and talk to you a little bit, if that's all right. I talked to Andrew last night, like I said." He didn't add that Andrew had been more than a little affronted at being asked to scale back his designs. It had taken quite a few arguments and finally a bald-faced challenge to get him to agree. He'd told Andrew that any dilettante could design a huge house but only a top-notch architect could create the kind of space he wanted on a smaller footprint. "I thought it would be helpful to get some more information from you. Why don't you point out what's most important to you about the property, so we can work out what to keep?"

"My grandmother's hands, and her grandmother's—and my sister's and mine—have nurtured every square foot of this land. You can't ask me to pick and choose."

"I have to. Like it or not, this is going to be my home." He remembered Mark's suggestion that he hint it could be hers, too, but he decided not to go there—yet. God knew he wanted to get closer to her, but it was far too soon to talk about moving in together. Far too soon to be even thinking about it. What was wrong with him?

"You're a one-man kind of woman, aren't you?" He

didn't realize he'd asked the question out loud until her eyebrows shot up.

"Are you asking if I sleep around? Because the answer is no. I don't. But you don't have the right to ask me that kind of question."

"I want to have the right," he told her frankly. "I want you to be mine." This conversation wasn't going at all the way he'd expected. He'd meant this meeting to be brief and practical, a fact-finding message so he could pass on parameters to Andrew. "Look, Emma, the thing is I'm up against a deadline. We need to get plans finalized so I can start building soon. I want this house done before November."

"Before the rainy season," she said faintly.

"That's right. And I want us to be friends. We're going to be next-door neighbors at the very least. I'm going to be honest—I want a lot more than that."

"Even if you weren't destroying something I love, it would be a bad idea to have a fling with my next-door neighbor," she said tartly.

"Who said anything about a fling?" He let that sink in. One thing Noah knew was that his gut instincts were good. He'd known from the minute Mark asked him to join his start-up in college it was the right thing to do. Knew instantly Mark had come up with a killer product. Knew instinctively when a deal would be beneficial and when they were getting played. Knew when he took a photograph if it would be the kind of image that magazines would kill for.

When he met Caitlyn, he'd been off his game, restless from waiting for his chance to pursue his real dreams. He'd wanted something fun and simple, and that's what he'd had up until the moment she'd complicated it with other men. He was right about Emma, though. Maybe it had taken Mark pointing it out to make it clear to him, but now that it was, Noah couldn't ignore it. It was crazy. He'd barely known Emma for a few days.

Didn't matter. He wanted her in his life—long term.

"Okay, this is getting too weird." Emma turned away, but Noah caught her hand.

"I need you to know what's on my mind." He let his gaze linger on hers until she flushed. "I'm going to build my house, but I'm going to do my damnedest to preserve some of what your family created. I think it makes sense to keep that area." He pointed to where the Trouble Bench was situated. Obviously, that was nonnegotiable. "I'll put the house over there." He pointed to the far back corner on the opposite side of the site. "To maximize the amount of garden that can stay. That means when you look my way from your place, you'll see garden first. My home will be tucked away behind it."

"The lot isn't that big," she said. "Your house is going to be front and center no matter what you do."

Someone called from the direction of the garden gate. Two women he'd seen her walking with before.

"Those are my friends. I have to go."

"I'll let Andrew know what we talked about."

"You really want to make this right?" she shot back. "Tell Andrew to talk to Ashley. Let her decide what parts of the garden to keep."

Noah didn't know what to think about that. Emma's sister was the one who'd sold him the garden. Why should she have a say about what would happen with it, and why did Emma keep deflecting her own love for the place onto Ashley all the time? She was the one who revered the history of the Cliff Garden, as far as he could tell. As for Ashley, he didn't understand her at all. She came off practical and hard-nosed, but she hadn't seemed pleased to meet him when he helped pick her up at the hospital. Was Emma right? Did she regret her decision to sell? Or did she simply feel guilty about disappointing her sister?

"Fine. I'll tell Andrew to talk to Ashley." He took Emma's hand, leaned in and brushed a kiss over her cheek.

"What are you doing?"

"Joining you on your walk."

"But—" Emma swallowed her protests with a shake of her head. Tried to disengage her hand from his and sighed when he wouldn't let go. "Oh, for heaven's sake."

Noah kept going toward the gate, leaving her no choice but to catch up with him if she didn't want him tugging her along like a child. When they reached her friends, he gave her hand a squeeze and released it. "Aren't you going to introduce me?" he asked.

"Ava, Penelope, meet Noah Hudson, my guest at Brightview," she said tightly.

Guest, huh? Had her friends seen his kiss? He hoped so.

"I guess *guests* are allowed to come on our sunrise walk," Ava said drily, looking Noah over head to foot, "if they can keep up with us."

EMMA THOUGHT SHE would burn up from embarrassment. Had Ava and Penelope seen Noah kiss her? They'd warned her against fooling around with guests.

"I can keep up," Noah assured Ava. As if to prove his point, he set off down the road at a fast pace.

"Typical man," Ava muttered as they all set off after him. "Look at him go. Sure we'll follow him."

"We are following him," Penelope pointed out.

"Like a trio of fools," Ava agreed. She nudged Emma. "What's the story?"

"I barely know him, and it's complicated." She didn't want to explain it within hearing distance of Noah.

"This walk is supposed to be for Cliff Sisters," Penelope said loudly. "That man doesn't look like a sister."

Noah slowed down until they caught up. "Sisters? You three aren't related, are you?"

"We're related by proximity," Penelope told him, not backing down. "We're neighbors, and we all live here on

Cliff Street. Cliff Sisters." She gave a little flourish as if that explained everything.

"Well, I'm going to live on the other side of Emma, so we'll be related by proximity, too," Noah said smoothly. "So I guess this is the Cliff Siblings sunrise walk now." He linked arms with Penelope and set off again.

Penelope cast a helpless glance over her shoulder, but she didn't pull away. Soon she was happily chatting away with Noah.

Ava sighed. "Here we go." She sent an arch look Emma's way. "But he's interested in you, not Penelope, isn't he? He was kissing you when we arrived."

"I honestly don't know how that keeps happening."

Ava laughed. "I imagine he keeps coming in for the kiss and you don't pull away."

"It's more like I can't pull away. I don't want a boyfriend, let alone one who lives next to me, and I definitely don't want one who's going to ruin the Cliff Garden."

Ava sobered up. "He's the one who bought the Cliff Garden?"

"Yep."

"I guess it could be worse." Ava studied Noah's back.

"I'm not sure how. He wouldn't even consider selling the land back to me when I thought I could afford to buy it."

"Buying it isn't a possibility?"

"No," Emma said shortly. She didn't feel like admitting how badly in debt she really was. She hadn't sat down and looked over the numbers again yet. Hadn't gone to Nana Angela's PO box to pick up her mail, either.

Avoiding reality, Ashley would say. Just like Dad.

"He's being really kind to Penelope," Ava said softly. She nodded to where Noah was steering her past several women walking with their small children.

"Does she need kindness?"

"She deserves it. She's been a good friend to me so far, and I think she's lonely. She really misses her uncle."

"How about you? Are you lonely?" Emma asked.

"I don't know. I thought I'd be married by now." They moved to the right to allow a boisterous family group to pass by them on the sidewalk. "I had a pretty serious boyfriend up until last year, but we had different visions for our future, and he found someone else."

"Ugh. I know what that's like."

"Suddenly my life is completely different. I'm living here full time instead of traveling the world, the way I did for years. I'm going to start a teaching job in the fall instead of selling my own curriculum online, like I used to do. Social media was my whole life back then. I was an internet celebrity, of a sort. Now that's all done. The teaching job is a pretty good gig, though."

"Sounds like things are working out?" Emma asked

tentatively.

"Except for finding the right guy to share it with. When is he going to turn up?"

"I hope it's soon."

Ava nodded. "Thanks." She jutted her chin toward Penelope and Noah. "We have your back, you know. Pen's on your side even if she is having a good time talking to him. If Noah gives you any grief, he'll have to deal with us."

A rush of gratitude swept over Emma. She'd never really had friends like that before because she'd rarely let anyone get this close. "Thanks," she said.

"Sisters have to stick together." Ava crooked an elbow, and Emma moved to link hers through it as they picked up the pace to follow the others.

NOAH FOLLOWED EMMA straight into the kitchen when they got back to Brightview, washed his hands and stood ready to help with preparing the breakfast buffet. He was afraid she'd boot him right out, but other than a soft sigh, she didn't react negatively to his presence.

"Get out some plates and silverware," she instructed him, and he did so, mimicking the arrangement he'd seen the previous day. "I'm making breakfast burritos today," she went on and got out the ingredients before getting to work.

Soon the female guests joined them, chattering happily on the sectional while they waited for breakfast to be ready. Noah was grateful it was such a comfortable group. If it had been a cranky family with small children, it could have been a nightmare to sort out things with Emma during their stay. Ashley appeared a few minutes later and joined the women. She looked brighter today, like she'd had a good night's sleep.

Andrew was the last to emerge. He shambled in from the deck, a little worse for wear from his night in the open air, and made a beeline for the hall bathroom. A short time later, he emerged again. Fresh out of the shower, judging by his damp hair, he fetched his tablet and sat at the high counter separating the kitchen from the rest of the room.

"I heard you were worried about your flower beds," he said to Emma. Ashley turned to listen to him. So did everyone else. Noah cursed under his breath, but before he could intervene, Andrew went on. "Don't be. You won't miss them at all when I'm done with that lot. I'm as good at landscape design as I am designing houses, and Noah's house is going to be spectacular."

If Noah could have dragged his brother right out of the room, he would have, but he could see the determined angle of Andrew's chin. Andrew was digging in. He might have heard Noah's request last night, but he didn't want to honor it. Noah had no doubt he'd spent an hour or two looking over his plans and decided he didn't want to give up one square inch of the marvel he thought he was building.

"If you come next door, I'll show you," Andrew offered.

Emma opened her mouth, but Ashley hopped over the back of the couch, touched Andrew's arm and cut her off. "Show me instead," she said. "Emma's busy. I'm the gardener in this family, anyway."

Hell—his brother was about to be ambushed, and he didn't understand the situation well enough to spot the attack. Did he hear the steely tone underlying Ashley's sweetness? Noah didn't think so, but it was definitely there, and for the first time, he thought he was getting a clear glimpse of her position. Ashley might have sold the garden, but she still cared about it. Possibly wanted it back, even if she hadn't admitted that to herself yet. This was getting worse and worse.

Andrew hesitated. "Uh… sure. I'd love to show you." He shot Noah a half-puzzled, half-pleased look. There was nothing Noah could do to warn him with everyone looking on.

"Let's go." Ashley gestured to the yard.

"What about breakfast?" Emma called after them as they left through the doors to the deck.

"We'll be back soon," Andrew assured her.

"Should I go after them?" Noah asked when they were gone.

"You'd better stay out of the firing line. You might be an only child when Ashley is done with your brother. Besides, I told you he should talk to her. He should have done that before he started bragging."

"Maybe you should get that loan and buy me out after all," Noah quipped.

Emma frowned and quickly got back to work.

"Emma?" Noah moved closer and lowered his voice. "Did you hear something from the bank?" She'd evaded his questions yesterday, and he'd assumed she'd gotten bad news, but she hadn't confirmed it.

She stopped. Braced her hands on the counter and closed her eyes. "I shouldn't even be telling you this."

"Yes, you should. We're not enemies. You know that." He wished they didn't have an audience and he could fold her into his arms.

She opened her eyes again and turned her gaze on him. "I thought I owned Brightview free and clear. Turns out I don't."

He stilled. "You have a mortgage you didn't know about? How's that going to affect your bottom line?" He cursed himself for going straight to the facts. He should be consoling her, not grilling her.

"I don't know how I'm going to make those payments on top of everything else. I need to be booked solid, and so far, I'm not."

"I'll look over things with you. Maybe I can offer a few suggestions."

"Maybe you can just go away," she snapped, then sighed. "Sorry. Don't do that. I need your rent money. It's just—I need to go to my grandmother's PO box today. I forgot all about it. Who knows what other ugly surprises are waiting for me there?"

"I'll come with you. It's always easier to face things with a friend."

She turned back to the food. "Don't you need to babysit your brother?"

"Do I even have a brother anymore?" Noah led the way to the window to look.

CHAPTER 7

EMMA BRACED HERSELF for what they might see, and it was as bad as she'd feared. Andrew and Ashley faced each other on one of the paths, both of them gesturing, their voices raised.

Noah undid the old-fashioned latch on the window and struggled to open it before it finally slid up with a groan. Since the huge sliding glass windows in the front opened wide to let in fresh air, Emma hadn't bothered trying to open any of the side windows since she'd taken possession of the place. She realized she needed to give them some attention.

"You can't improve on this," Ashley was yelling at Andrew, waving a hand to encompass the garden beds, the winding paths and the spectacular view. "The only thing you can do is ruin it!"

"This is just a mess of plants!" Andrew yelled back. "An unformed organic dumping ground! Architecture defines space. It enhances it. Raises raw materials to the divine!"

"Are you saying you can do better than Mother Nature?" Ashley demanded. "Is your ego really that big?"

"I'm saying my job is to take whatever is lying around us"—he gestured at the garden—"and turn it into art. You can't compare what I do to the poor attempts of the untaught. I'm sure there are a lot of pretty flowers here. That's very nice." His contemptuous tone said he didn't think it was nice at all. "But what I'm going to build here will be the kind of melding of natural and humanmade materials that transcends nice—that leaves *nice* utterly behind."

If Ashley ever thought Andrew worth flirting with, she'd changed her mind now, Emma thought. Beside her, Noah shoved his hands in his pockets.

"Hell," he said quietly.

"Hell, indeed," she agreed with him.

Out in Nana Angela's garden, Ashley lunged for Andrew. Emma sucked in a breath, thinking she'd have to run and stop the altercation, but instead of striking Andrew, Ashley grabbed his hand and kept going.

"What now?" Andrew demanded.

"I'm going to show you something you need to see."

Andrew dug his heels in. "I have plans to finalize."

"You're going to shut up and do what I tell you to do," Ashley cried, tugging him forward.

"I'd better get out there and help," Noah said.

"What's going on over there?" Ginni asked, looking up from her conversation with her friends.

"Nothing to worry about," Emma assured her as she

followed Noah to the street end of the house and out the door, where they met up with Ashley and Andrew, who were both fuming.

"Emma? Give me your keys!" Ashley demanded.

"Keys? You want to drive somewhere?" Andrew eyed the passenger van Emma had inherited with the house. "I'm not getting in that thing. If you don't kill me, it's bound to."

"Get. In. The. Car," Ashley told him.

"I'll drive." Noah spoke up. "Wherever you're taking him, I'm coming, too. Andrew is visiting me, after all."

"I'll come as well—but we all need to have breakfast first," Emma said. "Where *are* you taking him?"

"Santana Redwood State Park."

Emma's first thought was surprise that her sister even remembered the place—they'd gone there only once with Nana Angela. Then she remembered San Francisco was only an hour and a half away. Ashley probably knew the whole area much better than she could imagine. She'd always pictured her sister staying in the city, but who knew how Ashley spent her time? Maybe she visited state parks every weekend.

"You know what?" she asked. "That's actually a great idea. I think we should all go—after we eat. I'll pack a picnic lunch and ask the other guests if they want to come along. Noah, you can drive Andrew. I'll drive everyone else in Bessie." She nodded to the passenger van. "She's perfectly safe." Emma had driven her everywhere since she arrived.

To her relief, everyone agreed to the plan. An hour later, after breakfast was over and the kitchen clean again, they were on their way.

"I feel like we're getting a lot more than we're paying for," Kate remarked to Emma. "I didn't see anything about tours included in the price of the rooms."

"I'm glad to do it," she said. "Everyone should see where we're going once in their lives."

The road wound up into the hills until they reached the state park and turned into its main drive. A few minutes later, they climbed out of their vehicles. Annie shivered. "It's much cooler here."

"It is at this time of year," Noah said. "We're in the hills now, and the forest holds the chill in the air."

"Grab your jackets," Emma said. "We'll walk the loop trail first, then find a picnic table and eat."

Her guests spotted the nature center and gift shop at the start of the main trail, but Ashley was having none of that. "Work first, then play," she announced and marched Andrew onward, her hand gripping his bicep.

Emma watched her sister carefully, wondering if part of her was enjoying her proximity to Andrew in any way. She wasn't sure what to think of Noah's brother. He bragged a lot, but sometimes that kind of habit covered up insecurity.

It took only twenty steps down the trail before everyone in the party stopped, speechless.

"The redwoods," Andrew said reverently, and a weight shifted off Emma's chest. So, he was capable of awe. That meant he was redeemable. She met Ashley's gaze, and Ashley gave her a tiny smile. Emma noticed her sister's hand still curled around his arm.

Was Ashley falling for him? Heaven help them all if she was.

Noah moved to Emma's side and took her hand. "I've been here a bunch of times," he admitted. "It never gets old. Whenever I visit, I want to stay forever."

He squeezed her fingers lightly, and her breath caught. She knew exactly what he meant. Knew she couldn't fool herself anymore. She was just as lost as Ashley was.

Heaven help her, too.

THE GROUP FELL silent as they followed the trail through the giant trees, some of which Noah estimated to be more than fifteen feet in diameter. The forest itself seemed to dampen outside noises. They weren't far from the highway, but it was easy to pretend they were miles deep in the wilderness.

"I love the smell of it here," Emma whispered.

Noah took a deep breath. It was earthy, scented with cedar, and he wondered if the whole world had been like this once. Their party spread out, Ashley and Andrew taking the lead, he and Emma next, and the other women trailing behind them like the tail of a comet.

"What do you think they think of us?" Emma walked slowly with her head tipped all the way back to try to see the tops of the redwoods.

He tilted his head back, too. "The trees? Do you think they think about us?"

"When I was a kid, I imagined we left eddies in the air when we passed by them, traces of us washing up against their bark. They must sense us in some distant way, don't you think? A flicker of movement through their stationary world. I wonder if we're like colorful fish swimming by?"

He'd never thought of it like that, but her daydream reminded him of the kind of reveries he'd had when he was younger. In high school he'd had plenty of time to hike and climb mountains and camp, and he'd spent hours under starry skies, or alone in forests, or at the top of mountains, letting his mind wander where it would.

He'd done his best to keep active during his start-up years, but it hadn't been the same, and suddenly Noah had a sense of time drifting away. He wanted more of this. Much more.

Which was why he'd bought the lot in Seahaven to begin with.

He stopped in front of an enormous tree that had hollowed out as it grew, leaving a cave-like opening at the bottom of its trunk. "After you," he said.

Emma went in happily. "You should have seen Ashley and me when Nana Angela brought us here. We decided then and there we'd live in this tree someday. We had the space divided up and everything."

"I wish I'd known you back then."

She smiled. "I wish I could go back and start over. I'd do everything differently."

"Like what?"

"Like leaving Florida the minute I graduated from culinary school and coming straight out here to live in this tree. It would have been a much better plan than anything I came up with."

He didn't like it when she put herself down that way. Had someone else in her life talked to her that way? If so, she needed to leave them behind.

"What have you done that's so bad?" he asked. "Sounds like you had a business idea and took a shot at it. Maybe it didn't work out, but I bet you learned a lot that will inform your next attempt."

"What have I done that's so bad?" she echoed. "I think the real question is what have I done that's good? I figure you're only a few years older than me, right? You're a successful millionaire. I'm flat broke. I wasted years on a business that went nowhere. On a relationship that was doomed from day one. I was engaged, you know, before everything went bust. I lost my business and my fiancé all at once."

"That's rough," he said. "But we all have relationships that don't pan out, and nine out of ten businesses fail. That doesn't mean you can't start another one.

Besides, soon we'll both own a beach house in one of the most beautiful places in the world," he reminded her.

"If I can keep mine." Her words were so soft he had to lean in. Was she in that much trouble?

"Emma—"

"I see you two hiding in there," Annie exclaimed. "Probably making out!"

Emma scuttled out of the hollowed trunk. "We weren't making out."

"Wouldn't blame you if you were," Annie said wistfully. "Give us a try in there."

Noah came out, too, took Emma's hand and kept walking, leaving the women to explore the tree themselves.

"This is a magical place," he admitted a few minutes later, his neck already sore from craning to see the tops of the giant trees. He wished he could continue the conversation they were having and vowed to pick it up again another time.

"It really is, but all of Seahaven feels that way to me—like any moment, something out of the ordinary could happen here."

He nodded. He wasn't the fanciful type, but he knew what she meant. Cradled between the ocean's constant movement and the redwood forests' eternal stillness, Seahaven was… special.

Like Emma.

He tucked a lock of hair behind her ear, and she

turned his way. Noah couldn't resist. He drew her behind a tree, bent down and kissed her.

THE REDWOOD'S BARK was rough at her back, Noah's chest hard under her hands as she braced herself against him. He smelled as good as the forest itself, and the feel of his mouth on hers was wonderful.

Emma couldn't help it. She moaned as he pulled her in closer, enjoying the strength of his arms as he held her. Aware of him everywhere they touched, she felt desire kick in low and hungry inside her—desire that wasn't going to be denied no matter how she tried to repress it. Being with Noah didn't make sense, but she wanted this man. Loved the feel of him pressed against her and the giddy sensation she got when he kissed her.

"Someday we're going to be alone," he growled into her neck when the kiss ended.

"Not today," she reminded him. "Not now."

Being alone with Noah sounded terrifying—and fabulous all at once. She could easily imagine tumbling into bed with him. Had fantasized about it once or twice already, in fact.

"Let's keep walking," she told him.

He acquiesced but kept a firm grip on her hand that suggested he didn't mean to let go again.

They met up with Andrew and Ashley where the path made a circle around a particularly enormous tree.

"I'm not lying down in the dirt. I'm not a child,"

Andrew was saying.

Emma laughed. She thought this might be the reason Ashley had dragged Andrew here. This was what Nana Angela had made them do the day she brought them to the park. According to her, the only way to truly appreciate a towering redwood was on your back.

"Chicken," Ashley taunted him and dropped down to the dirt trail.

"I'm not chicken." Andrew watched as Emma joined her and then Noah did, too, more slowly. "Fine, but this is ridiculous." He removed the jacket he was wearing, some expensive brand Emma didn't recognize, folded it neatly and sat down beside Ashley with a disgusted sigh. When he lay back, however, like the rest of them, he fell silent again.

A soft breeze played through the canopy, making branches and leaves sway and flutter far overhead. They could hear the voices of other visitors, but they were muffled, as if at a great distance. Sunlight and shadow played over them, the sharp/sweet cedar smell pervading everything. Emma took a deep breath and relaxed.

That was the thing about redwoods—they were so calm. So enduring. So… huge. They'd already been here hundreds of years when she was born, and most of them would live long past when she died. While she scurried around conducting her everyday affairs, they stood here proudly, quietly getting along with things.

She heard Annie and the others approaching, but the

women didn't call out or ask for explanations. One by one they, too, dropped to the ground and lay back.

Emma didn't realize she was dozing off, mesmerized by the patterns made by the breeze through the canopy, until some minutes later, Noah shifted beside her. She opened her eyes to find him looking at her. "I bet some people are going to want to stop at the visitor's center before we eat," he said apologetically.

"You're right." Emma got up as slowly as if she were waking from a nap, her problems feeling as distant as the voices that echoed through the woods from time to time when other groups of visitors passed by. "Ashley? We should keep going."

They did so, but the group had lost its rhythm. When they finally finished their walk around the redwood loop, they didn't spend much time in the visitors' center or gift shop after all. They found a picnic table behind the gift shop, and the women chatted happily through the meal, but Andrew was quiet, his gaze distant as he ate. Ashley kept watching him from under her lashes. Emma watched her, concerned for her sister. Had she accomplished what she wanted with this little field trip?

What did Ashley want, anyway?

Sometimes Emma felt like she was the only one fighting to preserve her grandmother's legacy. Other times, she thought Ashley wanted to fight for it just as hard, even if she wouldn't admit it.

She figured Nana Angela had brought her and her

sister here when they were children to instill in them a sense of wonder and enough curiosity they'd always be interested in the natural world. Was Ashley trying to prompt some sense of humility in Andrew in his dealing with the Cliff Garden?

Would it work?

By the time they made it home, she was ready to be alone. Luckily everyone else seemed to be in a similar mood. As she parked Bessie in her spot, Andrew was already heading off for a walk. The women climbed out and went inside.

Noah met her at the door. "I guess Andrew needed some time to himself," he said with a shrug. "I don't know what's on his mind."

"Hopefully a little more appreciation for nature," Ashley said tartly, moving past him. She disappeared into her bedroom.

"Meet up at seven for dinner?" Annie asked her friends.

"That's a good plan," Ginni said. "I'm exhausted."

They made their way upstairs and, from the sound of doors opening and shutting, scattered to their rooms.

"I'm going to go catch some waves," Noah told Emma. "Let's meet up later, too."

"Sounds good."

Emma wandered around picking things up, doing some dishes and planning the following morning's breakfast, but soon found herself too restless to settle to anything. She poured herself a tall glass of juice and was ready to head outside as well, when she glanced through a window and spotted someone sitting on the Trouble Bench.

She took a calming breath and remembered what her grandmother used to say. "You need to give people a minute. See if the ocean breeze and the sun can cure their ills before you rush to give it a try. Sometimes that's all it takes."

Emma kept an eye on the young woman as she moved back to the kitchen, busying herself with unloading the dishwasher, a task she'd planned to put off until later. All the while, the woman on the bench stayed where she was. She looked to be in her early twenties. Her shoulders were hunched, as if she had wrapped her arms over her belly. Emma couldn't stand it anymore. She grabbed a plate, piled an assortment of cookies on it. Covered it with a linen napkin and filled a glass with water.

"Hi," she said a minute later as sat down on the Trouble Bench next to the young woman. "I don't mean to startle you," she went on. "I'm Emma Miller. I live at Brightview." She pointed toward the house. "You looked like you could use some company. Would you like a cookie?"

"Oh, I… I don't know."

"Don't worry, it's safe," Emma assured her. "It's tradition for the women in my family to bring snacks to people when they visit the garden. The Cliff Garden has been in the family for a hundred years."

"I heard something about that," the woman confessed. "But I heard the old lady who used to take care of it was dead. Sorry," she added a moment later. "That must be a relative of yours. I shouldn't have said that."

"It's okay. Angela was my grandmother," Emma told her. "She left me Brightview."

"You're so lucky." The woman tentatively took one of the cookies Emma offered her. "I'd love a house like that. I'm Aurora Bentley. I grew up in the Leaf."

The Leaf was a neighborhood on the other side of town whose streets approximated that shape. It was a solid, family-centric area, close to the tourist district with its boutiques and restaurants.

"Where do you live now?"

"I've been in San Jose for the past year, but I'm moving home. Twenty-four and going to live with my parents again. Yay, me." Aurora nibbled at the cookie, but Emma had a feeling she wasn't tasting it. "My boyfriend just dumped me," she said disgustedly. "I should have seen it coming a mile away, but I didn't. I feel so… stupid."

"You lived with him?" Emma thought about the day Jordan broke up with her—and she realized she was going to lose her home along with her fiancé.

Aurora nodded. She looked out at the ocean, watching the waves march toward the shore. "It gets worse.

I'm pregnant."

Emma straightened. "Congratulations!"

"Thanks." Aurora's voice cracked. "You're the first person to say that to me." A moment later, she began to cry. "I left school to be with him. He said college was a waste of money. He said I didn't need to work—he'd pay the bills. I thought we were going to get married. He said we would—someday."

"What happened?" Emma handed her the cloth napkin, which Aurora dabbed at her cheeks.

"When I found out I was pregnant, I told Ben. I thought he'd propose. Instead he broke up with me. He said he never wants to see me again."

"I'm so sorry." Emma handed her the glass of water, and Aurora took a long drink. It was Nana Angela's contention that most people were dehydrated and it contributed to their problems.

"I'm moving my things to my parents' house tomorrow. They don't know about the baby, and they're going to be so upset when they find out. They warned me about Ben, you know. Said he was immature and wouldn't stand by me when it counted. They were right." She scrubbed at her eyes with the sleeve of her shirt. "Why am I so dumb?"

"You aren't dumb. You're human. When people tell us things, we believe them. You wouldn't lie to Ben, right? Why would you think he'd lie to you?" Emma patted her arm. "And you're right; your parents might be upset—at first. But they love you and want the best for you. They'll come through for you in ways you can't imagine right now. You'll see."

"How will I support my baby?"

"For one thing, you'll file for child support when the baby is born. You'll find a job and go back to school, too," Emma said simply. "There are all kinds of ways to do that now. Night classes. Online classes. You'll find student loans and grants. Your parents will grumble, but they'll help. It'll be hard work for a few years, but you'll do it."

Aurora nodded slowly. "You're right. I will. I'm not going to screw up anymore. I'm going to make sure I can create the life this baby deserves."

"The life you deserve, too," Emma reminded her. "And someday you'll meet a man who's a true match for you, if you want one."

Aurora snorted. "I doubt that. I'm staying away from men from now on."

Emma remembered how she'd felt after Jordan's betrayal. "You don't have to try dating again anytime soon, but when you're ready, you'll do a better job at choosing a partner. You'll know you have to ask a lot of questions and spend a lot of time with a man before you make any long-term decisions."

"That's for sure. I won't be so easy to fool next time. Thanks," Aurora added, biting into a second cookie. "I feel a lot better than I did ten minutes ago. And these are really great."

"Come back any time you need to," Emma told her.

Then she remembered the Cliff Garden wouldn't be around much longer.

NOAH RAN INTO Greg getting out of the water when he made it to the beach.

"Hey, man, how's it going?" Greg high-fived him and set his board down on the sand. "You're right on time. There are some good sets coming in."

"Glad to hear it. I'm doing well. You?"

"Couldn't be better. Always stoked when I've had some time in the waves." Greg shook the water out of his hair and ran a hand through it to slick it back. "You look a little down, though. Something up?"

"You could say that." He explained his situation as briefly as he could. When he mentioned the Cliff Garden, Greg turned to look in that direction, although you couldn't see anything but the bluffs from here.

"I didn't realize that's where you were building. Lot of people around here love that place."

"I know that now. I didn't when I bought it. No matter what I do, someone is going to hate me. Either my brother or Emma and her sister."

"I'm not sure I understand how your brother comes into this," Greg said.

"That's a story for another time." Bad enough Greg knew he was going to ruin the Cliff Garden. Noah didn't need to give him another reason to dislike him.

"I'm sure you'll figure it out. There's always another way." Greg clapped him on the shoulder. "You coming to that barbecue I told you about?"

"Of course." Noah was grateful he was still invited.

"Good. Get out there and catch a few waves. That will clear your head."

Noah was counting on it.

An hour later, when he met up with Andrew at Brightview, he wasn't sure he had any more clarity about the situation, but he knew he had to set a few parameters with his brother. "Hey, we need to talk."

Andrew followed him to the Cliff Garden. When Noah spotted Emma sitting on the Trouble Bench with a young woman, he nearly turned back, but instead he led his brother to another corner and sat him down where they couldn't be seen.

"Look," he began, "I want you to build something really special here. I want you to win your awards and get those magazine covers, but when that's all done, I'll still need to live with my neighbors. Emma isn't the only one who's going to be upset when we mess with this garden. You need to situate the house over here." They were sitting in the farthest corner from Emma's place. "And you need to preserve as many of the trees, bushes, and flower beds as you can. Understand? I want Emma to barely see my house when she looks this way."

Andrew studied him, and Noah had a feeling he was

holding back a growing anger. "I get the situation," he said stiffly, "and I'm willing to change my plans, but I'm not willing to compromise on the feel of the place I'm designing. I can site the house where you want. I can have a garden on the side facing Emma. Now you need to back off and let me do it my way."

Noah thought about how stark Andrew's design was. Despite its size, the house was meant for a bachelor rather than a family. It was as if his brother thought he'd reached his apex and would remain like this indefinitely—a grown man acting like… a kid.

That wasn't what he wanted. Not after spending days in Emma's warm, comfortable home.

Before he could put any of that into words, however, Andrew added, "I've decided to fly home to Seattle tonight. I'll be back in a few weeks, and we'll finalize plans. Start pulling permits. Time to get this show on the road."

CHAPTER 8

WHEN EMMA RETURNED to the house, she poured herself a tall glass of water and took it outside to the deck, intending to sit on the swing and let the beautiful view and soft breeze calm her. She was pleased with the way things had gone with Aurora, who'd been happy to exchange phone numbers and planned to stop by the following week to check in, but she felt drained. She'd been so worried she might say or do the wrong thing. Now she needed a minute to herself.

To her surprise, she found Kate in the grassy area beyond the deck, on her knees near a flower border on the side closest to the Blue House. Was she weeding?

"You don't have to do that," she called out, hurrying down the steps toward her. It pained her to think one of her guests found the property so untended she thought she had to step in.

"Do you mind if I do?" Kate sat back on her heels and tucked a tendril of her hair behind her ear. "I've been… restless. I need something to keep me busy."

"I guess I don't mind," Emma said truthfully. "But it

seems like bad form to have a guest working on the property."

"I think you should advertise it as a perk. I'm living in a rental right now, and I don't have a garden to tend. I've missed it." She got back to work.

Emma, not knowing what else to do, crouched next to her and began to weed as well. So much for taking a break. She didn't mind Kate working on the border, but she wasn't comfortable with a guest working while she took it easy.

"You don't have to stay, you know," Kate told her with a laugh a few minutes later. "I'm perfectly happy working by myself. Not that I mind the company."

"It is kind of soothing, isn't it?" Emma asked her, finding she was enjoying the easy task, the sunshine and the company. "Ashley was the gardener growing up. I didn't have much patience for it, but I think… maybe I've gotten a little more patient with age."

"I think most of us do. Hang on." Kate crossed the yard to a small shed tucked in one corner and came back with a pair of gloves and a weeding tool for Emma.

"Much better." Emma got to work more efficiently, both of them tossing their weeds into a large plastic flowerpot Kate must have found earlier.

"There's a compost pile over there," Kate told her. "We can pile the weeds there."

It should be embarrassing to have a guest know her property better than she did, but Kate was so pleasant about it, Emma didn't mind.

"Where are your friends?"

Kate made a face. "Shopping. Again." She tossed a weed in the pot. "Don't get me wrong, I like shopping as much as the next person, but I wanted to be outside. After our trip to the redwoods… I don't know. I can't get it out of my head—a feeling that I'm not on the right path."

"What path should you be on?" Emma asked lightly. She wasn't sure if she was ready for another confidence so soon after talking to Aurora, but it seemed like she was going to get one.

"I've been playing everything safe for a long time. Working a job that doesn't exactly excite me, living in a city I used to love, but now… I don't know. I'm ready for something new."

"Like what?"

"Like—" Kate stopped herself. "Sorry. It's too soon. I'm afraid if I say it out loud, it will sound ridiculous, and that will be the end of that."

"I know exactly what you mean," Emma assured her. "Dreams are fragile things. You have to tend them for a while before they solidify. You know what, though? I spotted a whole bunch of art and craft supplies in the storage area on the third floor. If you help me carry them down, we can see if there's anything you might want to use while you're here. I don't know about you, but when I have an idea, I need to sketch things out."

Kate was looking at her.

"What?" Emma asked.

"I swear you read my mind. I was out here lecturing myself about how silly it would be to buy paper and pens and things when I'm leaving in a couple of days, but I've been itching to set down my ideas in a visual way."

"Whenever you've had enough weeding, let me know. We'll bring everything to your room."

Kate put down her weeding tool and threw her arms around Emma. "You're the best host ever. You know that?"

"Thanks." As Emma soaked in the sweetness of such praise, she realized that unlike Kate, she thought she was on exactly the right path. She belonged here at Brightview. She was good at this job.

She wanted to stay.

"I REMEMBER THIS place," Ashley said the following evening when Noah pulled into a parking space on the wharf in front of the restaurant where he'd booked a reservation. He'd invited both sisters to dinner, thinking it was time to soften Ashley's resistance to him if he wanted a future with Emma. The Pelican's Nest was a square building covered with weathered shingles that boasted a rooftop deck where local bands played.

"You've been here before?" he asked her.

"I think so. Emma? What do you think?" Ashley asked, getting out of the car.

"I think you're right. I do remember this place." Emma joined her, and they moved toward the front door. "Did we eat lunch upstairs once—and a seagull came and stole some of your fries?"

"That's right. I cried." Ashley laughed as she tugged open the door and waited for Emma to enter. Noah took over and ushered them both inside ahead of him. "I think Nana Angela ordered me more."

"She was so sweet," Emma said with a sigh. "Dad would have told you to suck it up."

"If he'd even noticed at all."

Noah saw the quick look that passed between the sisters and the way they abruptly turned in opposite directions. He filed away the conversation in his mind to think about later. What kind of father wouldn't get some more fries in a situation like that?

"What else did you order last time you were here?" Noah asked them when they were seated and looking over their menus, hoping to distract the sisters from whatever memories had made them both go silent.

"Fish and chips, of course," Emma said. "Nana Angela tried to get me to order something a little more sophisticated, but I knew what I wanted."

"I ordered crab legs with my fries," Ashley said. "I was definitely sophisticated."

"Sounds like the perfect combination to me." He thought about the photograph he'd seen in the living room. Two little girls riding bikes, one blond, one dark.

In that photo, they were both happy and confident. What happened in the interim? Both women had moments of guardedness that spoke of hard times in their past. "Emma told me you're buying into a partnership at your firm. Forensic accounting, right?"

"That's right. When something goes wrong, I pick through companies' financial records to find the threads that lead to what happened and who did it," Ashley said with satisfaction.

"Sounds interesting."

"It is." Ashley lifted her chin. "People always think accounting is boring, but numbers tell a story."

Noah wished he knew the full story behind Brightview's financial picture. He wanted to help Emma but didn't know how.

"Did you two grow up around here?"

Emma peered at him over her menu. "We grew up in Florida—on the Panhandle. Didn't I tell you that before?"

"You haven't told me much about your past, except about your business."

Ashley scowled. Emma looked down.

Uh-oh. He'd stepped in something there. "What's northern Florida like?" he asked, hoping to recover solid ground.

"Depends on where you live," Ashley said. "Some parts are paradise. Others are just hell."

"Ashley," Emma admonished her. "She thinks we

were hard done by," she told Noah.

"I know we were hard done by," Ashley corrected her. "Which is why I got out and I'm never going back."

The waitress came to take their order before Noah could press her further, and he bit back his impatience long enough to ask for a blackened mahi mahi dish that sounded fantastic. Emma ordered salmon. Ashley went with crab legs—and French fries—again.

Noah sat back when the waitress was gone and studied the women. Ashley was lining up her silverware with her plate. Emma was gazing at the other diners, deep in thought.

"You said your mother passed away when you were young?" he asked.

Both women lifted their gazes to him.

"Yes," Emma said softly. "I was eight. Ashley was six. She brought us out here for the summer that year, then slipped away before Christmas."

"I'm sorry to hear that." Now he had context for Ashley's earlier comment. If her father had raised them single-handedly after that, it would have been a big deal if he wasn't the kind of guy to give them a lot of attention. "What about your dad?"

"He's gone, too. Six months ago," Emma said.

Noah ran over the facts he knew about her in his head. She'd lost her mother as a child. Had lost her father this year—as well as a business and a fiancé? No wonder Emma was guarded sometimes.

"It was rough growing up, but we made it. There were plenty of good times, too," she said firmly.

"Were there?" Ashley asked. "I don't remember any of them."

"Come on, Ash. No one has an easy life," Emma chided her.

"I bet *he* did." Ashley jutted her chin Noah's way. "Millionaire child prodigy here doesn't know what it's like to be poor."

"Ashley." Emma shook her head warningly.

"She's right. I've never been poor." Noah stepped in before things could get out of hand. "But my parents passed away early, too," he told Ashley. "I was twelve. Andrew was eighteen."

Ashley's features went slack. "Shit. I'm sorry," she murmured, a faint flush edging up her cheeks.

"That must have been awful," Emma said.

"Andrew raised me." Noah shrugged. "Like you said, it was rough, but there were good times, too." And some really, really bad ones, but those were his own damn fault. "I bet your folks would be really happy with how you two turned out. Look at you running a B and B, and you buying into a partnership of an important firm, Ashley."

Ashley huffed out a breath. "Proud of us? Mom, maybe. I can't remember enough about her to know how she'd feel about my career choices, but at least she knew how to hold down a job. Dad…" She trailed off. Noah had a feeling Emma had kicked her under the table. "Well, Dad's another story," she finished.

Their dad had let them down, Noah mused, which gave them both a reason to be suspicious of men. How could he convince them he meant no harm?

"Maybe we should celebrate our own accomplishments," he suggested. "I, for one, am impressed with both of you. I've heard of Cotler, Tannen and Brindle," he added to Ashley. Emma had mentioned the company's name to him before. "It's got a fantastic reputation. If you've managed to work yourself into a position to become a partner at your age, you're the one who's a child prodigy."

Ashley settled down. "You know what? You're right. I set myself a bunch of goals when I was in high school, and I've achieved every one of them, or will soon."

"That's amazing."

"I haven't achieved any of my dreams," Emma said. "But Nana Angela has given me a second chance, and I'm determined to take it." She swallowed as if bracing herself for an attack, and for a moment, Noah thought Ashley might launch into one, but she restrained herself, smoothed her napkin where it lay on the table and adjusted her fork a fraction of an inch. He wondered what Ashley's beef with Emma was. She disapproved of something her sister had done. Was it the business Emma started?

"I hope you're successful with the B and B," Ashley

finally said. The words were a little forced, and Noah remembered what Emma told him before. Ashley thought she should sell the bed-and-breakfast and pay off her debts. If she'd changed her mind, that was a step in the right direction.

"Thank you," Emma said. She smiled impishly at Noah. "If we're celebrating, I should have ordered crab legs, too."

"It's not too late."

AURORA WAS BACK in the Cliff Garden when Emma met Ava and Penelope there the following morning.

"Hi," she said sheepishly. "I swear I'm not stalking you. I woke up early and couldn't fall back to sleep, so I decided to get out of the house before I woke my mom and dad, too."

"Is everything all right?" Emma asked her.

"It's fine. I told them about the baby. Mom cried, because she thinks things are going to be really hard for me, but then she cheered right up and started talking about baby clothes." Aurora shrugged. "You were right. It wasn't nearly as bad as I thought. My dad offered to help me pay for school."

"I'm so glad." Emma introduced her to Ava and Penelope.

"Want to walk with us?" Ava asked.

"Sure, as long as I'm not in your way."

"We'd love to have you."

They set out along Cliff Street as usual.

"How are things going with Noah?" Penelope asked Emma.

She got them up to speed on all that had happened the previous day.

"Noah is trying to get Andrew to situate his house so there's room for some of the garden to stay, but I don't think Andrew likes that idea," she finished.

"Isn't an architect supposed to do what you tell them?" Penelope asked.

"I'm not sure what's going on between Noah and his brother. He seems to be giving Andrew a lot of power in the equation," Emma said.

"Is Noah going to start a new business now that he's at loose ends?" Ava asked.

"I think he's going to focus on his photography. I don't think he ever needs to earn a dime again if he doesn't want to," Emma said.

"Lucky guy," Aurora said.

"Sounds like photography is his true passion," Ava said. "Even if I was rich, I'd need something like that to occupy me."

"What would you choose to do?" Emma asked her.

"I'd start a school of my own maybe," Ava told her. "I think the one I'm going to work for will be great, but I'd love to create a whole curriculum around science and nature. And adventure."

"I'd start a landscaping business," Aurora said, then

bit her lip. "Sorry. You didn't ask me."

"Don't be sorry. That sounds like a very practical plan," Ava said. "Are you good with lawns and gardens?"

"I'm great with them. I always took care of my parents' yard, and my grandma and grandpa's place. I used to mow lawns to earn money when I was a kid. I love gardens. I could come and help with the Cliff Garden sometimes," she suggested.

"Come anytime. You'll find everything you need in the shed," Emma told her.

"Have you told your parents you'd like to start a landscaping company?" Penelope asked her curiously.

"No," Aurora admitted. "Guess I should, huh?"

"I think so. Seems like it might bear on the choices you're making."

When their walk was over, the women parted ways, and Emma returned to Brightview energized by the sunshine and good company. She found Kate at the kitchen counter, scrolling through her phone. Emma washed her hands, tied on an apron and got to work on the breakfast buffet, handing Kate a cup of coffee and a mini muffin to tide her over.

"You're such a fabulous cook. Did you ever work in a restaurant?" Kate asked after swallowing a bite of the muffin.

"Lots of them. I went to culinary school, too."

"What did you do after that?"

Emma wondered how much she should say. These

days talking about the company she was once so proud of made her sad—and embarrassed. Which really was too bad, she thought. It had been a great idea.

"I'll show you," she said and pulled out her phone. She called up her old website. She'd disabled the order-taking part, but she hadn't had the heart to pull the whole thing down yet.

"Food to You Fast," Kate read. "Emma, your site is so pretty—and easy to navigate." She explored the different tabs. "You had so many meal choices. I bet people loved this. What happened?"

"Jordan happened." She'd never thought she'd say his name with such resentment. "I met him when I graduated from culinary school, and we dated for a few years while I worked at restaurants and he worked for his parents' chain of sporting goods stores. He hated working for his folks, and I was sick of working for other people, too. I got the idea for Food to You Fast, and as soon as we could, we quit our jobs. I moved in with him to save money. After a while we got engaged. Unfortunately, it turned out Jordan was a lousy businessman—and a cheat, too."

He wasn't always that way, though, Emma had to admit. He was funny when they first met. Sweet. A little goofy. If she was honest, he'd struggled to keep up with her right from the start. He wasn't good at his job when he worked for his folks, and he wasn't good at working with her, either.

Emma thought about that as Kate kept exploring her website. At the time she'd thought she was helping him escape his overbearing parents, but now she saw she'd only replaced them. Soon she was the one nagging and pushing him all the time. Had she pushed him too hard? Once, after he'd had a few beers, he admitted his real dream was coaching high school soccer. She'd laughed at him.

"That won't pay the bills," she'd said. Had his mother and father told him the same thing?

She remembered the way his face had fallen. "I know." Thinking about it made her a little sick.

"He stole your money?" Kate prompted, breaking into her thoughts.

Emma swallowed. Not quite. "He helped me lose my money—and broke up with me." She'd been telling everyone he'd dumped her. Walked out on her. Cheated on her.

That wasn't really what happened, though.

At the time she'd been frantic about the possibility she was going to lose her business. She was the one who'd told him he needed to work with Tricia Sedelman, the business coach she'd hired. She'd told him to figure out how to turn things around, and he'd tried. He had done the weekly calls with Tricia, first reluctantly and then enthusiastically. She'd thought she'd finally found the lever to make him produce in the way she needed him to.

She'd been wrong.

What had those conversations entailed? Had Tricia asked him what he really wanted to do? Had she listened to him when he said he didn't think he was cut out for business?

Did she encourage him to become a high school athletics coach? Was that all it had taken to lure him away?

"You know what?" she said to Kate. "He didn't lose my money. I did. I put him in charge of it, and when he told me he couldn't handle the work, I ignored him. Food to You Fast was my company, and I didn't take responsibility for it. I was overwhelmed, and I didn't know how. I really messed up."

"Do you miss him a lot?"

"Jordan?" Emma laughed, mostly in surprise at her visceral reaction to the question. She didn't miss him at all. "No, I don't. He was completely wrong for me—and me for him." Despite herself, her thoughts skipped to Noah. He was ambitious, smart, a go-getter, like she was.

Kate touched her arm. "Sounds like it wasn't the disaster you think it was. It was a learning experience." She gestured expansively. "Now you own a bed-and-breakfast, and you're fantastic at running it. I know I don't want to leave."

"Glad to hear it." She wouldn't mention the looming mortgage payment and all the repairs that needed to be done. She needed to make a new budget. Call the bank and set up another meeting. Try to refinance…

Kate took a sip of her coffee. "Is it harder than it looks, running this place?" she asked carefully. "You're still pretty new at this, right?"

"I am, but it's not that. It's… debt. I didn't realize how much is owing on this place when I inherited it, or how much it would cost to keep it up. I need to earn more money." She needed to go to Nana Angela's PO box. Why did it keep slipping her mind?

Kate brightened. "You should start by making a breakfast-themed cookbook. *Brightview Beginnings* or *Brightview Breakfasts* or something like that. It might not be the biggest money-maker, but it's a way to get your brand out there."

"I've always wanted to do that," Emma admitted. "I have a lot of recipes. What I don't have is a publisher or photographer."

"Did someone say they need a photographer?" Noah entered the room tugging a T-shirt over his head, giving them both a glimpse of his washboard abs. Kate shot her an amused look.

"Emma needs a photographer for the cookbook she's writing."

"You're writing a cookbook? That's terrific." He came to join them, bending down as if he meant to brush a kiss across her cheek but quickly straightening again. Was he worried she wouldn't want him to show affection in front of Kate?

Funny—if he had kissed her, she wouldn't have minded.

She was completely hopeless.

"Someday," Emma said, pulling herself together. She could not fall for this man. He was off limits.

"You need money now," Kate pointed out. "Why not get started? I'll help." She made an apologetic face. "I wanted to ask you about that, actually. I'd like to stay for a while after my friends leave, if you don't mind. I could work more on your landscaping. I'm kind of at loose ends right now," she added in a rush. "I know this is a really weird request, but I don't want to leave, and I don't know anyone else in Seahaven. I could rent another place, but I feel comfortable with you."

"I suppose that would be okay." Emma wasn't sure what Kate was asking. Did she expect to be paid for the work? She had no room in her budget for that.

"I'm not asking to be paid," Kate said, as if hearing her thoughts. "I… have a problem to sort out and I need something to do while I think about it. The art supplies you gave me are helping, but I need fresh air and physical work to focus my mind. I have tons of vacation time stacked up at my job. I thought I'd use it to give myself time to figure out what to do next. Does that make sense?"

"Actually, it does," Emma admitted. "When I need to solve a problem, I bake things. Usually by the time they're done, I've found an answer."

“Exactly.” Kate smiled and her whole face lit up. She was pretty, Emma decided. When Kate’s friends were around, she faded away into the background, but one on one like this, she shone.

“I’d love to photograph the food you make,” Noah said. “I’ve never done it before, so I’ll have to do a little research and learn some tricks, but I’m game to give it a try.”

“I don’t know if I’m ready…”

“You’re ready,” Kate assured her. “Judging by the weight I’ve put on this weekend. And I’ll tell you what, the cookbook is only the start. You need to create an online cooking course that people can purchase and take whenever they like. Basic recipes that taste great but use the kind of ingredients people like me already have, not bizarre things I have to run all over town to get. Do a whole series of classes, each one focused on a specific theme. You can keep adding new classes, and people will keep coming back. Set them up in a fun way, so people can get together with a few friends, follow the directions and make a fantastic meal to share.”

“Suggest wine and beer pairings,” Noah said.

“And ways to plate the food so it looks great,” Kate said.

“You could film right here in your kitchen—and advertise the B and B at the same time,” Noah suggested.

“You could put together vacation packages for people to come here and stay—and take live classes, too,”

Kate said.

"And put classes on for the locals," Noah suggested. "I bet you could team up with wineries around here to do special events."

"Enough," Emma cried. "That's more than I could do in a lifetime!"

"Start with the cookbook and the online classes. Noah and I will help every step of the way. Right, Noah?" Kate asked.

"Sure thing." He moved into the kitchen and found orange juice in the refrigerator. He knew where the glasses were stored. In fact, he seemed right at home.

"Are you serious?" Emma asked him.

"Absolutely. As long as I still have time to surf."

"Better get out there while you can," she told him. She needed him gone from her kitchen before she lost all her better judgment and went for that kiss he hadn't given her earlier.

"Yes, ma'am. Be back soon." He downed his glass of orange juice, whistled for Winston, who was lounging in his usual spot on the deck, and they both left.

"Well?" Kate said. "Are you going to thank me?"

"For the cookbook idea? Yes, thank you very much," Emma said, getting back to work.

Kate snorted. "For getting you the hottest business partner I bet you've ever seen."

Emma hesitated, then decided not to deny it. "Thank you for that, too."

THE NEXT FEW days went quickly, and soon everyone but Kate was gone. Noah made it a point to get up in time to meet Emma in the garden before joining her sunrise walks with the "sisters" or peeling off to get in some early surfing. Kate slept in a little later and spent her mornings working on the border gardens around the grassy area beyond the deck. Emma kept trying to get her to come along on the early walks, but so far Kate had resisted. Noah thought she was afraid she wouldn't fit in with the other, more flamboyant women, or maybe she was afraid to get too attached to the place.

He'd already lost that battle.

Ava and Penelope teased him mercilessly. The Surf Dads did, too, telling him he was burning through his probation period fast and he'd have to produce a child quickly or be thrown out of the club. "Then where will you go for cold beer and the best barbecue in town?" Greg had asked. Noah hadn't told him he could find both at Emma's place.

He'd connected with Will Jans and the Wilkens brothers—important names in the local surf scene who'd agreed to let him photograph them the next time the waves got big. He'd made a number of other acquaintances in the group, men he figured would soon be friends.

He spent his time with one eye on the forecast, the other on Emma, watching for any opportunity to surf or get close to her. Unfortunately, he wasn't the only one.

Every day someone showed up on the Trouble Bench. Luckily, Emma had lots of baked goods to spare.

She was spending all her free time in the kitchen, making test batches of the recipes she'd created over the years for her food delivery business, making changes and substitutions and jotting down new ideas as they came to her. He'd been watching videos about food photography, and whenever she brought a batch of treats out of the oven, he purloined some to practice with. It was hard to keep from eating her food long enough to photograph it, but he was getting better and had taken a few shots he was proud of.

"We'll have to split the proceeds from the cookbook," she said.

"No way," he told her bluntly. "Give me the photography credit on the book, but I don't want your money."

"It's only fair."

"If you have to sell this place, my new neighbor might be a real ass," he pointed out. "I want you next door. Nobody else."

She blushed, and he took advantage of the situation to steal a kiss.

He seemed to be kissing Emma all the time these days, but things hadn't progressed any further, and he wasn't sure why he was hesitating.

Maybe because he was afraid to ruin the understanding they'd come to. Emma was letting him kiss her now, but soon enough Andrew would return with new plans, and their arguments would start up again. He wanted this comfortable interlude to last as long as possible.

"Emma, can I get Ashley's number from you?" Kate asked later that day.

"Sure. Can I ask why?"

"The last time she was here we were chatting about border plants, and now I can't remember all the ones she said she liked. I was playing around with a design for sprucing up your border on this side of the lawn. Would you mind if I bought a couple of plants to add to it?"

"Mind? Of course not, but you shouldn't be spending your money on my property."

Kate waved her worries away. "It's my pleasure."

Emma gave her Ashley's number, and soon Kate was texting away happily. Over the next few days, "Ashley said" or "According to Ashley" began to pepper her talk, which was all about her design for the border. Noah wondered what Emma thought of that.

"I'm glad Ashley is talking about gardens again, at least," Emma said when he asked one evening. They were sitting out on the deck under a canopy of stars, wrapped in blankets against the chill, each drinking a bottle of beer. "When she sold the Cliff Garden, I wasn't just angry, I was worried about her. It was so out of character—she always kept a garden in Florida, and now she lives in a condo. I wish she would spend more time here."

"Do you think Kate will stay?"

"Maybe." Emma shrugged. "I think she's taken a shine to you."

"Well, I've taken a shine to *you*, so she can't have me," he assured her.

Emma studied him. "*Have* you taken a shine to me?"

"You haven't noticed?" He chuckled. "Yeah," he said. "I didn't mean to fall for anyone, but somehow here I am falling for you."

She let the stillness stretch between them until Noah worried she was about to brush him off.

"Ditto," she finally said. "I didn't mean to, but here I am."

He was unprepared for the effect her words wrought on his body. He'd been sleepy before. Now he was awake. Noah put his drink down. His voice was rough when he began to speak again. "Emma. Come here."

She hesitated, then slid his way, and he gathered her into his lap. When she relaxed against him, something in his chest loosened. He hadn't realized how worried he'd been that he could lose her.

He still could, he cautioned himself.

This was the lull before the storm.

CHAPTER 9

EMMA WAS GRATEFUL when April turned to May and a new party of guests came to stay, filling the rest of the second-story rooms once more. This time it was a mixed group of young couples from Las Vegas. The noise level in the house went through the roof. Kate began to slip around the edges of things, silent as a shadow but not unhappy, Emma thought. She'd introduced her to Aurora, after remembering Aurora's comment about wanting to start a landscaping business, and the two women soon became thick as thieves, working to implement Kate's border plan, looping Ashley in via text and video calls. Noah turned out to be helpful in a dozen ways, keeping the new guests occupied when she was busy in the kitchen, giving them lots of suggestions for local restaurants and bars, even inviting them to surf with him one morning.

Every time he came near, anticipation suffused her. She'd grown used to his kisses without noticing it and now caught herself rising on tiptoe to greet him when he came in from the beach or first thing in the morning, as if they were a couple.

She wasn't sure what they were. He hadn't formally asked her on a date—or made a serious move on her. Every night she braced herself for what seemed an inevitable question—would she like to come to bed with him? So far he hadn't asked. Emma wasn't sure if she was grateful or disappointed.

A little of both, she thought now. If he asked her, she'd say yes. Her desire for him nearly swamped her sometimes, and he was all she could think about at night before she went to sleep. On the other hand, she was afraid of the implications of falling for the man who would be her neighbor, especially once he ruined something that had been special to her family for generations. Could she really get past that, or would her anger grow? What if they had sex, things didn't work out and she had to live for the next fifty years beside a man who knew her intimately?

"Are you ready for tomorrow?" Ava called across at sundown from her third-story deck. She didn't invite Emma and Penelope over on days she had guests. Instead, she acted as a relay between the other two, passing on information.

"I think so. You're coming, right?"

"Wouldn't miss it for the world." She turned to catch something Penelope said. "Pen, either. We'll be there at six."

Tomorrow she was going to take her first crack at

teaching a cooking class. They would record the event as practice, and she would learn what did and didn't work about teaching both in person and online.

She was a little nervous and a lot excited. Kate and Noah were making the whole situation fun. They were full of ideas and energy, and the experience was so different from working with Jordan. How had she ever thought he was the one for her? Or that he'd make a good business partner?

"Incoming," Ava called. "It's from Penelope."

Emma set her glass down on the ledge and leaned over the side railing to pull in the message bag Ava was sending over on the clothesline between their houses. Inside, she found a soft rectangular package.

"Open it," Ava said.

Emma did so and pulled out a fuchsia apron with the words Brightview Bed-and-Breakfast emblazoned on it.

"Free advertising," Penelope hollered from two doors down.

"I love it!" Emma called back. "Tell her I'll definitely wear it tomorrow night," she said to Ava, who relayed the message.

"See you then." Ava toasted her. So did Penelope from where she stood.

Emma went inside smiling.

"You look happy," Noah greeted her when she reached the ground level.

"I am. I love it here," she told him.

"So do I." He tugged her in close, nuzzled her neck and slid his hands down to squeeze her bottom.

"Noah." She swatted him, but he caught her hands and kissed each one in turn.

"I'm being patient, but I don't know how much longer I can wait," he confessed.

"Me, neither." She didn't know why she always was so honest with him. Judging by the hunger in his eyes, he was pleased with her answer, which meant he might not wait much longer at all. What if they complicated everything by taking their relationship further?

Her phone buzzed in her pocket, giving her the perfect excuse to pull away. She answered it.

"Hello?"

"It's Ashley." There was a pause. "I'm in the hospital again."

"Ash—what's wrong?"

"Same as before." Frustration edged her sister's words. "I fainted at work."

"What did the doctors say?"

"Same as last time. They're running tests but can't find anything. They want me to rest. I can't rest!"

"Yes, you can. I'm coming to get you," Emma told her. Good thing she'd already prepared everything for tomorrow's breakfast—and the cooking class.

Should she cancel that?

"Don't you dare put yourself out for me," Ashley told her.

"I'm not." Emma decided to grab the bull by the horns. "But I'm holding a cooking class here tomorrow night. Do you think you'll be okay if I do that? I've got guests staying, too, and I can't keep kicking Noah out of his room. You're going to have to bunk with me this time."

"Of course. Just tuck me into a corner anywhere. I'll be fine."

When Emma hung up, Noah was jiggling his keys. "Another drive to San Francisco?"

"You don't have to come."

"I'm happy to. I just can't figure out your sister. She sold me her property, but it seems like she wants to keep an eye on it, at the very least," he joked.

"I don't think she's fainting for an excuse to come here," Emma chided him.

Noah grew serious. "No—I can't see Ashley faking an illness. She seems like a straight-shooter."

"I've never known Ashley to be sick at all. She's usually so dependable."

"Maybe she needs a break from that. You know, I don't mind driving up to San Francisco, but wouldn't it be easier for Ashley to hire a car to come down here? That's the way she went home the other day."

"My gut tells me she needs to be taken care of a little," Emma said. "It's making me nervous. Like I said, this isn't like Ashley at all, but if she needs some TLC, I'm going to give it to her. Heaven knows she used to pick me up when I fell down." When they were young, anyway. When Emma had chosen an entrepreneurial path rather than working for someone else's company, Ashley lost patience with her. "Don't worry—I told her she needs to share my room."

"Absolutely not. She can have *my* room again. If she stays more than a few days, we'll figure out something."

"Noah."

"Let's go." He whistled for Winston.

Emma was able to enjoy the drive to San Francisco this time, being more at ease with Noah and knowing her sister had pulled through this once before. They spent the time brainstorming ways to get the word out about her classes and cookbook, whenever she got that done.

Noah was more than happy to talk about this subject, unlike Jordan, who'd always complained if they spoke about Food to You Fast outside of business hours. In turn, she encouraged Noah to talk about his plans. He was focused on connecting with more surfers in the area and spending more time in the water where he could hone his skills.

"I can't rush this part," he told her. "I'm putting it out there that I'm looking for opportunities to shoot photographs of local surfers, but they're feeling me out as well, seeing how I behave out there in the water. How I act in the community, too."

"Do you think they like you?"

"For the most part," he said without arrogance, "but

I'm not winning favors by developing the Cliff Garden."

Emma didn't answer that. What could she say? She enjoyed Noah's company, and her body was very aware of his proximity, but he was right—his plans for the Cliff Garden complicated everything.

When they reached the hospital, Ashley was as pale as she'd been last time. Emma told herself if she needed to cancel her class tomorrow, she'd do it. Her sister's health came first.

"You brought Noah again?" Ashley asked her as Noah strode ahead of them to his parked car.

"He brought me," Emma corrected her. "Does it bother you I'm spending time with him? He's a paying guest—one who's going to sleep on the deck again so you can have your own room."

"He's still going to destroy Nana's garden."

As if Emma could forget that. She bit her lip and didn't say, "You're the one who sold it to him," but Ashley turned away as if she had, withdrawing into herself when she took her place in the back seat of Noah's car, until the silence became uncomfortable. When Noah turned on the radio, Emma breathed a sigh of relief.

She wasn't sure who was mad at whom anymore. Ashley had stopped telling Emma she should sell Brightview, buy something small and cheap instead and pay off her debts once and for all, but she wasn't exactly being a cheerleader for the bed-and-breakfast, either.

She'd sold the Cliff Garden to Noah, and yet she couldn't seem to forgive him for buying it. She claimed she planned to make a permanent home in San Francisco yet with each passing day became more involved with Kate and Aurora's projects in Brightview's backyard.

Emma decided to stop trying to figure out Ashley and concentrated on watching the scenery pass by instead.

When they reached Brightview, Noah grabbed his things from his bedroom, and Ashley slipped into it as soon as he was out. She stayed there until dinnertime, but even though she came out to join Emma for the meal, conversation between them remained stilted. Noah took himself off to the beach for some time in the waves before the sun went down. Winston went with him. Emma wished she could go, too. Instead she kept busy cleaning the bed-and-breakfast, prepping for the morning meal and keeping Ashley company.

The next day Ashley was up early. Emma found her in the Cliff Garden before dawn, weeding, when she went to meet her friends for her morning walk.

"You should be resting."

"I'm not sleepy. I swear, the minute I get to the coast I perk right up. Besides, this garden is getting out of control."

"I can't keep up with Brightview and the Cliff Garden, especially now that I'm trying to write a cookbook and learn how to run classes. Thank goodness Kate and

Aurora have been helping."

Ashley waved her off. Neither of them mentioned that the Cliff Garden wouldn't be around much longer, weeds or no. "Kate and Aurora both seem nice" was all she said.

"Morning!"

Ava and Penelope had arrived.

"Want to join us?" Emma asked Ashley.

"No. I'm happy right here." She had that dreamy look she got when she was gardening, one Emma recognized from when they were growing up. Ashley entered a kind of trance state when she worked, lost in thought so deeply it was hard to get her attention again.

She looked happy, Emma decided, joining her friends. That was what worried her most. The Cliff Garden was Ashley's introduction to a love of gardening. How would she handle it when it was gone?

"No Noah today?" Penelope asked her.

"Surf's up," Emma told her. "He's driven to Maverick's with some big-shot surfers. Going to take some photos."

"I wish I could see that," Penelope said enviously.

Emma wasn't so sure she wanted to. The waves got big there, and riding them was dangerous. Even taking photos would put Noah in danger, although he told her he'd be on a jet ski rather than a surfboard. She was relieved when he reappeared midafternoon, safe and energized, although a little pensive, too.

"It was amazing," he kept saying. "It's not November, when storms bring the biggest waves, but they were still impressive, and everyone was professional. They didn't cut any corners. Tightest operation I've ever seen."

He told them about the photographers lined up on shore. How he'd been one of the few in the waves. There was more than one off-duty EMT in the crowd in case there was trouble.

"Did you get some good photos?"

His exuberance dimmed. "I'm sure I did, but... I don't know. I felt a little flat. It's funny, I thought I'd be out of practice surfing, but I'm doing just fine when I get out into the waves. It's photography I'm rusty at."

"Guess you'll need to get more practice."

"Guess so."

"I'm glad everyone stayed safe," Emma said, but she was also glad she'd been too busy to worry too much about him today. She hadn't considered how nerve-racking it could be to date a man who spent his time documenting extreme sports. When Ashley joined their conversation, she was happy to see her sister seemed to have let go of her reticence from the night before. She'd spent all morning in the garden and finally come in exhausted and happy.

Emma's nerves grew taut as the afternoon waned and the time for her class drew near. Ava and Penelope arrived promptly at six, and other guests trickled in.

She'd found a local college student to film the proceedings. Tim O'Keefe's prices were cheap because he needed the practice. Since she didn't have much money to work with, she'd decided to give him a try.

"Everyone needs to find a partner to work with," she announced to the small gathered crowd, trying hard not to look in Tim's direction. He'd instructed her to act natural, and ever since she'd felt overwhelmed with stage fright. "Each group will make a version of the recipes I'm demonstrating, and we'll share the oven and stove." She waited for everyone to pair up and was happy when Noah, Ashley and Kate opted to work together as a trio. She'd been afraid Kate might slip away and hide in her room.

Tonight they were preparing chicken Marsala, roasted asparagus and the perfect fluffy rice, and for dessert, raspberry mini galettes with fresh whipped cream. As Emma demonstrated the proper way to prepare the chicken, Kate helped keep wineglasses full. When it was time for the groups to try the techniques, a happy buzz of chatter filled the room.

She'd situated the groups along the wide kitchen counter and large dining room table. She'd need to limit the number of students at any given class, but that made the whole experience more intimate and, to her way of thinking, more fun.

By the time all the dishes were lined up for their time in the oven, Emma's tension had eased. She served appetizers she'd made earlier in the day and let everyone know she'd included the recipe in the information packets they'd get to take home. Kate had helped her to design the recipe cards. In the future Emma planned to send them to a shop that could produce them on thick glossy paper.

"Where can I buy one of those aprons?" a woman named Madelyn asked. She was staying at Ava's vacation rental and had asked if she and her husband could come along when Ava mentioned the class to her. She was a housewife from Redding who sounded like she was the mainstay of her local church. When Emma had chatted with her before the class started, Madelyn listed half a dozen volunteer positions she held. Emma hoped her congregation knew how lucky they were.

"It was a gift," Emma told her. "Penelope made it."

"I can whip up some more," Penelope offered.

"I'd like one as a souvenir of our stay here. You should stock them in your gift store," Madelyn said. "Do you have a gift store?"

"No." Emma laughed. "I'm not sure where I'd put that."

"You could put some shelves over here," one of Emma's guests said, gesturing to the wall near the hall that led to the entrance.

As everyone talked over what other types of clothing and gift items she could carry, Emma lifted her gaze to Noah's. He was smiling proudly at her.

"Knew you could do it," he said the next time they passed each other.

"It's been fun," Emma said.

"You're a hit," Ashley told her later. "Maybe keeping Brightview won't be a complete disaster."

IT WAS LATE by the time the guests dispersed. Noah had enjoyed himself, but he was ready to be alone with Emma. She followed Ava and Penelope to the door, where they hugged her on their way out.

"Next time you have a class, give me enough advance notice so I can see if my guests want to participate, too. It was a blast and so convenient," Penelope told her.

"You did great," Ava chimed in.

"Good night," Ashley said on her way to bed.

Emma returned to the kitchen to clean up. Noah joined her.

"You seem to have charmed my sister," she told him.

"I'm not sure if charmed is the right word. I think we're just taking a break from hostilities."

"I hope it lasts."

"You and me both," he said with a grin.

It took more than an hour to set everything to rights. When they were done and she'd turned out the lights, he moved close and took her hand.

"Good work tonight." He captured her mouth in a kiss. As much as he wanted to spend more time with her, it was late, and she had a business to run in the morning.

He knew he should let her get some sleep.

"Thanks. I enjoyed that."

"I could tell."

"You know… you don't have to sleep outside tonight. It really doesn't seem fair when you're paying rent."

"I don't mind." He really didn't, but he was interested to know the alternative.

"You could… sleep with me."

He didn't need to be asked twice. He wasn't sure how he'd managed to hold back this long. "Lead the way."

Was she surprised that he'd jumped at the offer? She shouldn't be. He followed her up the two sets of stairs quietly, figuring she wouldn't want to alert her guests to this new sleeping arrangement. Once she'd shut the door of the attic room behind her, he moved close and took her in his arms.

Now he could take his time kissing Emma, and he enjoyed every minute of it. When he moved his hand to the hemline of her shirt, she didn't push him away. If anything, she gave a sigh of contentment.

Good. He'd never push Emma to do something she wasn't ready for. He was a grown man and could control himself.

But god, he wanted her.

She let him tug her shirt over her head and toss it aside. He spanned her waist with his hands, sliding them up to brush the underside of her breasts, still cradled in a silky, lacy bra. He couldn't wait to see what they looked like, but he was going to take this slow. Rubbing his thumbs lightly over her nipples through the fabric, he was pleased when she gave a low moan.

Noah delighted in teasing out the moment, caressing her until she leaned into his touch, nearly begging for more. When he finally reached around for the clasp and undid her bra, her breasts were soft and heavy in his hands. Only reluctantly did he let go to allow her to undo the buttons of his shirt. When it was off and she slid her hands across his chest, his skin warmed and his desire flared.

Time to get rid of the rest of his clothes. He had his pants off in a matter of seconds. Boxer briefs next. Emma was shimmying out of the skirt she'd worn tonight, and he helped her with it as best he could.

"God, you're beautiful," he told her. He picked her up and tossed her on the bed. "Brace yourself." He threw himself on top of her, and Emma laughed aloud.

"You're going to break the bed."

"I hope so." He meant to make love to her until he was spent. He wanted to show her what she meant to him. Prove that no land dispute was going to keep him away from her.

He settled himself between her legs. "Last chance to back out."

"You can't get rid of me that easily." She pulled him

down and met his mouth with hers.

As Noah pushed inside her, they both moaned.

And Noah knew he was lost.

THIS HAD TO be wrong, Emma decided the next morning, after they made love again. Even if it felt so right. Moving with Noah, filled by him, she couldn't get enough—last night or just now. Curled up with him, his arm around her possessively, Emma couldn't wait to do it all over again.

But soon her guests would be up and her friends would be waiting for her.

"You're thinking," he accused her softly.

"Time to walk," she told him.

"Time to stay and have a little more fun," he corrected.

"I'd love to—later." She sat up but shrieked softly when he bowled her over and covered her with kisses. "Noah."

"I know, I know. Come on, then." He got up, walked around the bed, leaned down and swung her up in his arms. He marched with her to the en suite bathroom and turned on the shower.

They spent far longer than necessary under the running water, and there was nothing for it but to satisfy themselves again before cleaning up and getting dressed. Emma didn't think she'd be able to think straight if they didn't.

She was having a hard enough time as it was.

Once she pulled on jeans and a soft long-sleeved shirt, and did her hair and makeup, she was ready, but apparently her attempts to look normal failed utterly.

"Oh my god, you two were together," Ava hissed when they met in the Cliff Garden just before dawn. She grabbed Emma's elbow and pulled her ahead of the others. "Tell me everything."

"How can you possibly know that?" Emma hissed back.

"You're glowing! He's glowing! We should harness you two to the electric grid."

Emma looked back to see Penelope's eyebrows lifted high. "Are you two a thing?" she mouthed. Emma sighed.

"Is there no such thing as privacy around here?"

"Nope. None at all. Pen and I are bored stiff, and you're our entertainment."

"Great."

Penelope took hold of Noah's arm and slowed her pace, keeping him well back while Ava pumped Emma for information.

"So is it the real deal, or are you trying to convince him to give you the Cliff Garden?"

"What?" Emma stopped in her tracks. Ava dragged her forward.

"If he falls in love with you, he'll give you the lot, right?"

She hadn't even thought about the lot since they'd slept together, but now she did, some of her excitement slid away. Would Noah be more amenable to selling the lot to her now that she was sleeping with him?

Not that she could afford it.

"One thing at a time," she managed to say.

"Just make sure you have a plan."

"You sound like Ashley." She glanced over her shoulder. Noah and Penelope were still talking. "Speaking of my sister, I want to take her to dinner tonight. Where should I go?"

Ava sighed, but she took the hint, and just as Emma hoped, soon all four of them were in a lively discussion comparing local restaurants. By the time they arrived home, she'd racked up a number of suggestions. She and Noah dropped off the other women at their houses and kept going. She hoped to have another minute alone with him, but Ashley was already up when they got inside.

"Morning." Emma tried not to sound disappointed. Noah, who'd come in right behind her, gave her hand a surreptitious squeeze and let go.

"Morning, Ashley," he chimed in.

"Good morning." Ashley looked from one to the other suspiciously. "I guess I missed the sunrise walk."

"I'll go again with you later, if you like," Emma told her. "How are you feeling today?"

"Better." She sighed. "Seriously, there's nothing

wrong with me. I should be at work."

"You fainted two days ago. Sounds to me like you need the break. What were you doing when it happened, anyway?" Her sister was still regarding Noah with narrowed eyes, and she wanted to distract her.

"Filling in all the paperwork about the partnership buy-in, which isn't even hard."

"Maybe it's stressing you out," Noah said. "It's a big purchase, right?"

Ashley's gaze kept skipping from him to Emma. Had she picked up on something? If she had, Ashley would find a reason to disapprove. She seemed determined to make Noah the enemy, when she was the one who'd created all the problems between the three of them.

"It's a big commitment," Emma said, alarmed when Ashley frowned. Her sister definitely knew something was up.

Ashley nodded slowly. "I guess I am worried," she confessed. "I've worked too hard to get here to make a mistake now."

"You'll be fine," Emma assured her, "and in ten years, you'll probably be running that place. You're great at your job, but Noah is right; it's still a big step. It's normal to feel nervous."

"Ten years sounds like forever," Ashley grumbled.

"Ten years is nothing."

Ashley shrugged. "Whatever."

At least Ashley wasn't focused on Noah anymore.

"Why don't you go work on the forms now while I'm making breakfast?"

Ashley hesitated, then nodded. "That's a good idea."

"Don't sound so surprised. I have a few of those now and then." Whoops. She hadn't meant that to sound so tart.

Ashley ignored her and disappeared down the hall.

Noah followed Emma into the kitchen. "You're a good sister," he murmured into her neck, sliding an arm around her waist and drawing her near.

"Shh. Stop." Emma pushed him away. "She's coming right back."

"Are we hiding our relationship?"

"I don't want to rub it in her face."

"She's not back yet," he pointed out, wrapped his fingers in her belt loops and tugged her closer. "But you're here, and you look delicious."

Emma didn't protest this time. Instead she let him kiss her until she was breathless and turned on all over again, wishing they could disappear somewhere and be alone for the rest of the day.

"Breakfast," she said decisively when they came up for air.

Noah looked like he'd argue, but he let it be.

She breathed easier when they broke apart and got to work. Ashley appeared again, carrying a laptop. She settled into one corner of the sectional in the living room area and got to work. Meanwhile, Noah's helping hands made the breakfast preparation go much faster. When everything was ready, Emma urged him to fill a plate and take it out on the deck with the other guests, who'd appeared in the last few minutes, drawn down from their rooms by the smell of the food. She filled another one and brought it to Ashley.

"Ready to take a break?" Emma asked her.

"I'm ready to push send. There wasn't that much more to do." Ashley eyed the food with appreciation, though.

"Want me to look it over?"

"No. Just witness this momentous occasion." She hovered her index finger over the send button. "Three. Two. One. There it goes."

Emma settled the plate on the nearby coffee table and hugged her. "You're going to be a partner!" She refused to acknowledge it was the final blow for the Cliff Garden. As soon as the escrow process ended and Ashley received her proceeds from its sale, she'd tie them up in the partnership buy-in and pay off her condo, too. Even if she had some money left, she'd already said she wanted to use it to start some retirement savings accounts—not to put a down payment on buying back a piece of property she'd just sold.

"I'm going to be a partner," Ashley affirmed. She lifted her chin. "It's working out exactly as I planned. You know that."

"You're right. I do know it." Who exactly was Ashley

trying to convince? "Come outside and join everyone else," she urged. Neither of them would benefit from overthinking Ashley's choices. "I'll put this on the picnic table for you." She picked up the plate again and was heading outside when a thump behind her made her spin around.

"Ashley!" She nearly dropped the plate when she saw her sister crumpled on the floor but managed to set it down on a console table without spilling anything before rushing to her sister's side.

Ashley groaned when Emma touched her shoulder. When her eyes fluttered open, Emma let out the breath she was holding.

"I did it again, didn't I?" Ashley lifted a hand to rub her forehead. "Why do I keep fainting?"

"Stay right there. You might have hurt yourself."

"I'm not hurt." She pushed herself up onto her elbows.

"What happened?" Noah appeared at Emma's side. The guests crowded in, too.

"Ashley fainted."

"Let's get you on the couch." Noah lifted her easily and placed her on the comfortable sectional she'd just vacated.

"I'm fine," she protested, but Emma was already tucking a light throw blanket around her. She went to fetch a glass of water.

"We should take you to the hospital."

"No more hospitals." The color was returning to Ashley's face, and Emma could tell she wasn't happy being the center of attention. Noah shoed away the guests.

"Let's give Ashley some air. Please, finish your breakfasts. It's such a lovely day."

They trailed back to the deck and were soon deep in conversation again, much to Emma's relief. Her sister had never liked being under the scrutiny of strangers.

"Maybe you haven't eaten enough." Emma retrieved the plate she'd prepared and placed it on her lap. Her sister picked up a poppy-seed mini muffin and took a bite.

"I don't think it's hunger," she said when she was done chewing. Emma took a seat next to her on the sectional, and Noah sat on one of the arms. "It's… stress or something."

"Maybe you should try seeing a counselor," Noah suggested. "She could help you sort out what's going on."

"You can always talk to me," Emma said.

"That's not the same thing," Noah told her gently. "Ashley needs to be able to say everything that's on her mind without being afraid to hurt your feelings."

Did Ashley ever worry about hurting her feelings? It didn't seem like it. Emma nodded, nevertheless. A professional would have distance from their problems and might be able to make some good suggestions.

"Counselors cost money," Ashley said.

Emma laughed. "You have money."

Ashley went silent, then laughed, too. "You're right, I do. Or I will, pretty soon. I'm so used to not having anything."

"And here I thought accountants got paid handsomely," Noah joked.

Ashley's smile disappeared. "San Francisco is expensive," she said defensively.

"Of course," Noah hurried to agree.

And then there were the debts Ashley needed to pay in addition to her mortgage and the partnership buy-in, Emma thought. Noah didn't know about those.

No one did.

Ashley met her gaze, and Emma knew exactly what she meant to convey: They didn't need to start telling anyone about those debts now. They'd kept them secret for years, and soon Ashley's would be gone. Emma needed to find her own way out of the dilemma.

She gave her sister a little nod. She'd keep that secret, for Ashley's sake. Somehow that part of the past hurt Ashley more than her, and there was no reason to disclose it.

"Are you sure we shouldn't take you to the hospital—or at least a walk-in clinic?" Emma asked again.

"I'm sure. I'm fine—it's probably excitement about the partnership buy-in. When it's all done, I'll have the life I always wanted. Everything will be perfect."

Except she didn't seem excited, Emma thought, and losing the Cliff Garden didn't seem perfect, either.

"WINSTON, COME ON," Noah called an hour later. Ashley was still resting on the sectional. Emma, at her insistence, had gone to run some errands. He figured he might as well get some surfing in.

"You're awfully comfortable here," Ashley remarked as he attached a lead to the dog's collar.

Noah stopped in his tracks. "Any reason I shouldn't be? This is my home for the next six months."

"You're pretty chummy with my sister."

"Is that any of your business?" Maybe he should be treating Ashley with kid gloves given her earlier fainting spell, but Noah had a feeling she wasn't the kind of woman who'd respect that sort of thing.

"I care about my sister, despite what she may think. That makes it my business. She isn't the best judge of character."

That was some plain talking. "You got something to say about my character?" He met bluntness with bluntness. He wasn't about to let Ashley think she could run the show when it came to his love life.

"I know you walked out on your business partner just when he probably needed you most."

He was unprepared for that line of attack. Had Ashley been checking up on him? She must have read about the sale of Maxwell Tech. "Mark is absolutely fine. I helped him out for more than a decade, and all that time he knew my real passion lay elsewhere. He's one hundred percent behind me pursuing it now."

"How understanding of him."

What was she getting at? "How about we stop playing games. What are you really worried about?"

Ashley puffed out an annoyed breath. "The last thing Emma needs is another man messing up her livelihood."

"I have no intention of doing that. In fact, I'm doing everything I can to help her, if you haven't noticed."

"For how long?" she demanded. "You'll play business partner for a while and then up and leave."

"You want me to buy her a ring?" He didn't back down. "It's a little early for that, isn't it?"

"I don't want you to break her heart!"

"I'm not going to break her heart!"

"Really?" Her sarcasm cut through him. "So you don't plan to build a house in the middle of our grandmother's garden?"

Now they'd reached the heart of the issue. He was sick of Ashley pretending to be an innocent bystander in this mess. He stepped closer. "You're the one who sold me that lot. You're the one breaking Emma's heart, not me."

He thought she'd escalate the argument. Instead she hesitated. Turned away, hugging her arms over her chest. "I know," she finally said. "Believe me, I'm well aware of that fact."

The pain in her voice sliced through his anger, leaving him unsure where to direct the frustration he was feeling. Was this why she kept fainting all the time? Did she care, after all, how her actions were affecting her sister?

"Why the hell did you do it? And why are you buying into a partnership it's obvious you don't even want?" It was a shot in the dark, but he wanted to hurt her. If she'd never listed the property, he wouldn't be in this position now. He and Emma were meant for each other, but that would change the minute the backhoes moved in to dig the foundation next door.

When she faced him again angrily, he knew he'd guessed right.

"What makes you think I don't want it?"

"You faint every time you take a step toward securing it. Maybe you're miserable all the time because you're not following your heart."

"Is that what you're doing? Following your heart?" Ashley demanded.

"Absolutely. With Emma—and my brother. You might not like what I'm doing, but you've got to admit I'm being true to myself." He stepped toward her. "Don't mess things up for me—or for your sister. You're the one with problems. Call that counselor and sort them out."

CHAPTER 10

EMMA WAS GLAD to see that Ashley was the only one in sight when she let herself in the door to Brightview later that morning.

"Is Noah still surfing?" She set her purse on the kitchen counter and rummaged through the fridge for a sparkling water. She'd finally stopped by Nana Angela's post office box this morning and been pleased to find only a handful of items that required any attention. Apparently Colette had picked up the mail regularly during her tenure running Brightview and paid the bills on time. The mortgage was the only thing to slip through the cracks. Emma made a mental note to set up online bill paying for all the utilities and to invite Colette to dinner soon.

"Guess so." Ashley shrugged and went back to reading a magazine.

"Why aren't you outside?"

"I was for a while, but I started to get sunburned, and I was too lazy to put sunscreen on." Ashley crinkled her nose. "Why are you looking so chipper?"

"Dodged a bullet." She told her sister about her fear that the post office box would be stuffed with unpaid bills. "Colette did a really good job running Brightview after Nana Angela was gone."

"Glad to hear it."

She didn't sound entirely glad, though, and Emma wondered if she'd somehow lost all the ground she'd gained in her sister's eyes after the cooking class. Before she could ask what was wrong, however, a knock at the door interrupted their conversation.

Emma went to see who it was, and when she spotted Mark on the stoop, she moved to greet him cheerfully. The moment she opened the door, however, her stomach twisted with a sharp awareness that something was wrong. He had adopted an overly casual stance, his mouth set in a smile that didn't reach his eyes.

"Hey, Emma, I'm looking for Noah. Is he around?" he asked jovially.

Too jovially, Emma thought. This wasn't a happy man.

Ashley had trailed her to the door, and she peeped around Emma's shoulders. "He's at the beach," she said when Emma didn't immediately answer. "If you want to come in and wait for him, you're more than welcome."

Emma wanted to kick her sister, but she chided herself for her reaction a moment later. Mark was an old friend of Noah's. Surely they had nothing to worry about, even if he did seem to be in a strange mood.

"Thanks." He allowed Emma to usher him in down the hall.

"Go right out on the deck," Emma told him. "I'll be out in a moment with some drinks."

"Beer if you've got it," Mark said.

"Sure thing."

Ashley followed her into the kitchen. "That's Mark Maxwell," she hissed. "He's Noah's old business partner."

"I know. I've met him before."

"He's worth a mint."

"Better get out there and start flirting, then," Emma said dryly.

"Ha ha. I think he's married." Ashley accepted a bottle of beer and another of sparkling water.

"Keep him company." She craned her neck to see what he was doing. "I think he's been drinking."

"Better bring out some food, too. It's fine," she went on when Emma hesitated. "There are two of us here. If he gets rowdy, we'll call the cops."

Emma relaxed. Ashley was right. Besides, Noah would be back soon, and Ava and Penelope were within shouting distance. She gathered some snacks and followed her sister as quickly as she could.

Ashley and Mark were deep in conversation by the deck's railing when she arrived, Mark chuckling at something Ashley had said, although once again, there was something off about his tone. She set the snacks on the nearby picnic table and went to join them.

"Thought I knew the guy. Turned out I was completely wrong." Mark pointed at Emma. "You'd better be careful. Last I heard he'd set his sights on you."

"What are you talking about?"

"Noah," Ashley informed her with a look that told Emma she wasn't all that comfortable with Mark's presence anymore.

"We're just friends," Emma lied. She didn't want to talk about Noah with a man who was obviously intoxicated.

"I thought we were friends, too," Mark said. "Turned out I was wrong. He was using me just like he uses everyone he comes in contact with."

"He doesn't seem that way to me," Emma protested.

"Of course not. He wants to jump in your bed. He's not going to show you his true colors." Mark took a long drink of his beer. "Don't think he'll marry you. He won't. He played this same game with my cousin last year."

"What game?"

"Pretending he was falling in love, then cheating on her with other women. He broke her heart." Mark waved the bottle expansively. "I came here today to sort him out." He took another swig of his beer and leaned on the deck's railing. "He was my best friend. My business partner. I introduced him to Caitlyn. Made him rich." He stared at the ocean a long moment before pushing back and holding his arms wide. "You know what it's like to go to a family reunion and find everyone pissed at you?" he asked them. "It was supposed to be my big moment. Just sold my company. I thought I'd get some high fives. Some congratulations." He shook his head. "Instead it was, 'Mark, why'd you set up your poor little cousin with that shark? Mark, we're so disappointed in you.' Fuck." He dropped his hands and began to pace.

Ashley exchanged a look with Emma. "That sounds rough," she told Mark. "Come on. Sit down. Eat some of Emma's wonderful food." She settled him in a comfortable chair and filled a plate for him. "What did your wife think about it all?"

Emma barely kept from rolling her eyes, but she understood that Ashley was trying to distract the man. She kept peppering him with questions until a half hour later, Mark got up. "I'm not waiting any longer," he announced. "Got to meet some friends. Some *real* friends."

"You can't drive," Emma told him. She couldn't prevent him from arriving at her house drunk, but she wouldn't let him leave that way.

"I'll drive," Ashley said. "Give me your keys, big boy," she told Mark. "I'll get you to the restaurant and take a cab back. Hand them over," she repeated firmly when Mark protested. "I want to hear more about your company, anyway."

"You should be resting," Emma protested.

"I've rested all morning. I'm fine—and someone's got to keep an eye on him."

She marched Mark through the house and out the door. When she was gone, Emma sank onto the sectional and thought about what he'd said.

Was Noah a player? Was he making a fool out of her?

Ashley got back before Emma expected her. "Now do you believe me?" she demanded when she bustled into the living room. "Noah knows you can turn the whole neighborhood against him if you want to. He's sweetening you up to make his stay here easier. Besides, he gets free meals, someone to share his bed… all under the same roof."

"He's paying me plenty to stay here, and he's sleeping on the deck because you're in his room. I don't treat him any differently than the other guests."

"Really?" Ashley held her gaze until Emma looked away. "Come on, Emma—I know you slept together. Face it, you're impulsive. You never look before you leap. He's just like Jordan. He's taking whatever ride you're willing to offer him. I told you this was going to end badly."

Emma couldn't think of an answer to that. Ashley was right.

And she couldn't stand it.

"I've got stuff to do." Emma went upstairs to her room, thinking she wanted to be alone, but as soon as she shut the door behind her, she found herself drawn to the balcony. She pulled out her phone and texted Ava and Penelope.

I need to see your faces.

Not long afterward each woman appeared on the balcony of her house. Ava shouted a hello. Penelope waved.

Noah is a player, she texted them.

No! Penelope texted back.

Are you sure? Ava wrote.

His business partner says so.

When she looked up, Ava had her back to her and was shouting something to Penelope. A minute later, she picked something up, crossed her balcony and put it in the pulley system delivery bag. She tugged the line, and Emma dutifully reeled the bag over to her house. When she looked inside, she found a four-pack of hard cider and a candy bar.

Thank god for friends.

She held them up for Ava to see. "Thank you," she called.

Ava held up her phone, and Emma set down the presents to check her messages. Both women had written again.

Make sure you have all the information before you go off half-cocked, Ava said.

But if he needs a good thumping, we're there for you, Penelope added.

She waved, took her treats inside and went back downstairs. She put the booze in the refrigerator and allowed herself a square of chocolate.

Then ate another one.

WHEN NOAH LET himself into Brightview, he was immediately struck by how quiet it was. He'd never been in the large house alone before and hadn't expected to be now, but there was no sign of the other guests, and Emma and Ashley were gone, too.

He'd noticed the passenger van was missing. Maybe everyone had gone on an adventure. He checked his messages, but there were none from Emma, and he squashed his disappointment at being left out.

Ashley would be involved, he reminded himself. She seemed determined to wreck what he and Emma had. What bothered him was that Emma might let her. He supposed he couldn't blame her. They hadn't talked about what they meant to each other or how they planned to proceed. From her point of view, they'd simply tumbled into bed together and had a little fun.

That was probably the way he should think about it, too, but Noah found he wanted it to be much more than that. The thought of moving on—the thought of another man in bed with Emma—made his fists clench. He wanted to know he was the only one she was thinking about when they were apart. He wasn't going to share her.

Which was funny because he hadn't seen another man anywhere near Emma. She didn't have the time to go out and flirt; she worked constantly.

She wasn't here now, though, and while he told himself she'd be busy keeping everyone else happy wherever she and the rest of the guests went, his thoughts kept sliding to an uncomfortable place as he waited. Could she fall for another man?

When he heard voices at the back of the house an hour later, Noah sprang to his feet and went to meet Emma, but it was only the other guests returning from dinner.

"Is Emma with Ashley?" he asked one of them.

"I don't know. Text her," she said brushing past.

He pulled out his phone and did so, using the number she'd given him when he rented his room.

She didn't answer.

Noah waited, trying to be patient, but as the minutes crept by, he began to get frustrated. It had been a beautiful afternoon, sliding into a beautiful evening. He wanted to be with his girl.

Was she his girl, though? He realized he hadn't asked her. Why hadn't he made his intentions clearer this morning when he had the chance?

Too restless to sit still anymore, he headed out for a walk. Catching sight of Ava and Penelope chatting over the fence between their houses, he hurried toward them.

"Do you know where Emma and Ashley went?" he

asked when he'd greeted them.

"Nope. Want me to find out?" Ava pulled out her phone and tapped at it. A moment later, she nodded. "They're grabbing coffee at Cups & Waves. Ashley is going home tonight. She wants to go to work tomorrow."

Why hadn't Emma answered his text?

"Thanks."

Ava was still reading her phone. "They're on their way home now," she added. "Better get back there and act casual."

Was he that transparent? "I don't have to act anything."

"I won't tell her you were checking up on her, Romeo." Ava wiggled her fingers at him. "See you later."

Hell. All the women in the world were ganging up on him. He made a show of going for a long walk down Cliff Street, and by the time he returned, the sisters were home. He let himself in the door and found Ashley sitting on the sectional, luggage by her feet, and Emma puttering in the kitchen.

"Hey, I was wondering where you got to." Noah wanted to smack himself the moment the words left his mouth. So much for playing it cool.

"What do you care?" Emma swiped at the counters with a dishrag.

Noah drew himself up. "What's that supposed to mean?" He was done with whatever games everyone around him was playing.

"There's any number of pretty girls around here, right? Hit on someone else for a change. You were going to do that anyway, eventually." She kept swiping.

Noah stared at her. He'd never been a player. It wasn't his thing. "You want to explain where all this is coming from?" He couldn't keep the edge from his voice.

"Your friend stopped by," Ashley said from where she was sitting. "Mark Maxwell?" She screwed up her face as if trying to remember. "Seemed a little pissed off. Something about a cousin?"

Mark was here? He was angry about Caitlyn?

Trepidation filled him. What was Caitlyn up to?

A little revenge?

"Where'd Mark go?"

"Surf Point." Ashley named a high-end local restaurant. "But that was hours ago. I doubt he's there now."

Emma slapped the dishrag down on the counter. "Maybe you should go track him down."

"Emma." Noah reached for her, but she backed away.

"No—we're done."

GETTING OUT OF bed the next morning was brutal.

Gone was all the joy of owning Brightview and the excitement she'd been feeling about running the bed-and-breakfast. Every aspect of living in this house was tied up in the time she'd spent with Noah. Even her bed contained memories of him—wonderful memories that had turned to regrets overnight.

Emma pulled back the covers and forced herself to stand up. Her body ached as if she'd done a kickboxing workout instead of simply tossing and turning all night. When she turned on the bedside light, it burned her eyes. As usual, she was up before dawn, but the thought of joining her friends for a walk felt impossible.

A shower helped a little, after she'd cried again with frustration. She allowed the running water to wash away her tears. Once dressed, her hair done, she made herself step outside, although she wasn't very good company on her walk with Ava and Penelope.

"You sure nothing is wrong?" Pen asked her when they dropped her back at Brightview.

"Everything's wrong," Emma said. "I just don't want to talk about it yet."

"That's okay," Ava told her. "We're here when you're ready."

Noah, who'd moved back into his room last night since Ashley had returned to San Francisco, was gone when she let herself inside, as was Winston. Probably out surfing, although she hadn't seen Winston on the beach. Emma continued with her routine, making breakfast for her guests and cleaning up when it was over. By the time her phone buzzed, she was numb with sorrow and regret, wishing she could go back to bed, fall asleep and sink into oblivion.

"Emma? It's Mark Maxwell."

"Oh." She didn't want to talk to him.

"Don't hang up. I owe you an apology. Your sister, too. When I stopped by Brightview yesterday, I'd had a few drinks, as I'm sure you're aware. I said a few things I shouldn't have."

"I appreciate the apology," she said carefully, "but you know what they say. In vino veritas—people tell the truth when they've been drinking."

"I didn't tell the truth, though." Mark sounded much more reasonable today—and embarrassed, too. "I didn't know the truth."

"I suppose Noah asked you to call and say that." It hurt to say his name. She hadn't realized how hard she'd fallen for him until she'd found out he wasn't the one for her.

"He did ask me to call, after telling me a few things I hadn't realized before."

"Which were?" She wasn't letting him off that easy.

There was a longer pause. "Look, I'm close by. Any chance we can meet for coffee? I need to do this face to face."

Emma nearly said no, given how awful her meeting with him was yesterday, but he sounded different today, and his rueful admissions seemed genuine. "Sure," she heard herself say. "How about Cups & Waves?"

"I know the place. I'll be there in five minutes."

When he hung up, Emma trailed into the bathroom, made an attempt to apply some makeup but gave up, tugging her hair into a ponytail and deciding that was good enough. She wished Mark was already gone. Noah, too, for that matter. How was she going to get through the next five months with him living in her house?

How would she stand him living next door for the rest of her life?

By the time Emma got to the little coffee shop, she was regretting her decision to come at all, but she figured she might as well go through with the meeting. Mark was already there. She thought she might be nervous to talk to him again, but he was sober today, his gaze searching hers when they said their hellos.

Emma relaxed a bit when she realized he was embarrassed after his performance the previous day. Besides, it was hard to be uneasy here. She loved Cups & Waves with its cream walls and broad plank floor. Plants graced every flat surface. A tall bookshelf near the door was full of paperbacks to borrow. Local art hung on one wide wall. Whenever she walked through the open door, Emma felt right at home.

"Let me grab something to drink," she said to Mark and made her way to the counter, where a young woman with a coronet of dark braids greeted her with a smile. "Chai latte."

"You got it," the woman said. Her nametag read Kamirah, and Emma knew her by sight, since she came here often. "You've been in here a few times now," Kamirah remarked as she got to work making the drink.

"I moved here about a month ago," Emma affirmed, grateful for the distraction.

"Really? Where are you renting?"

"Actually, I own Brightview. It's a bed-and-breakfast on Cliff Street."

"The one next to the Cliff Garden?" Kamirah asked. "And here I thought you were an Improbable. Turns out you're an owner. You're one lucky girl."

"What's an Improbable?" Emma asked as the younger woman finished making her drink.

"Someone like me. Someone who's hanging on here in Seahaven despite all the odds."

It took Emma a minute to catch up. "Because of the cost of rent?"

Kamirah nodded. "I've got a room at Vista Mar, so I'm not complaining, but I know a lot of people who are struggling to make ends meet."

"I don't know the Vista Mar."

"It's an old Victorian that's been cut up into a number of small apartments. It's only a few blocks from the ocean, so there's hardly ever an opening there. I got lucky."

"I'm glad you found such a nice place," Emma said honestly. "I remember my grandmother talking about housing costs when I was a kid. She lived in Seahaven her whole life."

"We Improbables make the place work," Kamirah said. "If it gets too expensive for us to live here, there won't be anyone to pour your coffee." She softened her words with a smile. "Welcome to Seahaven," she added. "I've always loved the Cliff Garden."

"Thanks." Emma said goodbye without addressing the garden. Would she be blamed when Noah built his house?

Probably, she thought glumly.

Mark stood up like an old-fashioned gentleman when she joined him and helped her scoot in her chair when she was seated.

"Thanks for coming." He was nursing a tall black coffee in one of the Cups & Waves signature mugs. "I'm really sorry I was such an ass yesterday."

"You said there were things you didn't know. What things?" She still wasn't in a mood to be very charitable.

"I think I need to back up a little. I'm not sure how much you know about Noah's past, but I met him in college. I convinced him to join my start-up, and we worked together for more than a decade."

She nodded. Noah had told her all this.

"A few months ago a bigger company started sniffing around. One with deep pockets. It was what we'd been waiting for—I built my business to be bought at some point, and it was going to be our big payday."

"All right."

"So it happened, just like I planned. What I didn't

consider was what would happen next." He took a long sip of his coffee.

"Which was?"

"Noah would leave." Mark considered her. "He's my best friend. He's been there every step of the way. It was a hell of a lot of work building Maxwell Tech—a lot of late nights—and then all of a sudden it was over. I stayed on after the transition—I'll be CEO going forward. He left."

"He told me you knew he would leave all along."

"I did. I just didn't know what it would feel like when he did."

She supposed she could sympathize with that. "What does this have to do with me?"

Mark kept his gaze on his coffee. "Like I said yesterday, Noah dated my cousin last year. They broke up about six months ago. When I introduced them, I thought it was another way we'd be connected. I imagined them getting married. Noah being some kind of relation as well as a friend." He heaved a long sigh. "Hell, I sound like a total asshole."

"You thought of him as a brother," Emma said. It made sense—they'd shared an intense experience together building their company. She knew what that was like.

Mark blinked. "Yeah. A brother." He shifted in his seat, leaned back, and watched through the window as a man rode a bike past the shop. "When he dumped

Caitlyn, I was pissed. I couldn't figure it out; they seemed so good together, and she said it came out of nowhere. Then the sale happened, and Noah took the money and ran. It didn't matter that I expected it. I still couldn't believe he actually did it."

"You thought he'd stay, despite what he told you—because of how well you worked together?"

"Yeah." Mark sighed. "I guess that's it. We had fun working together—and there's so much more money to make. So many more things to try to accomplish."

"So you were angry yesterday."

"Angry… and bummed out." He spread his hands wide. "Maxwell Tech isn't the same. He always used to be right down the hall. There was someone to talk to, go to lunch with, shoot the shit with. We'd play hoops in the middle of the day. Or bug off and surf, then work through the night to make up for lost time. I used to own my company. Now I'm working for someone else."

That was the heart of the problem, Emma suspected. She nodded. "It's a big change."

"It is. But that doesn't mean I should come and badmouth Noah to you."

It was her turn to shrug. "He dumped your cousin. Cheated on her, too, right? That's not very nice." She didn't want to get attached to a man who'd do that kind of thing.

Mark made a face. "Turns out I was wrong about that, actually."

"Really?" She took a sip of her coffee, trying to ignore the little leap in her pulse. "In what way?"

"In every way." He chuckled ruefully. "Turns out my cousin was the one who cheated—with multiple men. She admitted it after I talked to Noah last night and then called to confront her about it. I guess she had some regrets about their relationship falling apart when the sale went through and Noah became a multimillionaire. Smearing some dirt on his name was her way of taking him down a notch or two." Mark sighed. "My aunt and uncle are partly to blame."

"I'm not sure what you mean." It wasn't fair for her to pry this way, but she needed to understand what happened.

"I wasn't the only one who was hoping for a connection between them," Mark said bluntly. "Everyone knew there was a chance Maxwell Tech would hit it big, and they knew, as well, that if it did, Noah would come out of our venture pretty rich. I think some of my family thought a wedding between Noah and Caitlyn would keep Maxwell Tech's payday money in the family, so to speak, so when the two of them split up, my aunt and uncle came down on her pretty hard. Told her she was screwing up. Then the sale happened and proved them right. Caitlyn lashed out, lied to them about Noah… and the rest is history."

He studied his coffee as Emma tried to take it all in.

"I'm really sorry," he said again when she didn't

speak, finally lifting his gaze to meet hers. "I can't believe what Caitlyn did, and I can't believe I said all that stuff yesterday, either. It's like we're all in high school." He took a sip of his drink. "Tell me what I can do to make this right."

"Well, you came and apologized to me. That's a good start."

"I'm glad you feel that way. But what about Noah? I really let him down."

Emma had given up wondering why everyone thought she could solve their problems. Somehow it came with the territory these days. She thought about his question. "Seems to me Noah went out of his way to join a venture that meant a lot to you. Spent over a decade doing it, too. Maybe it's time you returned the favor. You surf, right?"

"Of course. I'm not all that into photography, though."

"Think about it. I bet there's something the two of you could spend time together doing. A new way to hang out. While you're at it, you need to decide how long you're going to stay at your company."

"What do you mean?" he asked sharply.

"I mean, you're CEO now, but you liked being an entrepreneur. You're not shackled to that job forever, are you?"

"Three years," he said. "My lawyer insisted they couldn't hold on to me any longer than that."

"Good. Take the next three years to tie up loose ends at your current business and train someone to take over. Then dive into the entrepreneurial pool again. Otherwise you're going to be miserable."

Mark rubbed a hand over his chin. "You're pretty good at this, you know that? You should write an advice column."

"I don't think so." The Trouble Bench kept her occupied enough.

Though it wouldn't for much longer, would it? The ache of losing it returned.

"Emma," Mark said. "I was completely out of line yesterday. Noah isn't a player. He doesn't fool around, and he's serious about you. I hope you'll give him another chance."

Emma sighed. "It's kind of hard to trust him again after everything you said."

"I will never forgive myself if I've ruined the best thing my friend has ever had."

"Best thing?" She picked up her cup.

"Definitely. I've known Noah for a long time. Despite what I wanted for them, he and Caitlyn were never serious about each other. He never looked at her the way he looks at you. First time I saw it I told him he'd marry you."

Emma nearly choked on the sip of coffee she'd just taken. "No one's talking about marriage."

"Not yet," Mark agreed cheerfully. "Figure it's a

matter of time, though. Put a good word in for me when he proposes, will you? I still want to be best man."

As she processed this an unreasonable hope took hold of her. Maybe she didn't have to give up Noah. Maybe they could go back to the way things were. "You're sure he's not a player?"

"I'm sure."

"And you think he's serious about me?"

"I know he is."

Emma decided right then and there to take Mark at his word. She didn't need to wallow in sorrow when nothing had actually happened. She had enough problems without inventing new ones. Setting her cup down, she asked Mark, "Do you like to eat?"

He laughed. "Does anyone not like to eat?"

"Noah has been helping me launch a cooking class. I'm doing them in person and filming them as practice for running online classes. Why don't you come to the next one? It will be fun."

A new thought struck her. Would Noah be angry about the way she'd reacted to Mark's revelations yesterday?

No, she decided. He'd understand.

He always understood.

Suddenly Emma couldn't wait to get back to Brightview.

"Sure." Mark pulled out his wallet and handed her a card. "That's my information. Call me anytime. I promise

I'll behave."

"Great. You can bring some friends." Maybe those friends would tell other friends and help spread the word about her new venture. If she and Noah were back on track, she could move forward with all her plans.

"Deal."

NOAH WAS RELIEVED to see Emma when she came home. It unnerved him every time he walked into Brightview and found it empty. It was as if the house was missing its heart.

"Hey. Can we talk?" he asked.

"I just had coffee with Mark," she told him. "He explained everything and apologized. I guess I should do the same."

He took her purse from her, set it on the counter and drew her into his arms. "You don't need to do anything except be here." He kissed the top of her head. He'd missed the way she fit against him, all soft warmth and wonderful curves.

"Noah."

"I mean it, Emma. I just want you." It was that simple. She made his days exciting, and the way they'd fit together when they had sex—

"Mark wants to spend more time with you."

Noah pulled back. "He said that?"

"He misses you. He's going to bring his wife and some friends to our next cooking class."

"Great!" He was impressed. Emma seemed to have sorted out everything. He'd already forgiven his friend for believing Caitlyn's lies. After all, she'd done a good job of fooling him, too, for a while.

"So the question is, can you photograph food or not? Teaching online classes is great, but I want a cookbook."

"You got it. I've been practicing, you know. Why don't you whip up a batch of your signature waffles, and we'll give it a try."

Once Emma had a batch of waffles on the go, they worked together to create a beautiful place setting and set up his camera equipment. An hour—and several batches of waffles—later, he had some photos he thought would work well.

"That one is perfect," Emma said as they looked through the photographs on his tablet. Two waffles sat arranged on a plate with several berries, a sprinkling of powdered sugar and a drizzle of syrup. It looked good enough to eat.

He should know—he'd consumed at least four of the castoffs during the process.

"We're going to get fat making this cookbook."

"But we'll be happy."

"You got that right." He kissed her, something he'd done at every chance all afternoon.

"I'm glad you're not a player," she proclaimed when she pulled back.

"Oh, yeah?"

"I like having you around."

"Good. Get used to it."

Emma ducked her head. Turned and got to work cleaning up.

Uh-oh. What was wrong now? "Emma?"

"This can't last. You and me." She gestured between them. "You're going to bulldoze Angela's garden."

He didn't even want to think about that. "Let's not worry about that today," he said gently. "Let's enjoy this." He pointed to the mess they'd made while they'd worked. "We took the first step in creating something really special together. Let's worry about tomorrow when it gets here, okay?"

After a moment, she nodded. "Okay."

But they both knew they were on borrowed time.

Casting around for something else to focus on, Noah remembered Greg's invitation. Maybe spending time with Emma away from Brightview would help.

"There's this barbecue coming up—the Surf Dads are putting it on. It's a chance to hang out and raise money for a local organization that sponsors beach cleanups and water testing. Would you like to come?"

She hesitated long enough he was afraid she'd say no. "Yeah, I'd like that."

CHAPTER 11

A WEEK LATER Emma shivered a little as she followed Noah to a covered picnic area at Farview Beach where several men were manning an enormous grill. The afternoon had been gorgeous, and the sun was shining when they'd left Brightview, but as they'd approached this side of town, fog had begun to roll in, and now Emma was regretting that she'd left her hoodie at home.

The fog obscured anything more than a few hundred yards away, reducing the world to their immediate surroundings. It fit her mood. These past few days she'd felt like she was existing in a kind of suspended animation. More guests had come and gone at Brightview, but otherwise things had stayed the same. Andrew was hung up in Seattle on some project, so no progress had been made on Noah's house. Ashley was back in San Francisco. Kate still remained, a constant, quiet presence at the bed-and-breakfast. She kept to herself for large portions of the day, working on the flower borders or tucked away in her room drawing and journaling. Emma gave her space, figuring Kate would speak up when she was ready to share more about her life.

Meanwhile, she was falling for Noah a little more each day. They had grown into a rhythm of time together and apart, working side by side on the cookbook and doing chores around the bed-and-breakfast, then splitting off to surf and garden and hang out with friends. Being with Noah was easy.

Too easy, she reminded herself. Soon Andrew would come back and start building Noah's trophy home. All this would end.

"You made it," someone called as they approached, a dark-haired man with a wide smile.

"We did. Greg, this is Emma," Noah said. "Emma, meet my friend Greg Nolan. He's the one who introduced me to the Surf Dads."

More people called out their greetings as they noticed Noah's arrival. They looked to be an active, happy bunch. Noah had explained about the Surf Dads—and moms—and Emma thought it was brilliant that all these people were helping each other with childcare so that they could still enjoy their sport.

"Do you surf, Emma?" Greg asked.

"Not at all," she said. "Noah keeps threatening to teach me."

"I'm surprised you haven't brought her out already," Greg chided Noah.

"I'll get right on that."

"Hi, Emma—I'm Reese Spencer," another man said.

"This is Marta, my wife, and that's Edie, Greg's better half."

"You finally working on getting a wife, Noah?" Marta called from where she was setting out stacks of napkins. "Then all you need is a kid and you can move up to full membership in the Surf Dads."

"It's about time," Reese said. "How long can someone stay a junior member?"

"Didn't even know we had junior members," another man joked.

"Had to invent the category for Noah, here," Greg told him, "since it was obvious he wasn't going to get lucky anytime soon. No offense, Emma."

"None taken." She laughed.

"Noah, dude, quit being such a slacker," Reese said. "I had my first kid when I was twenty-five. What are you, forty?"

"I'm thirty-two," Noah protested.

"You're ancient, that's what you are. And Emma's standing right there. She agreed to come on this date with you, right? Pop the question, dude, put a ring on it—fast—before she comes to her senses."

"You're the one who's going to scare off Emma," Noah told him. "At least let me get her on a surfboard a couple of times before I propose."

"No one is proposing to anyone tonight, thank you very much. Noah and I just met," Emma said tartly.

"Greg, you heard the woman. Get her a burger before she writes me off altogether."

"One burger, coming up." Greg winked at her. "You're a good sport, Emma. Don't mind us; we give everyone a hard time."

"I don't mind," she said and took the plate he handed her, moving down the table to where Marta and Edie were waiting for her.

"If you don't want a man to teach you to surf, we'd be happy to," Edie assured her. She was short but fit with a cap of dark hair.

"Sometimes the guy you're dating isn't the best candidate for surf instructor," Marta chimed in. "We moms are out on Tuesdays and Thursdays. Give me your phone and I'll put my number in." She was nearly a foot taller than Edie, a quintessential California girl with her bleached-blond hair and tanned skin.

Emma juggled her phone and the plate of food. Marta took it from her and entered a number. "There. You're all set."

"Thanks. I'll come out sometime soon, whether or not I'm ready for a lesson, just to see you surf."

"We'll catch up with you then."

"Sorry about all that," Noah said when they'd found a table to sit at. "Forgot you weren't an old friend."

"I don't mind teasing. It means people accept you when it's lighthearted like that."

"Exactly. I've really appreciated having these guys watching my back when I'm on the water."

"I'll bet." She took a bite of her hamburger. "God, this is good. Why is food always better when it's cooked out in the open?"

"I don't know, but I agree with you." He cocked his head. "You cold?"

"A little. I forgot to layer."

"Here." He set his plate down, stripped off his sweatshirt and handed it to her.

"Don't you need it?"

"Nope. I'm fine."

She set her plate down, too, and tugged the sweatshirt over her head, immediately enveloped in warmth. It was far too big, of course. She rolled up the sleeves so she wouldn't dip her cuffs in ketchup.

"Looks good on you," he said, getting back to eating.

"Thanks. It feels good."

They were quiet while they finished their burgers. The sun was setting, the fog eerie in the growing dark. When they were done, Noah set their plates aside, moved to sit beside her and wrapped an arm around her shoulders. She snuggled in beside him, content.

"I know we can make this work." He leaned in to kiss the top of her head.

"I hope you're right."

They watched the waves crash against the sand. A couple of kids ran by, giggling, caught up in a game of tag.

"Do you want to have children?"

His casual question made her straighten. Noah let her go reluctantly and sat up, too. "Didn't mean to ruin the mood."

"It's too serious a thing to answer all slouched together like that."

He chuckled. "I like being slouched together with you. But I'd also like to know your thoughts."

"The answer is yes. I want kids and I want—" She was taken aback by the strong emotions that welled up inside her. The fog was muffling the sounds of the people around them, and it reminded her of how lonely her childhood had been after her mother passed away. The slap of the water against the sand was too quiet. There was no ocean breeze. No stars visible overhead. Just a claustrophobic shrinking of the world to a few dozen square feet around them. Life had felt that way after her family had moved out of the peach house and she and Ashley had lost any means to fool the other kids about how poor they were. What few friends she'd gained, she lost again, leaving her alone with their shabby home, Ashley and their absent father. School and then work, work, work when she was old enough. "I want kids," she said again, more clearly this time, "but I want to be there for them. I… don't want to die."

Noah let out a long breath. "I don't want to die, either."

He knew how she felt, didn't he? His parents had passed early, too. "But you take chances out there in the waves," she said, remembering the day he'd gone to Mavericks, how antsy she'd felt until he came home.

"Is that how your parents died? Taking chances?"

"No." Neither of them had done anything risky like that. "My mom had cancer. Dad had liver problems."

He rubbed his chin. "I don't feel like I take unnecessary risks. Would my hobbies bother you if you were considering me for a long-term partner?"

It was a deeper conversation than she'd expected tonight. She thought it over. Would it bother her if she was with him and they were parents?

"It wouldn't stop me from being with you," she said honestly. "I've seen that you think things through before you do them."

"My risks are calculated," he agreed. "I know what my capabilities are, and I like to push myself to be my best, but I also value my life. I'm not going to throw it away for a thrill."

"I'm glad to hear that."

"We keep doing this, don't we?" he asked. "Jumping in the deep end before we paddle around in the shallows."

"It's too cold tonight to paddle around, period," she said, allowing him to pull her closer again.

"Deep end it is, then," he said and kissed her.

THE FOLLOWING DAY Emma held her second cooking class, which turned out to be even more successful than the first. Mark and his friends from San Mateo were fun, smart and enthusiastic participants. After Mark apologized to Noah again for being such an ass about his cousin, Emma forgave him everything. He'd obviously been overwhelmed by the process of selling his company and losing his business partner when he'd come after Noah. Now that they were friends again, she could let go of the whole affair, which meant she was able to enjoy the evening thoroughly.

It was a good thing she had that triumph to celebrate, because the news from the bank wasn't as good. After weeks of putting her off, Regina had been able to increase the size of the loan she could offer and again pressed Emma to fold her old debts in with her mortgage, but she still couldn't give Emma enough to make a last-minute bid to buy back the Cliff Garden.

She did get two more bookings for the bed-and-breakfast for upcoming weeks and several unsolicited calls from people interested in taking cooking classes. With Noah's help, she'd finished and photographed eleven more recipes for the cookbook, planned out two more cooking class evenings, and set up times with Tim O'Keefe, the college student, to film classes she'd sell online, now that she'd gotten the basics down. He'd gone through the footage he'd captured at her first class and given her suggestions for how they could improve things. For someone so young, she was impressed with how much thought he put into the project.

"This is what I want to do with my life," he'd told her. "Working with you is like doing a paid internship."

She was glad for his enthusiasm since she was a bundle of nerves every time the camera was on her, but both Tim and Noah assured her it would get easier and as the night went on, it did.

It was all coming together, so when Noah proposed they play hooky one afternoon and do something just for fun, she agreed, needing a bit of a break. "Let's take a picnic to the castle," she said. "I haven't been there yet."

They took Noah's car and hugged the coastline south to the far end of town where Seahaven Castle loomed over the shoreline. Built in the late 1800s by the wealthy family who had founded the town, for decades it had been the heart of tourism in the county, but family infighting in the last few generations had left it a shell of its former glory. A farmer's market operated on Saturdays just outside the main gate in the curtain wall, but the courtyard and bailey had been closed to the public for as long as Emma had been alive.

Emma directed Noah to the Dungeon, a pub close by where she remembered Nana Angela picking up sandwiches for a picnic like this one when she was a kid. She'd placed an order ahead of time, and it was waiting for her when she popped in to grab it.

They parked in the lot outside the enormous stone walls of the castle and found a spot on the bluffs in front of it. Soon they spread a blanket and began feasting on sandwiches while Winston basked in the sun.

"Have you ever had a tour?" Noah asked, nodding at the castle walls looming high above them. "I haven't. It was closed when I was a kid."

"It's never reopened. I remember Nana Angela telling me they used to have actual jousting tournaments on the back field when she was a girl. She said it was really something. There was even a castle watch—local men who took their positions very seriously. They'd get dressed up on holidays and play their parts. It killed Ashley and me to know we'd never get to see that."

"I wondered if maybe Angela got you in. Seems like she was well known in town."

"You're right. I guess she wasn't connected enough to get an invitation."

"Neither was I."

"Well, you wouldn't get one, would you? From what Nana Angela said, there's been no men allowed inside the castle for ages." Emma thought back to what Angela had told her. "I think there's a caretaker who lives there now. A woman. I don't know where the money comes from to keep it up without visitors."

"No men allowed, huh?"

"You must have heard that before if you lived here when you were a kid."

"I did," he admitted. "But I was only ten when we left. Thought maybe people were pulling my leg."

"Nana Angela told us there was a fight among the

family who owns it. The wife kicked the husband out, and that was that; no more men."

"No wonder it's falling down."

Emma snorted. "Don't oversell yourselves. Women can do maintenance, too."

He tilted his head back and stared up at the castle walls. "Challenge accepted," he called, giving the building a salute.

"Don't you dare break into the castle," Emma admonished him. "You don't want to mess around with rules like that. Next thing you know, you'll end up getting cursed. Or cursing the whole town. Either way, it won't be a good outcome for me."

"Because you want to be with me?"

"Because I need more guests like you if I'm going to pay my mortgage." But she allowed him to kiss her, a kiss that went on and on until Emma forgot everything else.

When they were done with their meal, they threw away their trash, packed up the remains of their picnic and wandered closer to the edge of the bluffs. Winston trailed them, snuffling in the grass, following invisible tracks that interested him. A triangular beach lay far below, and out on the water were the inevitable surfers. When Noah began to look from the waves to the castle and back again, it took Emma a second to realize he was figuring out the angles for a photograph.

"If I was in the water beyond those surfers I could

get the bluff and the castle in the background. I'd have to do it just right."

She could see the cogs of his brain working as he calculated where he'd have to position himself to get it all in. He caught her watching him and grinned. "I'll get the shot eventually."

"I'm sure you will," she told him. "You're happy here, aren't you? Living in Seahaven. Surfing and taking photos."

"And spending time with you," he added. "It wouldn't be the same without you."

"Really?"

"Really."

SEVERAL DAYS LATER Emma was kneeling in the Cliff Garden in the late afternoon, weeding around a salvia plant, when she heard soft footsteps approaching. She'd begun to make it a habit to spend at least an hour a day out here tending the beds.

"Hi."

"Ashley? What are you doing here?" Her sister looked pale again. She was wearing a sharp tailored suit, her pretty shoes sporting a skim of dust from the garden path.

"I fainted again. I know, I know." She put a hand up to forestall Emma's words. "I should have waited for you to come and get me, but I couldn't stand it there a moment longer. I didn't even go to the hospital this time. I just drove down."

"In your own car? What if you fainted on the way? You could have killed someone." Emma got to her feet and pulled off her work gloves.

"I only faint once. Then I get up, eat something, drink something, and I'm fine. You know that." She sat on the Trouble Bench with a thump, setting her bag beside her. "I needed to be here."

And then she dropped her head in her hands.

Alarmed, Emma rushed to sit next to her and wrapped an arm around Ashley's shoulders. "What's wrong?"

"I can't figure it out," Ashley groaned. "Why would Nana Angela leave me the Cliff Garden—now? Why now? Why didn't she come for us when we were kids and we needed her?"

Guilt stung Emma. She'd been so busy playing house with Noah, she hadn't relayed to her sister the information Colette told her.

"There's a good reason for that." She launched into a recital of what she knew. Ashley shifted away from her on the bench as she spoke.

"She thought Dad would end up losing Brightview and the garden if she passed it on to us when we were underage," Emma finished. "She understood what was going on better than we thought. She tried to help, but—"

"We made it impossible," Ashley finished for her. "I didn't know she'd sent that woman from CPS."

"How could we know?"

Ashley was quiet. "She loved us," she finally whispered.

"She loved us," Emma agreed.

Ashley pulled her feet up on the bench, wrapped her arms around them and pressed her forehead to her knees. A moment later her shoulders heaved, and Emma's gut twisted in concern.

"Ash?"

"I sold it." Ashley's voice was muffled, thick with tears. "I sold the garden."

"Oh, honey." She slid closer to her sister and rubbed her back. Here it came. Finally. She'd known Ashley couldn't be so cold about her inheritance, not when she'd loved this place so much the summer they'd spent here.

On the day they'd flown home at the end of their time in Seahaven, Ashley had spent an hour visiting each and every plant to say goodbye. Emma had trailed her around the garden, knowing her sister's heart was breaking and not knowing what to do about it.

"It's okay," Emma murmured to her now. She still couldn't make things right for Ashley, no matter how hard she tried, and it gutted her that they were careening through life hurting each other—and themselves—when each of them kept trying to do the right thing.

"No, it isn't." Ashley raised her head. Her cheeks were streaked with tears, her carefully applied makeup smudged. "It isn't. She loved us. She loved *me.* She gave me the best thing she had to offer, and I sold it."

"You had your reasons."

"Reasons." Ashley scrubbed her face with both hands, but her tears fell even faster. "I was so… angry at her. I thought she'd abandoned us, just like Mom did."

Emma understood. She'd felt the same way even if she hadn't admitted it. "Mom didn't abandon us. Neither did Nana Angela."

"I know." Ashley spread her hands wide. "But when I got the letter informing me of my inheritance, all I could think of was the day the dolls came and Dad took off."

"You told me he'd spend all the money if we got any back then. It was a good thing Angela didn't send it."

"You're right. He would have. I was angry when I thought we'd finally get the money we needed and he'd blow it." Ashley's face crumpled. "But then it didn't come and he… left. I never thought he'd do that. I kept waiting that night for him to come home, but he never did. I thought he was gone for good—and I thought it was all my fault." Ashley broke down and sobbed in a way Emma had never seen her do before.

Emma was taken aback. "It was only one night. He came home the next day," she protested.

"What if he hadn't?"

Emma had never seen her sister lose control like this and didn't understand why she was doing it now. Their dad's absence hadn't fazed her back then. Emma had been nearly eighteen. Dying to leave home and start her life. She'd always thought Ashley, at sixteen, had felt the same way. After all, it was Ashley who'd come up with most of their plan to escape the life they'd been leading. She was the one who'd kept a detailed list of the steps they needed to take. Graduate high school. Go to culinary school and community college. Save every penny.

"We were old enough to take care of ourselves," Emma told her sister. "We were already paying most of the bills. We would have been fine if he did leave."

"I wasn't fine. I was never fine back then!" Ashley's voice broke, and Emma's heart ached for her. "Don't you get it? I didn't want him to take care of us—I wanted him to love us."

"He did love us." But as the words came out of her mouth, Emma realized she wasn't sure that was true. Had he ever said so?

Had he ever acted like it?

Vertigo struck her, and Emma gripped the back of the bench seat. Ashley's sobs made it hard for her to think.

Was that why it had been so easy to fall into a relationship with Jordan? Because she expected so little from the people who were supposed to love her?

What about Noah? Was she fooling herself about what she thought she felt about him?

"I never felt loved by Dad," Ashley sobbed. "I didn't feel loved by Nana Angela, either, not after that first summer. When I learned I'd inherited the Cliff Garden, I didn't feel grateful. I felt… furious. I wanted to ruin something. I wanted to be done with debt and fear and worry—but I wanted to hurt someone, too. I wanted to hurt *her*."

Emma nodded, her own eyes filling with tears. She knew what that was like—wanting to lash out.

"All I did was hurt myself—and you." Ashley rubbed the heel of her hand across her cheek. "And it was all for nothing. Angela did love us. Now I've messed up everything."

"It's going to be all right," Emma said again, wishing she had more than platitudes to offer her sister.

"How?" Ashley demanded. "How is it going to be all right? The garden will be gone. I'll be stuck in San Francisco forever—at that stupid job for the rest of my life!"

"But you love your job."

"I love my job—but I don't love Cotler, Tannen and Brindle. I don't love San Francisco. I want my own company. I want to live here. I want my garden back. I want you back!" Her voice rose, and Emma glanced around to make sure they were alone.

"I'm right here." All she could do was let Ashley cry until her tears ran out.

"I fucked up so bad, Emma," she finally sobbed. "I

sold the Cliff Garden because I thought it would finally set me free, and it didn't. I feel like my cage got even smaller."

"Oh, Ashley." Emma hugged her. "Maybe we can still get it back if we work together—"

"There you are!" a hearty male voice called out. Ashley scrambled to her feet, scraping at her face with her shirtsleeves.

"Andrew?" Emma got up, too. She hadn't known he was coming.

"Don't let him see me like this!" Ashley ducked behind her. Emma tried to give her cover.

"Andrew, give us a minute, won't you?" she asked. "We'll meet you at the house. We were discussing something important." When he looked like he'd question her further, she added, "Are you joining us for dinner?"

"Sure, if that's an invitation." He beamed at her like a man who'd just summited a mountain—and wanted to share the photos he had taken to prove it.

"Go find Noah," she ordered him. "Let me finish up with Ashley. She's had a rough week."

He craned his neck to see, but she stepped in his way again. "Okay," he said reluctantly. "I've got new plans for the house. You're both going to want to see them."

"After dinner," Emma said firmly. Maybe she could shunt Ashley off to bed before then.

That wasn't the way it turned out, however.

When she tried to renew their conversation, Ashley wasn't interested in talking anymore. By the time they made it to the house, Noah had already ordered pizzas. The brothers were laughing and teasing each other as if Andrew's arrival was an anticipated treat, not the potential bomb that could blow up in all their faces. Ashley ducked into the bathroom.

"Noah says you've got a TV room upstairs?" Andrew asked.

"On the second floor." She wanted to whisk Ashley up to her bedroom, but when Ashley appeared again, Andrew and Noah both followed them to the second story.

"Come on," Andrew said. "You're really going to want to see this."

"Ashley," Emma began. "I don't think this is a good idea."

"Oh, I think it is," Ashley said in a dangerous tone. She flopped down on the sofa as Andrew began to connect a tablet to the large-screen TV. Emma, not knowing what else to do, sat beside her. Noah joined them.

Winston appeared a minute later and came to be petted. He settled on the floor in front of their feet.

"I took your suggestions to heart," Andrew told Noah when he was ready. "I shifted the house to the far side of the lot. Diminished the footprint." He flipped through some images, and Emma saw the house now sat in the far back corner, leaving quite a lot of room in front of it and to the side.

"And now for the new, reimagined urban garden," he pronounced and flipped to a new image, a 3D rendering of what the lot would look like from Brightview's back deck.

Emma's stomach dipped. There was Noah's house in the far back corner. There were the bluffs and the sea beyond. In between them was a garden… of sorts.

Ashley, silent until now, stood up. "No. No," she repeated. "What the hell is that?" She turned on Andrew. "What is that?" She pointed to the screen.

"The new Cliff Garden." He was still waiting for praise, confused by Ashley's reaction. Emma would have laughed if it wasn't so awful.

"That's a garden?"

Winston, alarmed at Ashley's raised voice, lumbered to his feet and whined.

"Of course it is." Andrew stabbed a finger at a series of cement planters set at neat right angles to each other in a kind of maze. They were of different widths and heights, their edges crisp and distinct. "See how the planters encourage the flow of visitors through the site?" he said. "They symbolize the complexities of modern life. The way we struggle to—"

"That is not a garden!" Ashley shrieked. "That's—"

"A statement," Andrew pronounced, puffing out his chest and moving to loom over her. "A statement fitting to the tone I'm trying to set. You know nothing about design."

The dog padded over to stand between them, looking from one to the other.

"And you know nothing about beauty. You're a destroyer, not a builder." Ashley's hands were balled into fists.

"I've created something stunning!" He pointed at the display again. "What have you ever made? You're a pencil pusher. A number cruncher. Don't talk to me about beauty. You wouldn't know it if it slapped you in the face!"

"Get out!" Emma didn't know when she got to her feet, but she was standing now, directing Andrew toward the door, fury making her hands shake.

Winston woofed.

"Emma," Noah began, slipping his fingers under Winston's collar and holding on to the dog. "Andrew, come on—you know that's not what I asked for."

"You're going to ruin everything!" Ashley shrieked at Andrew.

Winston barked again.

"Get out!" Emma roared at the men. "Both of you!" She'd had enough. Her sister had just sobbed her eyes out on the Trouble Bench in the garden they both loved. She wasn't going to let Andrew obliterate it with his stupid maze of cement planters.

Ashley was right: He was a destroyer, and what was

Noah? Someone who went along with destruction. He wasn't fighting for her. He was just using her. Sleeping with her. Trying to shut her up so she wouldn't complain.

She and Ashley had spent their childhoods trying to get attention and love from a man who hadn't even noticed they were there. She wasn't going to hand her heart to another man who didn't deserve it.

"Emma," Noah tried again.

"Out!"

He opened his mouth, shook his head and closed it again. Instead of speaking, he let go of Winston, lunged for Andrew, ripped the tablet from his hands and disconnected it from the television before marching Andrew down the stairs and out of the house, Winston hurrying after them. The rev of an engine a moment later heralded their departure.

"They're gone," Emma told Ashley. "It's all right. They've left." She was still shaking, cold even though the day was warm.

"But they're coming back, and they're going to pave over the Cliff Garden—and it's all my fault."

CHAPTER 12

"HAPPY NOW?" NOAH asked Andrew as they nursed beers on the outdoor patio at the Seahaven Brewery. Winston was visible sitting up in the back seat of the Range Rover, head resting on the open window, watching them mournfully.

"I show my plans, and everyone starts yelling. You think that makes me happy?" Andrew countered.

Noah bit back an angry reply. None of this was Andrew's fault. Not really. In fact, he wasn't sure whose fault it was. "I asked you to include the Cliff Garden in your plans. You didn't include it at all."

"It doesn't go with the vibe of the place. Shit, I tried. I drew up the house plans and then stuck those winding paths and overblown flower beds in there, and it looked ridiculous. That garden doesn't go with my house."

Noah stared at him. "Did it ever occur to you to make the house go with the garden?"

"That's not how you get magazine covers. That's not how you win awards."

"Really? You have to plow over the past to win prizes? I can't believe that's true."

They drank in silence for a minute. A band was setting up in one corner, and Noah knew soon the brewery would be too loud for talking.

"Come on. Let's get out of here." He settled the bill and led the way out to his car. He had no idea if Emma would let them back in the bed-and-breakfast, so he drove down Cliff Street to the end, where there were parking spaces and a lookout. He parked the car, got out and sat on a nearby bench. When Andrew joined him, he waved at the ocean before them. "This is what the Cliff Garden is all about. Framing the sea and sky. Making it human. Making it comfortable. All the houses you design are sharp and spiky—the opposite of comfortable. Why is that?"

"That's what sells." Andrew laced his hands behind his head and kept his gaze on the waves. "People don't want to blend into their landscape, Noah. They want to impose their will on it. 'I'm here.' That's what they're saying with their houses."

That wasn't what Noah wanted to say at all. His passion was photographing the confluence of people and nature. That's why he loved surf photography. It took a person and the ocean, a board and a wave to create the magic of the moment. Surfers rode the waves—they didn't control them.

He knew Andrew wouldn't understand that metaphor, though. You didn't win magazine covers by giving up control. That's what he'd say.

They sat in silence as the sun slipped beneath the horizon. Noah stood up, knowing he couldn't put things off any longer.

"Let's go. If Emma won't let us stay at Brightview, we'll have to find a motel." One way or another, he needed to find out where he stood with her.

"If she does, I'll give her a bad review," Andrew said.

"Like hell you will." Noah forced himself to count to ten.

When they got to Brightview, Emma met them at the door. He'd prepared himself for her to kick them right back out again, so he was grateful when she ushered them into the living room instead.

"Sit down."

They did so. Winston lay down at Noah's feet, ears perked up, waiting for more trouble, Noah thought.

"I've got something to say," she told them both. Noah noticed she didn't offer snacks—or even drinks. This was serious. "I want to formally offer to buy back the Cliff Garden. Together, I believe Ashley and I will be able to get a loan. We'll pay the full price you paid and enough extra to cover the expenses you've incurred while you waited to develop the land. It's a fair offer."

Noah swallowed, crushing the urge to look for his brother's reaction. At this point, if it weren't for his promise to Andrew, he'd sell the land to her in an instant.

"No way," Andrew said quietly. "Don't you dare. There isn't another waterfront lot available in Seahaven right now, and you know it."

"It's complicated," Noah told Emma. "Andrew is right—"

"I can't believe you." Emma crossed her arms. "You know how much this means to me, and you're going to talk about complicated? It's not complicated at all. Yes, you'll sell to me, or no, you won't. Which is it?"

He didn't answer quickly enough, and she pointed to the door they'd only just entered through.

"If you're going to build those stupid cement planters, you'd better build them twelve feet tall, because I never want to see you again, Noah Hudson. Pack your things, get out and never come back!"

CHAPTER 13

WHEN THE MEN were finally gone, Emma went up to her room and stepped onto the balcony, automatically checking the delivery system Ava had rigged up as she passed it. The bag was hanging low, which meant Ava must have sent something over earlier in the day knowing she'd find it eventually.

Emma leaned over the railing, fished for the bag and opened it to find a new batch of embroidered aprons from Penelope and a wrapped package that contained a scented candle from Ava.

The gifts cheered her but only a little. She ached to think of Noah out of her life, but if he was going to choose Andrew over her, it was only right she choose Ashley over him. In the end, family beat out everything else. Her heart broke for Ashley, too, knowing that forevermore she'd see Noah's new house and be reminded of something precious she'd tossed away.

She set the gifts on her bed and returned outside, hoping the fresh air would clear her thoughts.

Movement in the Cliff Garden caught her eye. Was

that Noah and Andrew?

No.

It was a young man in a black hoodie slouching through the garden, hands jammed in his pockets, shoulders high. He hesitated by the Trouble Bench.

Sat down.

"No," Emma whispered. She didn't have a thing to offer to anyone right now. Not after losing the man she'd hoped to spend the rest of her life with, she finally admitted to herself. Noah had seemed like someone she could truly open up to, a man who wouldn't run at the first sign of trouble, or shut her off, or let her down—

But he'd done just that, hadn't he?

The young man shifted on the bench, looking out to the ocean, then back the way he'd come. Was he waiting for someone?

He half turned on the bench to look her way.

Was he—waiting for her?

If he'd come on purpose to sit on the Trouble Bench, then he was her responsibility—at least for a few more weeks until Noah and Andrew bulldozed the land in preparation for building.

She didn't know how she got from the balcony to the stairs, but soon she was in the kitchen, automatically putting baked goods on a plate, covering them with a cloth napkin, filling a glass of water and walking out the sliding doors to the deck, down to the grass and to the shortest path to the Trouble Bench. If she only had a few more weeks, she was going to make the best of it.

"Hi." She dropped down next to the young man, startling him enough he jerked away from her. "Sorry. Didn't mean to scare you."

"That's okay," he said automatically. He scanned her up and down, his features hollow, eyes too big, ringed with dark circles.

"Have something to eat." She handed him the plate. When he wolfed down first a muffin, then a slice of lemon cake and a cookie, she wished she'd brought something more substantial.

She wordlessly handed him the glass of water when he was done, and he drank it all in one gulp.

"I fucked up," he said without preamble.

Emma thought of Ashley sitting here just hours ago, saying the same thing.

"Tell me about it."

"I fucked up," he said again. "I can't stop. I try… but I can't."

Understanding flooded her. The shadows as dark as bruises under the young man's eyes. The pallor of his skin.

"Drugs?" She didn't feel like beating around the bush. Didn't seem like beating around the bush ever helped. If she'd pushed Ashley for answers earlier, maybe they'd have been able to buy back the Cliff Garden.

He nodded sharply. "Nothing works. I stay clean a

day. An hour. Then I'm doing it again."

"There are places you can go to get help." She wished she knew more about addiction. Why hadn't she thought to gather brochures about the services the county offered for various problems—the ones too big for her to help sort on her own? What good was she to anyone if she couldn't even anticipate such an obvious situation?

She was spiraling, her fear and sorrow overwhelming her when what she needed to do was to concentrate on this young man. Her problems could wait. His couldn't.

"I know." His teeth were chattering, and Emma wondered if he was in withdrawal right now. "I fucked up," he said again. "I'm hurting everyone. My mom. My dad. They don't deserve this." He began to rock in his seat, and Emma forgot about the Cliff Garden—and Noah. What if this boy went into shock? Or tried to fling himself over the side of the bluffs? His gaze kept tracking in that direction. It was a long way down to the beach below.

"Your parents love you, and I'm sure they'll want to do everything they can to help."

"They've already done everything," he said. "They've tried everything. They deserve someone who listens. Who doesn't keep taking this shit and fucking up all over again."

He was rocking harder, and Emma knew she had to do something before the situation got out of control.

She took the plate and glass from his hands, set them on the grass by her feet and reached out, curling her fingers around his. He met her gaze, looking bewildered.

"What's your name?"

"Connor."

"Connor, I've got you, and I'm not going to let go." What else could she tell him? What would she want someone to say if this was her child on the Trouble Bench?

Emma wondered if she was qualified to be a parent at all, no matter what she'd said to Noah at the barbecue. Mom had died too young to be a role model for her. Dad had hardly noticed her at all.

She gripped Connor's hands and decided none of that mattered. She'd done her best to care for Ashley, even if she'd been a poor stand-in for the real thing. She had a heart. Knew what it was to love someone.

A breeze touched her face, and Nana Angela's wind chimes rippled the air behind her. Connor was waiting.

Suddenly she knew what to say.

"Here's the thing about parents, okay? They might look disappointed or angry when you tell them something they don't want to hear, but the truth is when they look that way, they're actually terrified."

His eyes widened. "What do you mean?"

"Your parents don't want to lose you. I know that for a fact." That's the way she'd feel if this was her child suffering the way Connor was. "Maybe they've told you in the past to excel at school or get a job or something like that, but you don't have to worry about that right now. Connor—are you listening to me?"

He nodded. "Yeah."

"Do your parents know you're struggling with addiction?"

"Yeah." He nodded again.

"Then all they want is for you to stay alive. That's it. That's the only thing you need to do for them right now. Understand? Stay alive."

A tear slid down his cheek. "I don't know if I can."

"You can." She gripped his hands more tightly. "I swear to god you can. And you don't have to do it alone. I'm right here."

He didn't look like he thought that would be enough, and Emma wasn't sure it would be, either. The breeze brushed her face again. There were the wind chimes, sending a delicate tracing of sound through the air.

She couldn't do this alone, Emma realized. She wasn't enough—not for a problem this big.

The surf moms, she thought, and relief flooded her. A group like that would know someone who had experience with a problem like this. Keeping a hold of Connor with one hand, she fished her phone out of her pocket with the other. "I'm calling a friend. She'll know what to do," she told him, hoping she was right. She found the number and made the call. "Marta?" she said when the other woman picked up. "It's Emma. Noah's… friend. I need help."

"I'll be right there."

"EVERYTHING'S OKAY," GREG said without any preliminaries when Noah answered his phone later that evening.

Noah's gut clenched. "What happened?" No one started a phone call like that if it wasn't bad news.

"Like I said, everything is okay. I was afraid someone might tell you about the excitement in the Cliff Garden—at your property, I mean."

"What excitement?" Noah's throat went dry. Had something happened to Emma?

"Emma needed help with a man who visited the Trouble Bench. A kid, really. An addict."

Noah's grip on the phone tightened. "What did he do to her?"

"Nothing," Greg assured him. "He was detoxing. Was suicidal. She called Marta for help."

Why hadn't she called him? Pain engulfed Noah along with shock, and he gripped his phone so tightly it was a miracle it didn't shatter. Why wouldn't Emma call him in a situation like that?

Noah stopped himself. She hadn't called him because he'd chosen Andrew over her. He'd hurt her, and she'd thrown him out.

"Is she okay?" he managed to say.

"She's fine. So is Connor, the young man she helped.

Reese works in the county's detox center. Emma made the right call. He pulled some strings and was able to get him in right away. They'll help him ease off the drugs. Support him in his recovery if he's ready for it."

"That's good." Noah paced the floor of the motel room he'd gotten for the night. Winston was asleep in a corner. Andrew was in the room next door. They'd needed a break from each other.

"I was surprised you weren't there," Greg said.

"I wish to god I was," Noah told him.

"I'm not going to pry. You're old enough to know your own mind. All I'll say is if you and Emma are having problems, you can't solve them if you're not in the same place."

"Point taken," Noah said, his voice rough. "I think I have to give her some space, though."

"Maybe so," Greg said. "Just don't give her too much."

"MOVE OVER."

Emma looked up from the Trouble Bench to find Ashley standing next her. It had been a long night. When Marta had dropped her home after they'd handed Connor over to people who could help him, she'd meant to go to bed. Somehow her feet had retraced their earlier route and brought her here, however.

It was late—long past dark. *Dangerous to be out here alone under the moon.* That's what Angela had always said when she and Ashley wanted to stay out past their bedtime. Her smile had given away her true feelings, though. Angela loved her garden at every hour.

"Are you okay?" Ashley asked. Emma had called her earlier from the detox center to let her know what was happening. "Sounds like you did a good thing tonight."

"I hope so."

Ashley sat down when Emma made space for her. In the leggings and oversize shirt she'd changed into, she looked like a teenager. "I honestly can't believe I sold this beautiful garden. What was I thinking?"

"You were thinking you didn't want to re-create our childhood." Emma understood that better now, and she was ashamed of how she'd shrugged off Ashley's pain previously. When they were kids, she'd never taken on their financial hardships as a personal indictment the way Ashley had. She'd understood that if she'd had nicer clothes, cooler toys—a mom—she would have been accepted by the other kids. It was their dad's fault they didn't have those things—not hers. When she'd reached an age where she could work, buy her own clothes and make a life for herself apart from her father, she'd been able to move on for the most part. She'd had boyfriends, a fiancé, a social circle of sorts she moved in, at least until Jordan left her and she'd had to take on two full-time jobs just to make ends meet. It was hard to maintain friendships in those circumstances.

With Ashley, it was different, she realized now. Ashley had worn their poverty like a brand on her forehead ever since the first time they lost their house. She couldn't stand rejection, so she didn't make herself approachable in the first place. Emma remembered her saying she had friends in San Francisco, but she hadn't seen any evidence of them. Were those people actually friends, or were they work acquaintances with whom Ashley had lunch or drinks sometimes?

Emma wished she'd been able to shield Ashley better from the ups and downs they'd experienced when they were kids. If their mother was still alive, would her sister be a different person? Happier? More self-confident? She didn't feel all that confident herself, but she bounced back more easily than Ashley did from financial upsets, which was what had allowed her to open Food to You Fast when the very idea of it gave Ashley hives.

"I thought what I was doing was going to make me happy," Ashley went on. "Instead I'm miserable."

They listened to the crash of the waves far beneath them on the shore.

"I've always been jealous of you, you know."

"Jealous?" Emma laughed. "Why on earth would you be jealous of me? I haven't accomplished much."

"But when you fail, you pick yourself up, dust yourself off and get right back to trying. You don't wallow in the past the way I do."

"Maybe it's because I got more time with Mom before she died—and I understood what was happening more than you could have. I think about that sometimes. One day you had a mom, the next she was gone. One day you had a loving father, the next he locked himself away and barely ever came out again. One day you had a Nana Angela, the next she disappeared and never came back."

"All those things happened to you, too."

Emma nodded. "But I knew Mom was sick and that she didn't mean to leave us. I knew Dad was grieving and couldn't function properly. That wasn't our fault. I knew Nana Angela loved us. It was obvious in everything she did the summer she had us to stay."

"Was Dad the reason there was a mortgage on the Cliff Garden when I inherited it?" Ashley asked.

Emma turned to her. "I didn't know the Cliff Garden had a mortgage."

Ashley nodded. "For about a quarter of the property's worth."

"The one on Brightview is even bigger than that. Big enough to even out the difference in the values of the properties, in case you were wondering." She'd been waiting for the right time to say that, afraid Ashley thought Nana Angela had been unfair.

"I assumed it was something like that." She was silent a minute. "How much money did Dad spend over the years, do you think?"

"You mean how much did he lose?" Emma corrected her. "A lot, I guess. I think his day trading might have been like a gambling addiction. That's what Nana Angela thought, apparently."

"That makes sense. We never really talked about that—the way Dad acted around money."

"Instead we did our part to cover up the problem," Emma agreed. "Does that make us enablers?" She thought of Connor. What had his family done when they realized he had a problem?

"I was so afraid when you started Food to You Fast," Ashley said quietly. "It felt too close to the way Dad always took risks when it came to money. I was afraid you were overspending. Getting in debt. I thought I'd have to cover for you, too."

Emma sighed. "I know, and I'm sorry. I should have kept you in the loop more. Let you talk through your fears and show you why I thought I had a good plan."

"No, I'm sorry. You're not like him at all, and I should have trusted you."

"Food to You Fast didn't make it," Emma pointed out.

"If you'd had a different partner, would that have made a difference?"

"I think so. Not that it was all Jordan's fault. He just wasn't the right man for the job."

Ashley nodded. "I wish I'd been there to help."

"That's okay. Shutting it down meant I was available when I inherited Brightview, and I'm so glad of that. I really like it here."

"I do, too."

"I think I can make a go of it if I work hard," Emma went on. "And you're going to do great things at Cotler, Tannen and Brindle."

Ashley's lip trembled. "Except I don't want to be a partner at the firm. I don't want to live in San Francisco. I want to live here and run my own business, even if the idea of it scares me to death. Emma, what am I going to do?"

Emma let out a shaky breath. What would Nana Angela tell her sister?

She scanned the dark ocean lapping at the shore down below. Took in the stars twinkling overhead. When life felt overwhelming, it was good to be outside to see that the universe went on running through its cycles, unfazed by any of it.

"You know what you're not going to do? You're not going to make any decisions tonight. Tomorrow you're going to call your boss and tell him you're taking a vacation," she announced, thinking of what Kate had done. "I'm sure you have weeks of time banked from all the years you've worked at your firm. Why not use it? Rest. Play. Think everything over. If at the end of a month, you still feel the same, call your boss again and tell him you've changed your mind. I know you, Ashley. If you decide the partnership isn't for you, you'll help find someone else to take your place and you'll make the transition as easy as possible on the other members of the firm. It will all work out."

As she talked Ashley straightened, and by the end she was nodding. "You're right. That's exactly what I'm going to do. The other partners aren't monsters. They'll understand, and they'll appreciate that I'm not compounding my mistake by sticking with a plan I know won't work."

"When you've fulfilled your responsibilities in San Francisco, you can start fresh doing anything you want."

"Can I live here with you? I could pay rent."

"Of course." That would certainly make paying the mortgage easier, Emma thought. "It will be too late to try to get back the Cliff Garden," she added. "I think we have to accept that ship has sailed." She found her sister's hand and held it tight. To think this beautiful space would be gone still broke her heart, but knowing Ashley wanted to move in made up for that—a little.

"We'll just have to garden every square inch of Brightview," Ashley said determinedly. "There's a lot more we can do with it. It won't be nearly as big a garden, but it could be lovely."

"We've made a good start. Kate's been a big help."

"She has."

"We'll have friends here," Emma went on. "Good friends. Ava, Penelope, Kate and Aurora, Regina at the bank and Kamirah at Cups & Waves."

"And Noah next door," Ashley said.

"Forget him. I already have."

IT WAS THE longest week of his life.

Noah thought it only fair to Emma to give her time to grieve the Cliff Garden before coming back to try to persuade her to give him another chance, but he couldn't wait any longer.

He parked in his usual space at the bed-and-breakfast, noting Ashley's car was present, as was the passenger van, but no strange vehicles were in the small lot. Good. This would be easier if there weren't guests around. He let Winston out of the car, and the dog padded alongside him to the door. He hadn't been back since the night Emma threw him out.

"Oh. It's you," Ashley said as she opened the door. She disappeared inside, leaving him to follow. She must have scampered up the stairs, because the main room was empty when he entered it from the hall. Steady footsteps soon came down the stairs, however.

"Noah." Emma stopped short when she caught sight of him. "What are you doing here?" She was beautiful in shorts and a T-shirt, her hair pulled into a high ponytail. She must have been cleaning something. She still held a duster in one hand. Winston headed straight for her, and she bent to pet him automatically.

"I was hoping we could talk."

He thought she'd refuse. She sure looked like she wanted to. Instead she gestured out onto the deck. "Go and sit." When she put the duster away in the laundry room, returned to the kitchen and pulled a sparkling water for herself and a beer for him from the refrigerator, he relaxed a little. She couldn't still be furious with him if she was offering him a drink.

"I don't suppose you've come to tell me you changed your mind and want to sell me the Cliff Garden?" she asked as they took their seats on opposite rattan couches on the deck. She sat cross-legged and unscrewed the top of her bottle of water.

"No. Sorry." He wasn't sure where to start. He owed Emma an explanation. Should he just launch into it or make some general conversation first?

"What do you want?"

Right to the heart of things. He wanted to touch her badly, but he knew she'd push him away if he did. "If it were up to me, I'd sell you the Cliff Garden in an instant and find somewhere else to build."

"Why isn't it up to you?"

Another direct question that deserved a direct answer. He supposed it was time to come clean. "Because I owe Andrew—big time. Look, I'm an asshole. A real fuckup. You just don't know it yet. I hoped you'd never have to know."

"I don't think I follow."

"When Mark asked me to join Maxwell Tech, at first I wanted to say no. All I cared about was surfing and photography and having fun. I didn't even want to be at college, let alone taking on any extra projects. Mark really needed the help. He was on to something—obviously.

Had a product that was going to go the distance, we could all see that, but he didn't have any connections or a way to get funding...." He was getting too deep into details. "Anyway, he needed me, and he asked me to make a commitment. He asked for a decade."

"That's a big ask." Emma looked impressed—with Mark, not him.

It still blew Noah away Mark had been able to see the whole trajectory of his start-up back then. "It felt to me like he was asking me to sign up for a lifetime. I wanted to say no, but I didn't know how to do that to a friend like Mark, so I went to visit Andrew to get out of there for a while. Andrew was already out of school and had been working for Regis & Stratford for a few years—an architecture firm near Seattle."

Emma nodded, but he had the feeling she would lose interest if he didn't get to the point.

"They made Andrew lead on a project on a major college campus, and he came up with this really innovative design. The building was supposed to be a gathering place. He decided that since the college was built on traditional Native American territory, it should reflect that. He collaborated with a young architect from the Native American nation in question, and together they produced something that was a mixture of ultra-modern and Native American influences. It was amazing, Emma. When you saw it, you felt like a breeze was washing over this organic building—or washing through it—like the structure itself was under the influence of the weather and local natural forces. I can't explain it, but it was beautiful. Just beautiful." He trailed off, knowing the next bit was going to be excruciating to put into words. At the time it had gone down, Noah had thought the event would haunt him forever. That his life was over, not to mention any career he might have—with Mark or anyone else.

"What happened?" Emma asked softly.

"The building was almost done. In a couple of weeks there was going to be an open house where everyone on campus and in the community would get to walk through it for the first time." He broke off again. Mark had helped him wipe almost every trace of what had happened from the internet. He lifted his hands out wide in defeat. "I destroyed it."

Emma's jaw dropped open. He couldn't blame her. He still couldn't believe what he'd done.

"Destroyed it?" she echoed.

"I didn't mean to. I mean, no one ever sets out to be a self-absorbed asshole." He put up a hand to stop her when she began to protest. He wouldn't let her minimize what he'd done. He'd never paid the price for it—until now.

"I stole Andrew's key. He went to bed early back then. Did all this health shit before the sun came up. Going to the gym. Running. Juicing. You name it. He was on the top of his game. I was bored. Restless. Still didn't know what to do about Mark's offer. Was mad as hell Andrew had gone to sleep before ten on a Friday night and hadn't taken me out to some club or party so I could forget about everything for a minute."

He remembered the adrenaline coursing through his veins. The god-awful fear of a desk job tying him down and consuming his youth.

"I headed to the campus. Ran into some kids coming home from a party. Invited them to the gathering place. We stopped and got more beer—a lot more beer. They asked if they could invite a few friends. I figured why not."

"Oh, Noah."

Emma obviously saw where this was going.

"There was this girl with them. She was pretty cute. Pretty wasted, too. I let them in and we all got drunk. More and more people kept coming, and we were all having a good time. At some point the girl and I left the others and found a room."

He'd lost himself in her arms for an hour or two. Hadn't even noticed what was going on outside.

"Guess Andrew built those walls pretty solid. Or else I was too damn preoccupied. I didn't hear a thing." It wasn't funny even after all these years. The pity in Emma's eyes was the worst of it.

"Three hundred people showed up, best we were able to estimate later. It got totally out of hand. Someone brought some spray paint. Inside, the walls were this perfect white—curves everywhere—the ceiling and floors all wood. People couldn't resist. They tagged everything. Spilled booze. Someone set a fire. By the time I came out, the cops and firemen were there. People were screaming, breaking windows, getting out any way they could. Luckily there were sprinklers installed and the fire got put out—but by then, the place was a complete mess. The first photos splashed across the local papers were of the aftermath—not the pristine piece of art Andrew had built."

He was prepared for the shame but not for the anguish that welled up inside him when he told Emma. He'd never forget opening the door of that room and finding mayhem on the other side. How the girl he'd been fooling around with had run off without looking back.

How he'd faced the cops—and Andrew—alone.

"Andrew's company fired him. It took him nearly ten months to get another job and then he was stuck designing commercial building upgrades, working for a mom-and-pop establishment, not an award-winning firm like he had been. It took years before he was able to work his way up to something creative again, let alone to be lead on a project. He should have been a star. Instead his career was crushed—by me."

Emma didn't say anything. Did she hate him? Was that disgust in her eyes? If it was, he couldn't blame her. It still made his skin crawl to think about what he'd done.

"Mark was the one who saved my ass," he went on, needing her to know all of it. "He was the one who paid for the best attorney he could find, who was able to get me off the hook as a first-time offender. Then he got his hacker friends to erase every trace of the story from the internet."

If Emma was surprised by that last bit, she didn't show it. "And in return, you committed to ten years at Maxwell Tech," she said.

"That's right. Ten years that turned into twelve. And I didn't begrudge one day there," he added. "It was a fantastic experience, one I didn't deserve, and now I'm filthy rich."

"And you're finally paying back your brother."

"And hurting you in the process." He lifted his hands. "I don't know, Emma. I'm beginning to think I will never pay this debt. I'm trying. I've been trying for years. I actually thought I was going to succeed, but now it's transforming into something worse. It's like it's in me. Like I'm the thing that's rotten—"

"No!" Emma crossed to him and took his hands, sitting down on the rattan couch beside him. "That's not true. You're not rotten. You're human. We all are. We all screw up."

"But I want to marry you." She had to know everything in his heart. "I don't even want that damn house Andrew is going to build. But I can't take it away from him—not again."

Did she understand? If anyone could, it was Emma.

"Of course you can't take it away—he's your brother."

"And you're the woman I love. Can you be with me if it means losing the garden?"

"I… I don't know."

CHAPTER 14

EVEN AFTER NOAH left, Emma stayed out on the deck. The moon was full. She'd missed sundown with Ava and Penelope and hoped they'd understand. She could use a drink, but she was too emotionally exhausted to get one.

She still didn't have a good answer to the question Noah had asked her. She understood now why it was so important to him to allow Andrew to design and build a house on the Cliff Garden lot, but that didn't make it hurt less to lose Nana Angela's legacy.

"Emma?"

She tried to shake off her gloomy thoughts as Ashley set a glass of wine in front of her and took the seat Noah had vacated an hour ago.

"Can I join you?"

"Of course."

"I think it's my turn to offer a little advice."

"I'll take any you can give."

"There's no fixing the fact I sold the Cliff Garden. What's done is done."

"Noah explained why he feels he has to let Andrew build his house." Emma relayed the information as briefly as she could. Ashley listened, nodding now and then.

"It's a wonder any of us survives to adulthood with all the trouble we get into." She swirled her wine in her glass, gazing at the garden. "So, like I said, we can't change the fact I sold the Cliff Garden, and Noah can't change the fact he damaged his brother's career and wants to make up for it. He's right; he bought the lot fair and square, with no indication there were any extenuating circumstances."

"Okay." Emma wasn't sure where her sister was going with this, but she figured starting from the bare facts was sensible.

"We can't go back—any of us. We have to move forward."

"How?"

"You need to patch things up with him."

"He's going to ruin Angela's garden." She was keeping Noah at arm's length for Ashley's sake. Didn't she see that?

"I'm the one who ruined Nana Angela's garden," Ashley said. "I'm the one who needs to bear the consequences, not Noah. Not you. Look," she added. "I've been telling you for years you have lousy taste in men, but much as I hate to admit it, I think Noah is the exception. He's a good guy. He's loyal. Now I understand he's been fighting for the Cliff Garden in his own way, even if Andrew refuses to go along with his requests. I think he really cares about you, and I don't want to be the one who stands in the way of you having a relationship like that."

"I don't know if I can look past what he's going to do," Emma said honestly. "I like him. I really like him," she corrected herself. "I want to be with him, if I'm honest. But it's going to hurt so bad when the garden goes under."

"I know." Ashley studied the moon. "I'm sorry—for not believing in us. For giving up so fast and choosing safety over family."

"It was the only sensible choice for someone who's had to take care of herself since she was a teenager."

"No matter what happens next, I'm going to be here for you now. I'll help you make the bed-and-breakfast a success."

"Thank you."

Ashley stilled. Pointed to the Cliff Garden, where two small lights bobbed and flashed next door. "Someone's visiting the garden." It looked like they were using their phones to guide their way through the paths.

"Are they going to the Trouble Bench? Should we look?"

"No." Ashley touched her hand. "They're past it already. Besides, you need to rest. Let the garden take care of itself for one night."

"WE'RE NOT GOING to be able to figure out anything in the dark," Andrew said.

Noah spread the rough blanket he'd brought with him on the ground near the Trouble Bench. He'd gone back to the motel, fetched Andrew and Winston, who was now sleeping in the Range Rover, and driven straight back. "Sit," he commanded. "Let's just hang out awhile."

"Fine." Andrew collapsed on the blanket beside him.

"You used to tell me you had to listen to a place before you knew how to design what should be built on it. You talked about letting the surroundings speak to you."

Andrew made a dismissive sound. "That was before I spent a decade designing strip-mall storefronts. Listen to a few dozen parking lots—see what they tell you."

Someone else might think his brother was as jaded as he sounded, but Noah heard the pain in his voice. Andrew was an artist—he cared about what he did. He'd poured his heart into the Gathering Place building, then saw it destroyed. It had crushed him.

His spirit had taken a second blow during those long years of cramped creativity. Noah could tell he didn't believe in his abilities the way he once had. Was probably bracing himself for this opportunity to be whisked out from under him again. If he went back on his word, he'd deal Andrew's confidence a death blow.

"Let's just listen," he said again. "I've been rushing around for over a decade working for Mark, and I need to relax. I'm struggling with my photography. It's like the ocean has been driven out of my veins. I don't know the rhythm of it anymore. I can't anticipate when to take my shots."

Andrew stirred beside him. "You've got to get in that water every day," he said. "Be down at the beach at all hours until you've memorized the angles of the sun again and the colors of the water at different times. It's just a matter of showing up, day after day, hour after hour. You know this stuff."

Noah stifled a grin. If only Andrew listened to his own advice. "I know. I think… I got used to having a partner," he said. "I got used to someone else telling me what to do. Now I'm in charge, and it's weird. I don't trust myself."

Andrew nodded in the dark. "Yeah, I get that," he said finally, his voice husky.

"You're an incredible talent," Noah told him honestly. "And it kills me that I'm the one who nearly ruined that for you. I don't want you to build a storefront here, you know."

Andrew laughed, but Noah pushed on.

"I want the best design Andrew Hudson has got to offer. I want a house people will talk about for decades. I want it to grow right out of the ground the way it was meant to be, shaped by your understanding of the property. I want the kind of place you would have built before I destroyed your career. You hear me?"

His brother nodded again, more slowly this time. "Yeah. I guess I do," he said.

"Want me to sit vigil with you?" That's what Andrew used to call it when he took the time to connect to the land on which he meant to build.

After a long moment, Andrew shook his head. "I think I need to do this alone. Should have done it when you first bought the lot."

Now they were getting somewhere. "Okay. You know how to reach me." Noah got up. He needed to talk to Emma again.

When he knocked on the door, she let him in and led him to the kitchen. If she was surprised to see him again, she didn't show it. Ashley was there, too.

"I'm going to bed," she told them a few minutes after he arrived, purloining a cookie from a container of them on the counter.

"Don't leave on my account," Noah said, but Ashley just waved and disappeared down the hall.

"She thinks I should give you another chance," Emma told him.

"Really?" Noah straddled a barstool at the high counter. "I thought she wanted to drum me out of town."

"She's taken full responsibility for what she did. Selling the Cliff Garden to you," Emma clarified. "I think we're both on the way to making better choices in the future."

"Glad to hear it. What about you? Have you put any thought into giving me a second chance?" he asked casually.

"It's only been an hour. The jury is still out," she said.

Noah stifled a grin. At least there was a jury. The judge could have booted the case before he had a chance for a trial.

"What if we take a night off—from everything?" he suggested. "Just be friends for twenty-four hours. Let's go do something. Catch a movie or some live music."

"April Sunset is at the Pelican's Nest tonight," she said. "I was going to go to bed, but I guess we could check it out. Dance a little, maybe."

"Sounds perfect. Let's go."

"MORNING."

"Morning." Emma smiled up at Noah, who sat leaning against the headboard in bed beside her. Light was spilling in through the gaps in the curtains. She must have missed her walk with the Cliff Sisters already.

"It's late," he said, reading her mind. "But not as late as you think."

"Good." She stretched and sat up, too, hiking the sheets around her for modesty. So much for keeping things casual. Dancing with Noah under the stars last night had made that impossible. Every time he touched her, her body hummed with desire. She'd found herself resting her head against his chest, appreciating the way it felt within the circle of his arms. She'd meant to hold back from him. Instead she'd invited him up to her room when they got home.

They took turns in the shower. Emma slipped on a bohemian skirt and soft blouse, and made up her face. She wanted to be ready for whatever the day threw at her. Downstairs she found Ashley up, too, sipping a cup of coffee and tapping away at a laptop.

"I'm looking for office space," she announced as Emma raided the coffeepot. "The firm granted my vacation request. I let them know I was having second thoughts about the partnership, and they reacted better than I anticipated. I guess those fainting spells were sending up red flags. They agreed to give me a month to consider my options and get more tests done. I think they'll be willing to work with me if I decide to stay in Seahaven." She smiled a little. "Which I already have. The thirty days is really just for due diligence."

"I'm glad they're being so reasonable. Want some breakfast? I'm thinking about omelets today."

"I already had some toast. I think I'm going to take a walk."

Noah emerged from the stairway, his hair damp from the shower, and Emma's heart warmed at the sight of him. Ashley raised her brows a fraction but made no comment.

When a knock came at the door, Emma hurried to

get it and was surprised when a rather disheveled Andrew greeted her. "Andrew. Come in."

"Thanks. I could use a clean-up."

"Uh… sure." She ushered him into the bathroom off the hall and kept going. "It's Andrew," she told Noah and Ashley.

Noah didn't seem surprised. Ashley sat down again. "Maybe I will have some eggs."

Emma got to work on breakfast and had it well underway by the time Andrew reappeared.

"Thank you," he said—not to Emma but to Noah.

"You had a good night?"

"Best one in years."

Emma glanced at her sister, who seemed equally baffled by the men's conversation.

"I stayed in the Cliff Garden last night," Andrew explained. "Slept under the stars. I needed to hear it—to feel it—before I could design the right house for Noah. That's why I was having such a hard time before. I hadn't put in the time on the property."

"I see." Ashley's voice gave away nothing. Emma wasn't sure how she felt about what he was saying. On the one hand, maybe he'd design something better than the plans he'd come up with so far. On the other hand, she wished he wasn't designing anything at all.

"It's important," Andrew told Ashley. "The land needs to want what you build on it, or the site will never be harmonious, and that disharmony affects everything and everyone around it."

Emma thought she knew what he meant, but she was surprised to hear the sentiment from Andrew. It was something her grandmother might have said.

A whisper of wind floated through the open windows. In the distance, the chimes in the Cliff Garden sounded. Ashley exchanged a look with her. Had she heard them, too?

Was Angela near?

"Did you get a feel for the site?" Noah prompted him.

"Yeah." Andrew smiled in a lopsided way, and Emma thought she could see what he must have looked like as a boy. "It doesn't want anything built on it."

It took a moment for his words to sink in. "Doesn't want *anything* built on it?" Emma repeated.

"What do you mean?" Ashley asked him.

"I've never gotten such a strong read on any piece of land. It was adamant. No houses. No nothing. And I tried to change its mind—believe me."

Noah was staring at his brother like he'd gone mad. "You… had a conversation with the land?"

Emma almost pitied him. You couldn't spend a summer helping Angela in her garden without hearing similar sentiments.

"I can't describe what I do. It isn't talking. It's… knowing," Andrew said. "At first I didn't want to believe what I was hearing, but no matter what kind of house I envisioned building there, all I got was a big, fat no."

"So what did you do?" Ashley asked.

"I gave up. Just sat there. I need this project, you know. I wasn't happy with how things were going out there, but then… I don't know. Everything got quiet, and the wind changed direction. There were these chimes."

Emma had to swallow down a sudden thickness in her throat. Angela.

She *was* here.

"You'll think I'm nuts, but I felt… like I wasn't alone."

"You're not nuts," Ashley said softly. Emma held her breath. Noah watched his brother silently.

"I heard words in my head. *Let go. Just let it all go.* So that's what I did. I let go of everything. My fears. My worries. My ambitions. I just sat there all night long—empty. When the sun rose, I felt better than I've felt in years. Who cares what happens next? I'm still young. Healthy. I'm damned good at what I do. I'm not going to starve if I don't design a house on the Cliff Garden lot. Why the hell was I making such a big deal of it all?" He ran a hand through his hair. Smiled a little. "Then I got a text. It was from a friend of mine I met in grade school—a guy I reconnected with a couple of years ago on social media. We've been meaning to get together for coffee since I've been coming to Seahaven. Anyway, he knows I'm an architect, so when a friend of his bought a property down the street from here recently, he passed my information to them."

"You're kidding," Noah said. "I tried to buy that property. It sold before I could even talk to the realtor. That's why I bought the Cliff Garden the minute I heard about it."

Andrew laughed. "Really?" He rubbed the back of his neck. "Well, we talked a few minutes ago, and they're really excited to work with me. They want me to start right away. They're tearing down that old wreck of a cabin that's sitting there now and building a house big enough for their whole extended family. They want everything top of the line. They love the sound of an outdoor kitchen and an infinity pool." His smile spread to a grin. "I walked down there just now. I can see the whole thing. I know exactly what that land wants me to build." He moved near to Noah and clapped a hand on his shoulder. "Sorry, man. You're going to have to find another architect. I'm out."

Noah didn't have time to respond before Ashley hurled herself across the room and leaped into Andrew's arms. As Andrew caught her, she wrapped her arms around his neck, her legs around his waist.

"Good architect!" she cried.

"Take it easy," Andrew protested, although he looked pleased at this development. "I'm not a dog. You sound like you're talking to Winston."

Winston woofed.

"No, you're definitely not a dog." Ashley cupped Andrew's chin with her hands and kissed him. "You are a wonderful man who's finally doing the right thing, and I'm so happy! It was killing me to hate you."

"I don't want you to hate me."

Ashley buried her face against his neck. Andrew closed his eyes and held her. Emma bustled around the kitchen, wanting to give them the moment to themselves. Noah joined her there, touching her hand when their paths crossed.

When Andrew set Ashley on her feet, she straightened her clothes.

"I want to hear everything about the house you're going to build," she told him.

"Want to go see the place?"

"Definitely."

Andrew held out a hand, and she took it.

"What about breakfast?" Noah asked.

"I'll pack you two a picnic," Emma said hurriedly. "It's a beautiful day, and that way you can take your time." She got to work and soon was able to hand a full hamper to the couple.

When they were gone, she turned to Noah, who was leaning against the counter, looking down the hall to the door through which Andrew and Ashley had just disappeared. She couldn't read his emotions. Was he relieved at Andrew's change of heart? Sad that he'd bought a property for nothing? Would he sell the Cliff

Garden back to her?

He turned her way. Met her gaze full on.

"Emma, would you marry me?"

WHEN EMMA'S MOUTH dropped open, Noah could have kicked himself. Why didn't he do this right? Pack a picnic of his own—take Emma somewhere breathtakingly beautiful? Get down on one knee?

She stared at him. "W-what?" she faltered.

"Would you marry me?" There was no turning back now. "I don't want to lose you. I want to spend my life with you, here in Seahaven. I'm not ruining your grandmother's garden anymore, so that's a vote in my favor, right? God, Emma, I don't know how to do this. All I know is I want you to be mine. What do you say?"

"I… I don't know what… yes." She blinked. "Yes, I want to marry you."

They stood there a beat, then Noah crossed the space between them and took her hands. "Yes?"

"Y-yes," she stammered. "I mean, it's reckless, but—"

"It's not reckless. It's the smartest thing either of us has ever done." He lifted her up and set her on the counter, bracing his hands to either side of her. "You're the best thing that's ever happened to me. I've hated hurting you."

"No," she said. "Remember? Ashley and I are taking responsibility for ourselves now. We're not blaming anyone else for the problems we created."

"I hope you'll let me be responsible for a few things now and then."

"Maybe. Do you really want to marry me?"

"Damn straight." He wanted to whisk her upstairs right now and show her how he felt. "I didn't think I was going to do this, you know. Fall for a woman. Make it forever."

"Me, either. I'd given up."

"Don't ever give up on me, okay?" He stole a kiss and then another.

"I won't. But—Noah?" She pulled back a little. "I want to stay right here. I don't want a fancy new house."

"I don't want a fancy new house, either. Brightview is the best home I ever had. I thought I was going to be this bachelor who ate out of take-out cartons for the rest of his life. Now all I want is to be right here helping you in this kitchen. And that's not all. You know what else I want to do?"

"What?" She was smiling now, and that made him happy.

"I want to mow your lawn. Hell, I want to wash your car. I want to pick up groceries for you on my way home. I want to make a life with you right here." He thought about the Surf Dads. How long until he was one of them for real?

"What about the Cliff Garden?"

Was she bracing herself? For all her talk about letting go of the past and accepting things as they were, he knew she loved the garden with all her heart.

"It'll be my engagement gift to you." He moved to stand between her legs and wrapped his arms around her waist. "The Cliff Garden is yours. And when we marry, I'll pay off Brightview's mortgage. Your roots run deep here. This is where we belong."

Her lips parted with surprise, and he kissed her again, not able to resist running his hands up under her blouse and brushing the underside of her breasts. Emma leaned into his touch, her eyes bright with tears.

"You don't have to do that," she told him. "You own the garden. Brightview's bills are mine. I've got a plan to pay them off."

He pulled back and looked at her. "All those things are both of ours," he corrected her. "Emma, I don't want to do this half-assed. No separate bank accounts or prenup. If you want me, I'm all in. I mean that. Be as ambitious as you want. I won't stop you. Just work because you love it, not because you have to. Now, tell me again." He moved his hands higher, tugging at the fastenings of her bra. "Do you want me?"

"I want you. God, do I want you."

Relief flooded Noah. He hadn't lost her. He was going to get to spend a lifetime with her.

"Then you've got me." He picked her up and carried her up the stairs.

CHAPTER 15

"WHERE ARE WE going?" Emma asked the following morning. They had parked Noah's Range Rover near Seahaven Beach and were walking along Esplanade at the base of the Leaf, an area full of boutiques and restaurants.

Noah gave her hand a squeeze. "We're almost there." He stopped in front of Ashbury Jewelers. "See anything you like?" He pointed to the display in the window.

"I don't need any jewelry today," Emma said.

"Are you sure? Maybe a ring?" He laughed at her perplexed expression. "Hello. We're engaged, right? It's tradition?"

"I… guess."

"It's definitely tradition," he asserted. Emma was engaged once before. Hadn't Jordan bought her a ring? Knowing Emma, she'd dutifully returned it when they'd split up.

Noah ushered her into the little store, where a man built like a linebacker with a thatch of blond hair sat behind a row of glass cabinets filled with jewelry of all kinds.

"Hello," he greeted them. "Can I help you find something?"

"We're looking for an engagement ring."

"Got lots of those." The man fished out a bunch of keys, opened several cases and brought out trays of rings. "White gold, right?" he asked Emma, pushing a tray her way.

"For heaven's sake," a voice trailed out of the back room, "I can see from here she needs platinum!" A moment later another man pushed through the beaded curtain that separated the front from the back. "Don't mind Lance," he said apologetically. "He's a Philistine when it comes to matching metals to people. I'm Gary."

Gary was as short and slim as Lance was tall. Lance shook his head but pulled the tray of white-gold rings toward himself and pushed a new tray forward.

"I'm Noah. This is my fiancée, Emma."

"See anything you like?" Gary asked.

Emma leaned over them. Noah slid his hand up and down her back. "Take all the time you need." He wanted to cherish this experience with Emma. Build memories that would last them a lifetime. "What about this one?" He pointed to a ring with a line of diamonds set flush into the band. "With all the work you do with your hands, maybe it would be a good choice?"

"That's a princess-cut channel-set ring," Gary said. He popped it out of the tray and handed it to Noah, who lifted Emma's hand and slid it on her finger.

"What do you think?"

"It's lovely." Emma touched it with a trace of awe.

"Oh, that's it—that's the look. Good job," Gary said to Noah. "You got it on the first try."

"The look?" Emma asked.

Noah thought he understood exactly what the man meant. Emma had softened—and brightened, too—as soon as he slipped the ring on her finger.

"You ever think of going into the jewelry business?" Gary asked Noah.

"No, can't say I have." Noah fished out a card and handed it to the other man.

"Sports photography, huh?" Gary shook his head. "Have I seen any of your work?"

Lance elbowed him to the side and pushed another tray in front of Emma. "Come on. You can't just try one ring. Try them all on!" He began to pull out one after another and handed them to her.

EMMA STIFLED A smile and tried on each of the rings as Lance passed them over. Gary kept grilling Noah about his photography.

Lance leaned in toward her. "He collects people. It's an addiction," he said with a jerk of his head at Gary.

"That's okay. Are you the owner?"

"We own the place together. I design the rings, Gary does sales and paperwork."

"They're really beautiful." She hoped she was hiding her surprise. It was hard to imagine Lance's football player fingers creating these delicate pieces.

"Been doing it since I was a teenager. My teachers kept trying to push me into auto shop classes, but I kept returning to metalwork. Finally bought the equipment and started working at home. Taught myself everything I know."

Emma picked up the first ring again.

"Your fiancé is right, you know," Lance said. "That's the one. When a woman lights up like you did, she's found what she's looking for." He smiled gently. "Kind of the way you light up whenever you look at your fiancé."

"Do I?"

"You do. Here, let's get your size." He jotted a note on a pad of paper when he'd measured her ring finger. "It'll take a few days to resize whichever one you choose." He leaned in again. "Can I give you another tip?"

"Sure."

"Let him spoil you a little. You're a modern woman. I bet you're independent. Bet you've been hurt a time or two before, too."

"You can tell all that by just looking at me?"

"Been doing this a long time," he said. "Looks like you've got a keeper there. Someone who really loves you. Remember, you don't have to do everything yourself."

"Are you speaking from experience?"

He laughed. "Yeah, guess I am. Took me a long time to realize I've got someone on my side these days." He sent an affectionate look toward Gary. "So how do you like running Brightview?"

"She's a natural at it," Noah broke in. He must have caught Lance's last sentence. "Her guests love her. She's developing a cookbook and an online cooking class."

"Noah. He doesn't want to know all that," Emma chided him.

"Sure he does. You're amazing," Noah told her.

"See what I mean? You've definitely got a keeper there," Lance said.

"I guess I do." Her heart was full.

"Is this the one?" Noah held up the first ring he'd picked for her.

Emma nodded. "It is."

"I CAN'T REMEMBER the last time I surfed Castle Beach," Greg told Noah late one afternoon a few days later. "I don't come over here as much as I should."

"Thanks for humoring me." Noah checked his equipment as they stood on the sandy crescent, the high bluffs behind them, the castle far overhead. He had no idea if he'd be able to get the shot he wanted, but he was going to do his best.

"We'd better get out there if you want to catch the light."

"Let's do this."

Unlike Greg, Noah didn't have a surfboard, and he wasn't photographing from a boat today, either, the way he sometimes did. Today he'd be in the water. He slipped his feet into a pair of fins, sloshed awkwardly into the surf and began to swim.

All his equipment was waterproof, made for conditions like this. He swam out past the breaking waves and ducked under the water when the swells passed overhead. When he'd cleared them, he swam into position, communicating with Greg between sets.

As the sun edged down the horizon behind him, it lit up the castle walls at the top of the bluff, towering over the surfers in the foreground, Greg included, who had just caught a wave.

Scissoring his legs to keep himself afloat, his wetsuit helping to make him buoyant, Noah caught the action with his camera, but he already knew the conditions weren't quite right.

"Again?" Greg called out when he'd paddled back out past the waves.

"Again!" Noah appreciated Greg's cooperation, but he knew now that his friend had a taste of the waves, he'd stay here as long as he could. Noah didn't blame him. He was itching to get on a board himself.

Greg caught another wave, and Noah got as many shots as he could, but it still wasn't right.

Greg didn't ask this time when he paddled past. He

got himself in position, jostling for space with other surfers, calling out jokes and taunts—Greg knew everyone in the surf scene here in Seahaven.

The sun was slipping behind the horizon now. Noah caught a few photos of a line of pelicans flying past it, knowing it would make a pretty composition. He was getting that edgy, irritated feeling that happened when conditions for the right shot were fading away.

He turned to Greg poised for action and readied his camera but spotted another man edging in on a surfboard to catch the incoming wave, too. Noah swore, knowing Greg would stand down if this other man pressed his claim to the wave.

He was too experienced a photographer not to be ready when the action started, however. Greg leaped to his feet just as the other man did. A cry died in Noah's throat when the collision he thought was imminent didn't occur. Both men caught the wave but veered apart to miss each other. Noah followed them as best he could, the zing in his veins telling him this would be the one.

He'd have a cover shot for sure.

Noah didn't know how many times his camera's shutter clicked, but when it was over, all too soon, he swam for shore, knowing he'd gotten what he needed, excitement fizzing in his veins as he splashed out of the water onto shore. He figured he'd have to wait for Greg, who'd want to surf until it was too dark to see, but a minute later, Greg met him on the beach.

"Do you know who that was?" he asked as Noah pulled off his fins.

"No, who?"

"That was James Kane. The man's a legend. Did you get all that?" He waved at Noah's camera.

"Of course I got it." He nearly laughed at Greg's excitement. "I'll need Kane to sign off on the shot, though."

"I'll introduce you. Don't know him well. No one knows him well."

"A mystery man, huh?"

"He's the heir." Greg led the way to where another surfer was toweling off down the beach.

"The heir?"

"To Seahaven Castle. One of them, anyway. I wouldn't mention it, though. Touchy subject since his side of the family was banished two generations back."

"No men allowed." That's what Emma had said.

"Exactly." Greg kept going. "Kane! Got a minute?"

The man lowered his arms and tossed his towel aside. His wetsuit was unzipped to the waist, his arms out of the sleeves. He slicked back his wet hair with one hand and watched them approach.

"Greg. Good to see you."

"Good to see you, too, man. It's been ages." Greg gestured to Noah. "This is a friend of mine, Noah Hudson. Noah, meet James Kane. Noah is a photographer. He was getting footage of me out there today."

"Sorry I stole your wave." James grinned suddenly, a smile that transformed his sharp, formidable features. Now he was just another surfer.

"Figured you were defending your territory."

"Yeah, get back to the north side, bluffer."

Noah chuckled. He'd heard that term before. Surfers were apt to get territorial, and there was a rivalry between those who lived to the north and south of the Seahaven River, which cut through town.

"Shut up, serf," Greg drawled.

James winced, his smile gone in an instant. Greg made a face.

"Shit, sorry about that."

Noah knew why he was embarrassed. Bluffers were people who lived to the north of the Seahaven River in the neighborhood called the Bluffs—where Brightview was situated. Serfs were people who lived near the castle. Shops near here sold T-shirts and swag items with all kinds of variations on the words *serfs* and *surfing*.

But if Kane was the heir…

"No worries." James waved it off, but it was clear his good mood was gone.

"Could I get your permission to use a shot of you from your last ride if one of these photos turns out?" Noah asked. Technically he didn't need permission, but it was good form to get it.

James hesitated. "Don't like a lot of publicity," he

said.

"Oh, come on, Kane," Greg said. "It'll be an amazing shot. No one outside Seahaven knows who you are, anyway."

"Guess that's okay, then."

"What brings you back?" Greg went on. "I haven't seen you in years."

"Had some time. Wanted to surf."

That didn't seem to be much of an explanation to Noah, but it seemed to satisfy Greg, who held out a hand. "Well, I'm glad you're here." Kane hesitated a moment, then shook it.

"Yeah, good to be back in the old neighborhood."

"You going to stay?"

James shook his head. "Nah. Nothing to keep me around."

"I've got a form set up on my phone," Noah broke in, worried Greg would ask too many personal questions before he got a record of James's permission to use the photos. "Do you mind?"

"Sure."

"Greg, can you grab it for me? It's with our stuff." Noah had left his phone with their things on the beach.

Greg shot him a puzzled look but said, "Yeah. Sure," and loped off.

"I appreciate this," Noah told James honestly. "I got some good footage out there just now. It'll probably land me a cover."

"I've seen your work," James said. "If it turns out the way you want, send me a copy."

"Will do." He wasn't sure why the request made him feel proud. James was the perfect heir to a mysterious American castle, he decided. Aloof yet approachable. Troubled but sincere. He wondered if it would be possible to arrange a feature story with him. He wasn't a reporter, but he'd done in-depth interviews with other surfers before and had a friend who'd help him spiff up his writing before submitting it to a magazine.

Before he could even ask, though, James shook his head. "No," he said. "You can have the shot, but that's all."

"How did you know what I was going to ask?"

"You had that reporter look," James told him. He glanced up at the bluffs looming over them, and Noah knew he was thinking about the castle on top of them. "Best to let sleeping dogs lie."

"It's a shame for the castle to be closed. Local businesses could use the revenue from the tourists who'd come to see it."

James shrugged. "I can't do anything about that."

Greg returned with Noah's phone.

"Thanks," Noah said. He pulled up the app he used, and James signed some paperwork digitally, giving Noah the right to publish his photograph, then entered his address. "I'll send you a copy as soon as I can," Noah told him.

"I appreciate it." James turned away, signaling an end to their conversation, and Noah led Greg down the beach before his friend could push his luck.

"Can't believe he's really here." Greg turned back to look at James one last time as they gathered their things and prepared to leave. "Haven't seen Kane in Seahaven in years."

"Must be rough being close to the castle without being able to go into it—especially if you think you have some title to it," Noah said.

"He hasn't had it easy," Greg agreed. "So what about the photos? Think you got anything good?"

"I know I did."

"THAT'S NOT A weed, that's a flower!" Ashley said in exasperation.

Noah sat back on his heels. "Which ones are the weeds, then?"

Emma, working in another flower bed close by, suppressed a smile. She and Noah had come home from coffee at Cups & Waves a half hour ago to find Kate and Aurora hard at work installing six new shrubs in the borders around Brightview's lawn, and Ashley bullying Andrew into helping her in the Cliff Garden. As soon as Ashley had spotted them, she'd waved them over to help, too. Emma had followed along willingly. It was a fresh, sunny, breezy day, perfect for blowing the cobwebs out of your brain, as Angela used to say.

"That's a weed. And that. And that." Ashley pointed them out, and Noah attacked them.

"How long is this going to take?" Andrew surveyed the huge garden.

"We won't do it all today. Another hour and we can take a break."

Andrew groaned. Noah laughed.

"Here's a cheerful group."

Emma looked up to see Colette had wheeled her bike into the garden and propped it against the picket fence.

"Come and join us if you like," Ashley said.

"I'll do that."

"She was joking," Emma rushed to say. "Ashley, you can't order everyone around."

"She didn't order me," Colette assured her, "and I can't think of anything better than to get my hands in the dirt."

Emma went to get her a kneeler and another pair of gloves. She thought Colette would come and work by her, but instead she joined Ashley, who cast her several puzzled glances before getting back to her task.

In time, Emma forgot about the others, engrossed in cleaning up the flower bed she was working on. When she stretched her back later and looked around, she noticed Ashley and Colette sitting next to each other on the Trouble Bench.

Noah came to join her. "Looks like Colette really

stopped by to talk to Ashley."

"Looks that way."

"Any idea what they have to talk about?"

"Mom, probably. Dad, too. Maybe Nana Angela. Ashley was angry at her for a long time, but that's because she didn't know the truth about what happened. I told her what I know, but Colette can fill her in on the details."

"It's good to get closure about the past."

They worked together a moment before Emma gathered the courage to say, "I've been thinking about your childhood. You must have been devastated when your parents died. I know you had Andrew, but a teenage boy isn't a substitute for a mom and dad."

"He did his best," Noah said. "But you're right, it wasn't enough. Nothing has ever been enough." He frowned as if surprised by his own words. "I screwed around a lot when I was younger. Pretended to be tough. That nothing could touch me. I think the only thing that saved me from getting into even more trouble was how active I was. In high school I joined this photography club with members of all ages, and we went everywhere. Hiked, camped, explored. It kept me busy, and there were enough grown-ups in the group that things didn't get out of hand on those trips. I guess… I guess some of those people became stand-ins for my parents in a way. I really messed up things for Andrew in the end, but it could have been so much worse."

Emma nodded. She didn't want to break the flow of his words, but she was thinking of Conner, the young man who'd come to the Trouble Bench for help with his addiction. The line between safety and danger was so thin in this world.

Reese had let her know Connor was still in detox, getting ready to transition to a longer-term facility. "He's doing well," Reese said. "It was lucky he ran into you that night."

Beside her, Noah was lost in thought. "It was a good thing that when I did get in trouble, Mark was there with a way out—and a job that kept me even busier than ever. I knew I needed to work hard to pay him back, and by the time I did, I was in up to my eyeballs in the company's business. I just kept going."

"Did you like the work at all?"

"It was interesting, and I got to meet a lot of people, talk to them, negotiate. From day one I had a vital role in the company. That was good for me, too."

"And now you get to pursue your passions full time."

He smiled a wicked smile. "Damn straight."

Emma met him halfway when he moved in for a kiss, but there was something else she had to tell him.

"Noah, I should have brought this up sooner, before I agreed to marry you." She took a deep breath and plunged on. "I… have debts," she said. "I would like to settle them before the wedding."

Noah eyed her warily. "There's a mortgage on Brightview. You told me about that. I already said I'd pay that off."

"I have some bills for start-up costs for the B and B. I bought some new towels and sheets and filled the pantry. That kind of thing."

"Okay." He waited. "Why do I get the feeling there's more?"

"Because there is. There's something I haven't told you." Something that seemed so trivial now compared to the problems they were just discussing.

"About Food to You Fast? Were there expenses you couldn't cover when you shut down?"

"No, I was able to pay those." She was proud of that fact.

"Then what is it? You do remember I'm rich, right?" He bumped his shoulder against hers. "You're not going to shock me."

She hoped that was true. She'd been shocked years ago when she'd discovered how much she owed. Even now, it was hard to talk about what had happened.

"When my grandmother died a decade ago, my father was convinced we were saved," she began, then stopped. "You know what? I need to go back further or you won't understand." She took a moment to compose herself. "Before my mother died, my parents both worked. Together they got by, but when she passed and my father was grieving… well, I think he lost the will to go on. He lost his repair shop, which was probably struggling already, and we eventually lost our house. We moved into a crappy little rental on the wrong side of town, and we all suffered."

"Sounds like a rough time," Noah said.

"When Ashley and I were eleven and nine, my grandmother gave my father a large sum of money, hoping to provide us with the kind of childhood she thought we deserved—and buy her way back into my dad's good graces so she could see us. They'd become estranged." She didn't go into the details. Time enough later to fill everything in.

"Okay. What happened?"

"Dad bought us a beautiful house, then blew the rest of the money on day trading. We skimped along for a few years until he went too long without making a mortgage payment, and we lost our house again."

"Hell."

"Exactly," she said. "By that time, Ash and I were old enough that social standing mattered to us—a lot. Especially to Ashley. We got really good at hiding our true situation and keeping people at a distance. We moved into another crappy little rental house in another crappy neighborhood, but now Ashley and I were old enough to do something about it. We went to school, but we worked, too—all the time. We bought ourselves clothes, paid for haircuts, that kind of thing. We paid the bills when Dad eventually stopped bothering to. We saved enough for cooking school for me and a couple of years of community college for Ashley. It was hard—really hard—but we pulled through. Thought we'd finally made it out of all that hell. And then I tried to get a loan and found out what my father had done."

She found it difficult to go on. Even after all this time, even with her father dead and gone—no one around to care about her family or judge them—she wanted to be proud of him.

And she couldn't be.

"Emma?" Noah watched her, his concern clear.

"It turned out my dad had opened credit cards in our names. He started with one in Ashley's name and one in mine, then got more and more. He juggled them around, paying off one with cash advances from others, from what we could figure out later. He was still day trading, and once in a while I guess he made some money, paid the debts down and got the limits raised. By the time I discovered what he'd done, the debts he'd racked up were enormous. We each owed well in excess of a hundred thousand dollars."

"How on earth did it go that far?"

"Apparently my dad was a genius when it came to moving money around—just not when it came to making it," she said bitterly.

"Did you report him?" His whole expression changed when she didn't answer. "Hell, Emma, tell me you reported him!"

"He was our father."

"You told the credit card companies what happened, though, right? What he did was fraud. You didn't cover for him, did you?"

"Of course we covered for him. We'd covered for him since we were children!" Emma fought down a rising tide of pain. "We didn't even talk about it—there was never any question that we wouldn't take on his debts as our own."

"Why would you pay for something you didn't do?"

She remembered Ashley sitting on the Trouble Bench, her wail of anguish. How could she describe what it felt like to learn a thing like that? To stare into your father's eyes and see no remorse—only frustration that he'd been caught?

"Because if we admitted to ourselves what he did, we'd have to face the truth." She could tell Noah still didn't get what she meant. "Come on. What kind of father racks up hundreds of thousands of dollars on credit cards he's fraudulently taken out in his daughters' names?" She was losing patience. Why was he forcing her to spell it out? She didn't want to think about it. Had tried for years not to think about it.

"I don't know. You tell me."

They stared at each other. Was he really going to make her say it out loud?

"The kind of father…" She swallowed and tried again. "The kind of father who doesn't… who doesn't love…" The horror of it all threatened to overwhelm her, and she stumbled on the words. It hurt so badly to say them. "Noah, he didn't… he didn't love us. He couldn't love us. Whatever human kindness he'd ever had was gone. He might as well have been dead." She'd never said that out loud. The truth of it shocked her. It laid bare the reality of her childhood in a way she'd never faced before.

She always told everyone her mother died, but she never said her father abandoned her. He'd always been right there—and so far away at the same time. Pretending to be present but as out of reach as if he was buried in the ground.

She had no idea how his demons got a hold of him like that, and now she saw there was nothing she could have done about it. Someone else needed to see what was happening, step in and take control. Nana Angela had tried, but she'd failed.

Noah pulled her into his arms. "I'm sorry. I'm so sorry, Emma. I love you. I will always love you. I don't care how many debts you owe. I don't care what your father did or didn't do. I'm never going to leave you. I'm going to be here for you for the rest of your life. I won't even die."

Emma laughed, although she was still close to tears. "You can't promise that."

"I'll try not to," he amended. "I mean it, Emma. I love you. Just the way you are. Your past. Your present. I already love the woman you're going to be, as well."

"Even if I fail at running the bed-and-breakfast and everyone hates my cookbook? Even if I never pay off the money I owe?"

"Even if we lose everything except each other." He held her tight, as if he never wanted to let go. "I'm going to be that one person who sticks by you through thick and thin."

Emma began to cry. Noah tightened his arms around her and let her tears dampen his shoulder until her sobs faded into hiccups and she let out a long, shuddering breath. She'd held all that in so long, she hadn't realized what a heavy burden she was carrying around. Now she felt empty but in a good way. Like there was room inside her for something new. Pain giving way to love.

"You promise you'll stay?" She settled against him, his heartbeat a reassuring sound. Noah seemed like a man who had a lot of love to give, and she was ready to accept it.

"I promise."

"I want to clear my own accounts, though," she added softly, pressing a hand to his chest, marveling that this man had decided to link his life to hers. "Can you understand that? My family went so off the rails. It's important that Ashley and I get back on them ourselves."

She could see he didn't want to understand—but he did. "I can't enjoy pursuing my dreams if you're struggling to pay your bills," he finally said. "And I'm selfish—I want to marry you now." He sat back on his heels, thinking. "How's this?" he asked. "I'm a photographer, and I'm going to need some gallery space soon. You let me use the walls of Brightview's rooms for the next ten years, and I'll pay the fee for all of it up-front." He named a number, and Emma rolled her eyes.

"That's ridiculous," she protested. He was trying to make things too easy for her. "If we get married, it'll be your house, too."

"You think the fee should be higher? You drive a hard bargain, Emma Miller."

"It's too high already," she tried to say, but he was kissing her again, and Lance's voice was in her ears. *You don't have to do everything yourself.* Maybe this was a compromise she could live with.

"Too bad. That's the rate," Noah said. "I'll have paperwork for you to sign tonight."

"Shouldn't I be the one coming up with the paperwork?"

"If you like." He tucked a lock of her hair behind her ear. "Will that be enough?" he asked more seriously.

"More than enough, and it's—"

"It's done," he said. "You help me, and I help you. Your guests will snap up my photos. I'll be rich."

"You're already rich."

"You got that right." He pulled her close, and somehow Emma knew he wasn't talking about money anymore. She looked over his shoulder to see Andrew had joined Ashley and Colette by the Trouble Bench, and now the women were hugging. She tightened her arms around Noah's neck.

"I think everything is going to be okay," she whispered against his neck.

"I think so, too."

"I'VE GOT SOMETHING to show you all. Be right back," Noah said when they gathered on Brightview's deck a while later. Kate and Aurora joined them, and Colette agreed to stay for lunch, too. Emma ducked into the bathroom to wash her face, then brought out sandwiches, chips and fruit slices, and soon everyone was eating happily.

He grabbed an envelope from his room and hurried to rejoin the others.

"What is it?" Kate asked.

He drew a photograph from the envelope and passed it to Emma, who wiped her hands before she took it. "Oh, Noah—that's lovely."

"That's going to be the next cover of *SurfWorld*."

Emma passed it to Ashley, who studied it and looked up at him. "You took this shot?"

"That's right."

Ashley passed it to Andrew, who said, "That's Greg, right?" He pointed to one of the surfers skimming the waves in the foreground, the bluffs and castle looming far above him.

"Yep."

"Who's the other man? Do you know?" Kate asked, leaning in to see.

"That's James Kane."

"James Kane?" Colette reached over and plucked the photograph from Andrew's hands. "*The* James Kane?"

"The heir to the castle," Noah confirmed. "Hell of a shot, isn't it?"

Colette straightened, eyes wide. "I'll say."

"Who's James Kane?" Emma asked.

"The rightful heir to Seahaven Castle," Noah told her. "But he's been banished, just like the men before him. Quite a story, huh?"

"You didn't tell it to *SurfWorld*, did you?" Colette asked.

"I wanted to."

"James would hate it."

"You know him?" Aurora asked, bending close to Colette to study the photo. "I've seen him only once, when he was taking part in a surf competition. That was years ago. He's never here."

"I knew his mother," Colette said.

"I thought about writing an article to go with the shot," Noah admitted, "but James wasn't interested. I did some sleuthing and finally found a phone number to call to ask questions about the castle, though. It doesn't even have a website," he complained. "I talked to a woman named Euphemia Harper." He gave a chuckle. "Thought she'd be about a hundred years old but turns out she's young. From the sound of it, Fee runs things."

"Fee?" Ashley asked.

"That's what she said to call her."

"Fee Harper is an amazing young woman," Colette said. "I'll introduce you one of these days."

"Anyway," Noah went on, "she confirmed what you said, Emma. The castle has been closed for years. There's no plan to open it to the public any time soon. Sometimes she'll give a private tour, but she's bound by the rules. No photography inside the walls, and no men allowed."

"No men? They can't do that!" Andrew said.

"They can if it's not open to the public," Colette told him.

"I think it's a shame," Emma said.

"I'm not giving up," Noah told them. "Someday I'll see the inside."

"I hope we all get to see it someday," Ashley said.

"WHAT'S THIS?" EMMA asked when Ashley handed her an envelope a few days later.

"Open it and see." Ashley perched on one of the stools by the counter, crossing one leg over the other.

Emma did so and drew out a bank statement. "What is this for?"

"Escrow cleared. Noah owns the Cliff Garden now,

and I informed my firm I'm not buying into the partnership. I took some of my proceeds and paid off the debts Dad racked up—all of them, your share as well as mine."

"Ashley! That's your money. You can't spend it on me."

"Of course I can. You got me through community college and did so much more than that," Ashley said. "I've never thanked you or paid you back."

"I didn't expect you to."

"Because you're the best sister a woman could have." Ashley hugged her. "Think of it as a wedding present."

"You really shouldn't have," Emma said. She read the statements again. All those zeroes.

No debts.

"I wanted to. We're free, Emma. Really free."

Emma met her gaze. "Noah is giving me the Cliff Garden as an engagement present. He's going to pay off Brightview's mortgage, too. Of course, once we're married, we'll own both jointly. You'll always be welcome to stay with us, you know. I still feel like the Cliff Garden should be yours."

"I'll come take care of the garden," Ashley promised, "but I need my own home. I'll figure it out."

"What will you live on?"

"I've still got plenty left over from the sale of the Cliff Garden, plus equity in my condo. I'm in great shape."

"What about the other partners in your firm? They were okay that you decided not to buy in?"

"I think they were relieved, honestly. They're all convinced I have some terminal illness because of my fainting spells, and they thought they were going to be on the hook for my medical insurance. There's another woman, Maisey Woodman, who is thrilled to have the chance to take my place."

"I'm so glad it all worked out." Emma had an idea. "Hang on a second." She ran upstairs, looked through her closet and returned with a doll under her arm. "I don't know if you want it, but I thought you should know I have it."

"Mom's doll?" Ashley took it from her.

"Her Ashley doll. I still have the Emma one. I've been hiding them for years. I was afraid if you ever saw them, you'd make me throw them out."

"I thought they were long gone." Ashley held the doll reverently. "I miss Mom. I always have. I miss Dad, too, despite everything. The way he was when we were little."

"I know." Emma wrapped her arms around her sister, and they stayed like that a long time, pulling apart only when the door at the street end of the house opened and Noah came in.

He looked from one to the other. "Am I interrupting something?"

Emma explained about Ashley paying their father's

debts.

"And Emma gave me something I thought I'd lost a long time ago." Ashley held up the doll.

"Does this mean you're going to rent your gallery space to someone else?" Noah asked Emma when Ashley went to her room a few minutes later, after giving Emma another hug.

"Never. You're the only photographer for me." She went up on tiptoe and kissed him.

"Good." He took her hand and slid something on her finger. Her engagement ring, Emma realized. He lifted her onto the counter and kissed her. "How does it fit?"

"It's perfect."

"Health department," Andrew hollered, coming in from the deck and startling both of them. "Unsanitary conditions in the kitchen!"

"There's going to be some unsanitary conditions in your head in a minute," Noah warned him, but he didn't make a move to go after his brother. Emma was grateful. She loved having her arms wrapped around him. Loved it when he was this close.

"I can't wait to marry you," she said, marveling at the beautiful ring on her finger.

"Can't wait to marry you, either."

CHAPTER 16

"YOUR GRANDMOTHER WOULD be so happy for you today," Colette said as she adjusted Emma's veil. It was a stunningly beautiful July morning. Ashley, Ava, Penelope, Kate and Aurora were all gathered at Brightview to help Emma prepare for her wedding day. Colette had arrived just minutes ago and presented her a pair of vintage earrings Angela had given her years before. "You need something borrowed," she reminded Emma.

Now they stood in front of a large mirror in one of the guest rooms, which Emma had set aside to use for the occasion.

"I wish she could be here. Mom and Dad, too." Emma meant it. She'd forgiven her father for his sins. He'd been such an unhappy soul, and she wished she could have done something to ease his suffering.

"I'm sure they're with you in spirit," Colette said. "By the way, I wondered if you've ever seen these." She took an envelope out of her purse and withdrew two photos from it, handing one to Emma. "This was from Angela's wedding."

"No, I've never seen photos of her wedding." Emma took the photograph reverently. Ashley crowded close to see. Their grandmother stood next to a tall, handsome man Emma knew was her grandfather, Theodore. She'd never met him, since he passed away before she was born. Flanking them were several other people, including two older couples. Her great-grandparents, she realized.

"That was Adelaide, Angela's mother," Colette said, touching a finger to the woman on the right, whose dark hair was swept up high on her head. "She tended the garden before Angela. And that's Andrea, Angela's grandmother."

Beside Emma, Ashley let out another small sound. "A whole line of women," she whispered. "Andrea, Adelaide, Angela. And Audra," she added, naming their mother.

"Don't forget Ashley," Emma said. "See, you were destined to tend the garden."

"What about Brightview?" Ashley asked. "Is there a line of women who tended it?"

Emma's heart squeezed. Ashley wanted a legacy for her, too, but she didn't need one. She knew she belonged at Brightview.

"Sometimes one woman tended both; sometimes there were sisters." Colette pointed to another woman next to Andrea, and Emma could see the resemblance. "That's Teresa, Andrea's sister. They shared Brightview and both raised their families here."

"Do we have cousins?" Emma asked her, memorizing Teresa's features, noticing the broad smiles on her and her sister's faces. They were both happy.

"I'm sure you do. I'll help you track them down if you like."

Emma nodded, her vision of family suddenly expanding. Even if she didn't have cousins, she had all her new friends, and the Surf Dads and moms.

"Here's a photo I'm sure you've seen before." Colette pulled out the next one.

"Mom and Dad," Ashley said. Their father had kept a version of this photo in a frame in his bedroom, but Emma rarely saw it until he passed away and she'd packed up his things.

Now she looked at the photo with new eyes. Her mother and father gazed at each other with palpable love, and she knew that was how they felt about each other in real life, too. Her family had been happy before her mother died. It was only when she was gone that their world fell apart.

"This is how I want to remember them," she said to Ashley.

Her sister nodded. "Me, too."

"They loved you. Your grandmother did, too." Colette hugged Ashley, then turned to Emma. "We'd better put these away for later and get ready for your big moment."

"Don't forget your bouquet," Kate said shyly, handing her a beautiful arrangement of flowers. Kate and Aurora had worked closely with Ashley to provide all the flowers for the occasion.

"I won't," Emma assured her. "I'm so glad you could stay for the wedding."

Kate smiled. "I'm so glad I'm staying for good." She and Aurora were going to open a landscaping business. Kate had found an apartment near the Leaf and was already making arrangements to get the rest of her things sent out.

"I hope I can be your first customer," Emma told them. "Ashley's too busy with the Cliff Garden to pay much attention to Brightview's borders."

"We'd love to have you on our client roll," Kate said.

Aurora slipped out of the room and came back a few moments later. "It's time," she said. "Noah is waiting for you."

Emma's heart filled as the younger woman slipped out to find her seat. Noah was waiting—for her. She'd spend the rest of her life with him. No matter how short or long a time she got with him, she promised herself she'd make the most of it.

Ashley took her place by the door. Ava, Penelope and Kate followed behind her.

"I'll see you on the other side," Colette said and kissed her cheek. She slipped past the other women, as well.

Emma gave her a minute's head start. When she was

sure Colette would have made it to her seat, she nodded at Ashley, who started the procession.

Slow and steady, she reminded herself. She knew she could have asked Colette to stand in for her father, or maybe Andrew—or even Ashley—but Emma had decided to walk down the aisle on her own. She'd chosen to come to California. She'd chosen to make a go of the bed-and-breakfast. She'd made the decision to spend her life with Noah. She was her own woman, and she'd make her way to the altar alone.

Then she'd never be alone again.

When they descended the stairs, crossed the living room and paraded out to Brightview's deck, where her friends and family were seated on folding chairs, Emma's heart grew full. This was what she'd always wanted. A home. People to care about and care for her.

A man to share it with.

Noah smiled as she approached and took her hand when she drew near. Winston sat at his feet, tail wagging.

"Ready?" Noah asked.

"Absolutely."

NOAH HAD NEVER spent much time thinking about weddings or vows or any of the trappings of such a ceremony, but standing on Brightview's deck, under a flower-garland-wrapped arbor, telling the woman he loved that he'd respect and honor her, he had to admit there was something to all this pomp and circumstance.

When he slid a wedding band on Emma's finger, he felt like it contained his love tied up in a promise and understood why people wore their wedding rings as a daily reminder.

"You may now kiss the bride."

Noah didn't need to be told twice. He swept Emma into an embrace and didn't want to let her go, knowing that from here on, he'd spend his days—and nights—by her side.

Mark clapped him on the back when they finally turned to face their friends and walked up the aisle to a chorus of congratulations, Winston trotting happily along behind them.

Inside, alone for a minute, they embraced again.

"Happy?" he asked Emma.

"So happy," she assured him, going up on tiptoe to meet his kiss. She looked so lovely in her slim, pale gown that flowed over her curves like a ripple of water.

Out on the deck, people were moving chairs and tables into place for a meal. Later, they'd clear the space again for dancing. It was a small, sweet affair.

"It's all perfect." She sighed.

"You're perfect," he told her, letting go reluctantly as people swarmed in around them to take the buffet lunch outside.

"Don't you dare try to help," Ashley warned her when Emma moved toward the kitchen. "You two go upstairs for five minutes. Let us worry about the food."

“Sounds good to me,” Noah said, taking his wife’s hand. Winston went to a favorite spot near the sectional, out of the way, and lay down with a doggy sigh of contentment.

“We expect you’ll qualify for full membership in the Surf Dads any day now,” Greg called in passing as he lugged a cooler full of beer to the deck.

“We’ll work on that.” Noah ushered Emma to the stairs, tugging her up the first flight, then swinging her into his arms for the second. He carried her into her third-story bedroom and tossed her on the bed, launching himself on it after her, just like he had the first time they were together.

Emma shrieked and laughed. “Don’t ruin my dress.”

“I’m going to destroy that dress—later tonight,” he warned her. “But for now I’ll be good. Sort of.”

He bent to the task of worshipping every inch of his new wife’s body as best he could without tearing the delicate garment she wore, until Emma was moaning with pleasure beneath him.

“We’d better stop,” he panted some minutes later, “if we’re going to make it to lunch.”

“Don’t you dare stop,” she said, pulling him back down. “Just be quick.”

“I can be quick,” he promised her and proceeded to show her, soon forgetting everything but Emma as they joined together.

Later, when they'd put themselves to rights again, Noah led the way downstairs and was happy to see their guests enjoying themselves far too much to notice their long absence. They lingered at the bottom of the stairs, their hands entwined.

There were Ashley and Andrew, sitting side by side on the swing, their intimacy unmistakable. Over the past weeks, they'd grown closer and closer and finally decided to rent a small building together with an apartment on top and office space on the ground floor. Andrew was moving his architecture business to Seahaven, and Ashley was opening her own forensic accounting firm.

There was Colette, seated with her daughter and granddaughter at a table packed with other locals. Noah and Emma had visited them for dinner one night recently and seen how the three generations of women lived harmoniously together on their organic farm several blocks from the castle.

There was Kate and Aurora talking animatedly in a group of other young twentysomethings.

Mark's wife was sitting on his lap, an arm around his shoulders as they snacked on appetizers.

The surf moms and dads were everywhere, laughing, joking and chatting. Winston was fast asleep curled up where they'd left him.

Beyond them all was the restless ocean and the bright blue sky.

"This is everything I've ever wanted," he said to Emma.

She leaned against him contentedly. "It's everything I've ever wanted, too."

The End

Read on for an excerpt of Beach House Vacation.

Beach House Vacation

by

Cora Seton

CHAPTER 1

"I'M NEVER LEAVING Seahaven," Ava Ingerson said, fighting down a rising panic. "Why would you ask that? Do you think I should?" She stood with two of her closest friends where the ocean met the sand, foamy waves sweeping around her feet. She held her sandals in one hand and impatiently brushed away a strand of hair from her face with the other. It was barely dawn on a day in late July, and a light breeze was blowing, making her glad that she'd grabbed a light jacket on her way out the door.

"Not forever," Penelope Rider assured her. "I meant like on a vacation." She stood in the surf, too, her thick, dark hair piled high on her head, her shorts leaving her long legs bare. Wading in the waves was a tradition they'd recently added to their morning walks as summer unfolded in Seahaven. "I know I could use to get away for a bit. Maybe head down south. All I've done this past year is work on my house. I'm getting restless."

Ava relaxed a little. The subject was a touchy one for her. She'd been in Seahaven less than a year and settling here had cost her the man she'd thought she'd spend her life with. It was no wonder Penelope's innocent question about future travel plans had hit her wrong.

"I'm not restless at all," she asserted. "I'm staying right here. Forever, I hope."

"You have to travel sometime, though, right? I mean, you did it for years before you came here," Emma Hudson said. Her blond hair was in a ponytail and she wore a light blue sundress, its long skirts bunched in her hands to keep them out of the water. "Don't you miss it?"

"Not at all." That was mostly true. She didn't miss moving around from place to place, but she missed having a partner—a lot. Todd's betrayal was still a fresh wound after all these months. She'd gotten over the man himself, but without the sense of purpose she'd thought they'd shared, something was lacking in her life. Of course, Todd hadn't really shared that sense of purpose after all, had he? He had traveled for the sheer adventure of it. Nature was his playground, but that was the extent of his interest in the world around him. She felt a kinship with the plants and animals, the sea and sky. She was fascinated by the tiniest details. Todd was a big picture kind of guy, and the focus of the picture was always himself.

It had hurt a lot when he left, but it helped that she loved this small, seaside town where she'd come to settle when she'd inherited the Blue House from her aunt

Laura. She eyed the other women curiously. She'd met them after she moved in. Penelope had grown up in San Jose but had spent summers with her uncle at Fisherman's Point, the beach house that sat to the right of hers. He'd offered bare-bones accommodations to the people who went on his fishing charter trips but Penelope was aiming for a different type of customer. She wanted to provide a venue for small, boutique destination weddings. Emma had inherited Brightview, the house to the left of Ava's, from her grandmother, and ran a bed and breakfast out of it, showering her guests with comfort and yummy baked goods. Ava had always assumed her new friends were here to stay. Did either of them yearn for more exotic adventures?

"I was just curious," Penelope said. "Don't worry, I'm not going anywhere. Too much work to do."

Ava thought she looked discouraged. Pen always said she was grateful for inheriting her beach house from her uncle, but beneath her enthusiasm for fixing it up was a trace of discontent Ava didn't know the reason for. Maybe she was simply missing Dan and her time with him on his fishing boat.

"I need to belong someplace," Ava told her emphatically. "Todd made sure we never stayed more than a week or two anywhere, and usually less than that. I never meant to travel for that long, and now that I've got a home I plan to stay."

"I didn't realize traveling wasn't your idea." Penelope

shifted her weight as the waves pulled back and spun in again. The water was only ankle deep here, but it still exerted a tremendous pull, sucking the sand away from under their feet and washing it back over them with every return.

"I was teaching when Todd and I met," Ava reminded her. "We were only supposed to be gone one year. He promised after that, we'd pick a place to settle, get married and start having kids."

"What made you keep going then?" Penelope asked.

"Pen," Emma chided her. "Maybe Ava doesn't want to talk about it." Newly married to the handsome millionaire who'd been one of her first guests at her bed and breakfast, Emma positively glowed these days and Ava couldn't help being a little envious.

"I don't mind the question," Ava assured them. "Todd kept putting it off. He kept coming up with new countries we hadn't visited yet. New sights we hadn't seen. I went along with it. I thought that was what couples did—supported each other." She made a face. "I was wrong."

"That's what couples should do," Emma said. "Noah and I support each other."

"You're lucky." Ava squared her shoulders. She was tired of feeling like a victim. Shouldn't she be comfortable with the single life by now? "Anyway, here I am living my dream." If her words rung hollow, neither of her friends pointed it out.

"I wish I was living my dream," Penelope grumbled.

Ava exchanged a surprised glance with Emma. "I thought you were. Pretty soon you'll have your house fixed up and there'll be a wedding there every week. Besides, Seahaven is your home. You have a huge, extended family close by."

"But now my uncle is gone and my mom is in Costa Rica with her new husband." Penelope ticked off her sorrows on her fingers.

"You own a beach house that you're getting to fix up exactly the way you want. You live in the best place on earth." Ava didn't have an extended family at all now that Aunt Laura was gone. Her parents and brother lived outside Philadelphia and that was the extent of the family she'd known. Her mother's parents had died young and Aunt Laura was her only sibling. The rest of her father's family lived in Belgium. He'd come to Philadelphia to go to school and had refused to go home again. He kept in touch with his family, but she'd only met them once or twice.

"I guess I saw my life going differently." Penelope shrugged. "The grass is always greener, right?"

"You're just cranky because of all the construction at your place," Ava said. "I'd offer to put you up, except I've got a big party arriving today."

"Me, too," Emma chimed in. "Tell us if there's any other way we can help, though."

"You're right," Pen said. "I am cranky and I'm going

to shake it off." She shaded her eyes to look out at the surfers farther out in the water. "I'm spending too much time in my house and not enough time out here. I don't have anyone to go out fishing with anymore, so maybe I should take up surfing. Maybe I'd meet someone as nice as Noah and I wouldn't feel so out of sorts."

"That's not a bad idea," Ava agreed.

"Next time the Surf Dads and Moms have a barbecue, you two need to come along with us," Emma said. "The Surf Moms love to teach newcomers."

"Sounds good." Ava made the resolution right then and there that she would do just that. She needed to be braver about exploring her new home and all the activities that were possible here. In a few short months she'd be a science teacher to kids ranging from first grade to eighth, and she'd need to lead them on day trips all over the county to illustrate the concepts they'd be learning. This was no time to be a wimp. Besides, she'd traveled the world, climbed mountains, camped out in deserts and jungles, navigated the biggest cities, faced all sorts of dangers—with Todd by her side.

Ava bit back a groan. She didn't need Todd to try new things. In fact, she felt braver these days than she had when he was around. It wasn't until he'd been gone that she realized how much he'd taken over her life. He'd been the one who always made the decisions. His whims guided their travels and their activities when they reached a new place. Seahaven was all hers. She could do whatever she wanted here, which more than made up for the fact she was without a partner.

At least, that's what she told herself.

"I'm so glad I met you two," Penelope said as they trooped out of the water onto the sand. Winston, Emma and Noah's dog, who'd been roaming the beach nearby, trotted up to join them. The retriever submitted to a thorough head patting and scratching behind the ears from each of them in turn.

"I know what you mean," Ava said, taking her turn lavishing love on the dog. Ever since she'd met Emma and Pen, they'd walked at dawn every morning and saluted the sunset in the evenings from their top floor decks with a glass of wine—or soda or chocolate—when the weather permitted. Ava wondered if Noah's constant presence in Emma's life would eventually put a stop to either of those traditions. "It's okay if you want to go on vacation now and then," she added to Penelope, straightening again, "but don't you dare ever move away. Seahaven is where I'm growing roots and I want both of you nearby."

"I'm not going anywhere," Emma declared.

"Me, neither," Penelope said, "despite my whining. I want an adventure or two, but I love Fisherman's Point. I mean, EdgeCliff Manor," she corrected herself with a shake of her head. "I swear, it doesn't matter how much I fix up my house, it's always going to be Fisherman's Point in my mind. I wonder what Uncle Dan would think if he could see the place now?"

"He'd love it," Ava told her stoutly, even though she'd never met the man and from the sound of it he hadn't been one for fancy touches. "He obviously doted on you since he gave you the place. He had to know you'd change a few things to make it suit."

Penelope made a face. "Actually, right up to the end he thought I'd marry a fisherman who'd take over the business as it stood. He was always asking about my boyfriends. Always trying to fix me up with one of his clients. I was so sure he'd leave the place to one of my cousins since I hadn't married, you could have knocked me over with a feather when I found out he left it to me after all."

"Why didn't you take over your uncle's business, then? You still have his boat, right?" Emma asked.

Penelope kept her gaze on the sand. "Women don't run fishing charters. The customers are too rough. Too male. I'm no use in a brawl. That's what Uncle Dan always said and given that he was in the business for over fifty years, he ought to know."

Were there a lot of brawls on fishing charters? Ava had no idea: she'd never been on one. She sensed this was a sensitive area with Penelope and skirted the conversation. "You're doing a great job with your house and soon you'll have a booming business," she said, but in truth she had her misgivings. Pen was fun and capable, but Ava wasn't sure how well she'd get along with the fussy, high-end clientele she was targeting.

"I'd better." Penelope caught their concern. "Don't worry about me. Like I said, I'm grumpy today. And hungry. And ready for coffee. Let's get going."

Their conversation turned to the guests Emma and Ava were expecting and they made their way home, slipping on their sandals when they reached the stairs that led to the street on top of the bluffs. Winston followed dutifully behind them, investigating interesting smells now and then. It was only a few hundred yards from there to EdgeCliff Manor, the Blue House and Brightview. Ava said her good-byes and went inside.

Once there, she spent the rest of the morning bustling around readying the first two floors for her guests, turning music on when the place began to feel too big and lonely. She told herself she'd feel better as soon as everyone arrived and meanwhile she should enjoy the quiet, but after five years of spending almost every moment with Todd, she was still adjusting to living alone. The Blue House was spacious and made the most of its ocean view, with an open-concept floor plan on the first floor, its kitchen, living room and dining area all surrounded by windows and sliding glass doors. There were several bedrooms at the back of the house, and more on the second level. The guests had the full use of those two floors, along with a deck and two second-story balconies that all faced the ocean. She was able to accommodate parties up to fourteen people, but today's group had only nine.

That was plenty, to Ava's way of thinking. She was a little worried about this particular group. For one thing, Chloe Spencer, the woman who'd booked the rental, had made it clear she was the type of picky guest who was going to find fault with something. For another, they were staying for two weeks, which in Ava's experience would be about eight days too long. People thought they wanted extended vacations until they actually took them, then they got bored being away from their homes and possessions. She might not have to interact much with her clients but living on the top floor of the house as she did, she overheard plenty of conversations—and arguments.

Usually, on the first day, people were tired from their traveling but thrilled with the house, the view and its proximity to the beach. Days two and three generally went well, too. Everyone fought on day four, however. Kids were sick of being dragged to boutiques and galleries. Adults were sick of the beach. Married couples were sick of each other. Day five could be sullen, but by day six of a weeklong trip, people realized their vacation was nearly over and they rallied, often drinking on the deck until the wee hours of the morning. On day seven there was the scramble of packing up, and by noon they were gone, leaving Ava to hurry and clean everything before a new party arrived.

Add a whole extra week to that equation, and you

got chaos. Not many people attempted it and, thank goodness, some who did had a strategy in place. Those were the digital nomads who worked on their laptops part of the day or the retired couples on golfing vacations who'd made a science out of traveling together.

It was the extended families and groups of friends who tended to overestimate just how much they really liked each other. Ava had a list of possible activities on hand to offer them, not that it helped much, but she hoped this time would be different. Chloe seemed extremely organized, and Ava would bet she had a plan for every day she and her friends would be in Seahaven.

Besides, it wasn't any of her business what her guests did. She was there to change lightbulbs or fix a clogged sink if necessary. Otherwise, they were on their own.

When she was done with the guest floors, Ava used the separate outside staircase to reach her third-story suite. Ready for a break, she picked up the photo album her aunt had sent to her one summer, when Ava had been traveling with her family in West Sumatra. Knowing Ava was desperately homesick and lonely, Aunt Laura had created a compendium of photos that captured all the places and people she routinely encountered during her days in Seahaven. That way Ava could better imagine the homey stories which filled her letters and emails. There were images of every room in the Blue House and the view from the back deck. The Cliff Garden and Sunset Beach were documented, as were the

Santana Redwoods and Sunset Slough, two places Aunt Laura loved to explore.

There were pictures of the grocery store where she liked to shop and the farm stand she visited every Wednesday and Saturday at Heaven on Earth farm, photos of the bank, the post office, the library and more. There were images of all her friends and acquaintances, too.

Aunt Laura had sent her new photos to add over the years as people came and went from her life and every summer, when Ava travelled with her family, Laura wrote to her often, comforting Ava with funny little stories about the town and the people in it. When Ava moved to Seahaven last December, she'd missed her aunt horribly, but she'd found herself meeting the same people whose photos she'd been staring at for years. Aunt Laura had given her a big head-start in making Seahaven feel like home. She had several good friends and many acquaintances. If only she could find someone who loved the place as much as she did—a man who thought of Seahaven as his home.

Someone who loved nature. Who loved being outside and learning new things. Someone who cared about the world, who could see the beauty in a rainstorm and the way water flowed across the land. The kind of guy who could slow down and watch a spider spin a web or stop traffic while a duck ushered its ducklings across the road.

Did men like that exist? Men so at ease with themselves they had something left to give to others?

Ava wasn't sure anymore, or rather, she wasn't sure those men were attracted to her. Noah struck her as filling those criteria, but Emma was special, the kind of woman everyone loved. Noah couldn't keep his eyes off his new wife. He spent much of his day supporting her career choices, photographing the dishes for her cookbook, helping her with videos and social media. Todd had participated in Ava's videos, but he'd always had to be the star.

She'd been lucky to have him.

Ava shook the thought away, increasing her pace as she finished her chores and prepared to run some errands. That's what Todd had always told her. So had her brother, Oliver, who'd been Todd's friend before she'd started dating him. Ava hadn't dated much in high school. She traveled with her parents too much over every break and summer vacation to be in the popular crowd and by the time she reached college, she'd been awkward and shy. Todd liked to tell her he'd seen the potential in her. "What would you do without me?" he always asked, then kissed her before she could answer, confident she wouldn't have one.

He was right about that much at least, Ava thought. He'd seen something no other man seemed to. She hadn't been asked out since he left, not that she'd met many single men. She'd been too busy getting her new business up and running to go out much and her new friends, Emma and Penelope, were too busy, too, to do more than their morning walks and evening salutations to the sunset.

She needed to go to parties and clubs. Maybe download a dating app.

She didn't really feel like doing any of those things.

Ava ran errands that afternoon, catching sight of several people who figured in her photo album, ate dinner in her suite and at seven o'clock that night donned a pretty sundress and took a batch of cookies out of her oven. She planned to leave them on the kitchen counter downstairs, inspired by the way Emma always showered her guests with home-baked treats at her bed-and-breakfast next door, but when she took a good look at the cookies, she wondered why she'd bothered.

Who was she fooling? She wasn't a natural hostess like Emma, all warm and welcoming. She'd kept the treats in the oven a few minutes too long, and now they looked hard and crispy instead of soft and chewy. Should she still serve them or simply throw them out? Standing in her tiny kitchen, contemplating the baking sheet she'd just set on top of the stove, she felt exactly like she did when her sister-in-law, Marie, had sent photos of the family Christmas celebration back in Pennsylvania last year. Surrounded by the feast she'd prepared in her lavishly decorated kitchen, she'd looked like a diminutive

Martha Stewart. Ava, in Heathrow airport on her way to Seahaven to take possession of the house she'd just inherited, had promised herself next year she'd be the one whose house looked like a magazine spread. She'd imagined her family flying out to spend the holiday in her new home, friends flocking to her place for a fabulous holiday party.

That had been before Todd had left her and before she'd fought with her brother, Oliver, who'd taken Todd's side of things. She didn't care if Oliver and Todd had played together on a soccer league before she'd dated Todd, or that Oliver was the one who'd introduced them. He was her brother and he should have backed her up. Instead, he'd told Todd he wished his parents would dump Ava and adopt him in her place. Todd had made sure Ava heard about the comment and when Ava confronted her brother, he didn't deny it. "You're never going to meet another guy like him," he told her. "What are you thinking letting him get away?"

Ava suspected his hostility toward her stemmed less from the fact that she'd split from his old friend and more from his anger that Aunt Laura had only left him a bequest of fifty-thousand dollars. When questioned about the discrepancy—the beach house was valued at well over two million—Aunt Laura's executor had told them the money she'd given Oliver was all the cash her aunt had left. She'd bought the beach house late in life and had only recently paid off the mortgage. She only made enough from her guests to live on, not enough to stack up a new set of savings. Ava's parents were the beneficiaries of a small life insurance policy she had and that was that. "Besides, Ava is the only one who had a relationship with her, as far as I can tell," the woman had concluded.

She was right. Her mother had never been close with her sister and Oliver never bothered to keep in touch with anyone. No one had suggested Ava sell the house and share the proceeds with her brother, but Ava had sensed a distinct coolness from all the members of her family, not just Oliver, in the last few months. Not that they'd ever been what you could call close.

She shook the ugly thoughts away. She'd done without much contact with her family for years. She could keep going without them. Still, she sighed with relief when she heard a vehicle pull up outside and people's voices a moment later. No time to arrange the cookies prettily on a serving dish—or to wallow in guilt over the uneven inheritance. She left the cookies where they were, hurried downstairs and threw open the door to her guests, a greeting on her lips. She nearly choked on the words, however, when she took in the size of the passenger van parked outside. It barely fit in the spot she reserved for guests, and she wondered if she'd be able to get her Rav4 out around it.

"Welcome to Seahaven," she called out when she recovered herself. A pretty woman with straight ash-blond hair, who was holding a clipboard, waved back and started toward Ava.

"Hello." She stuck her hand out, and Ava shook it. "I'm Chloe Spencer. That's my fiancé, Ben Heyward." She pointed to a tall blond man with football player shoulders, who was stacking luggage by the oversized van. "And these are my friends, Julian and Naomi, Carter and Elena, Gabe and Hailey." Chloe pointed to each person in turn, then craned her neck. "Where's Sam?" She gave a little sigh of frustration. "Ben," she called. "Where's Sam?"

"I'm right here."

Another man got out of the van, lugging a duffel bag. He bypassed the pile Ben was amassing and came Ava's way.

"I hope you're not going to spend the entire trip keeping us waiting," Chloe said to him when he drew near.

"Give it a rest, Chloe. I've apologized five different times for being late this morning. In fact, I'll do it again. I'm sorry, I'm sorry, I'm sorry, I'm sorry, I'm sorry. Now I'm at ten apologies. Are we good?"

Ava knew she shouldn't be staring, but it was hard not to look at the man who stood in front of her. Where Chloe's fiancé was fair, Sam was dark, his hair nearly black, his eyes walnut brown. He had none of Ben's linebacker-style stockiness, but he was well-built all the same. Ava figured under his urban clothing, he was ripped. He had an athlete's confidence and despite the edge to his voice, there was a tinge of humor to his tone that Chloe clearly didn't appreciate.

"No, we're not good. Don't sabotage my pre-wedding friend-group bash," the blonde hissed at him. "I've worked for months to set up this trip. You should be grateful you're even here."

"I wish I didn't have to be—" Sam broke off, catching Ava's eye. He squared his shoulders and sidestepped Chloe. "Hello. I'm Samuel Cross."

Ava's hand tingled when he shook it, and a curl of desire woke low in her belly as she stared into his eyes. It was a darn good thing she wouldn't have anything to do with these people as soon as she'd ushered them inside. It had been too long since she'd been with a man, and this man was—

Something.

"H-hi," she managed. "I'm Ava Ingerson. I own the Blue House. Come on in. I'll give you a tour."

Too late, she remembered Chloe, but the blonde had rejoined her fiancé and was giving him directions about the luggage. The rest of the guests were milling around, talking and finding their bags. Ava led Sam inside, knowing she was playing with fire. There was no reason for her to single him out for special attention.

"Have you been friends with the happy couple long?" she asked conversationally as she showed him the main floor. She noticed Chloe had listed the other guests in couples, but no one seemed to be paired with Sam. If he was single, maybe he should take one of the smaller bedrooms on this floor. No, she decided, she'd steer him toward the bunk bedroom upstairs. It had a view and none of the couples would want it.

He gave a low laugh. "You could say that. Ben's been my best friend since grade school. Chloe—well, she was my fiancée before she was his."

Ava stumbled but quickly caught herself. "Why on earth are you here on vacation with them?"

He shrugged. "Just keeping an eye on things." He must have seen the look of surprise on her face. "Ben isn't just my friend," he explained. "He's my business partner. And Chloe is a very ambitious employee of ours."

Ava took that in, wondering about all the details he hadn't supplied. What had happened to break him and Chloe up? Did he still love her? What did he mean when he called her ambitious? "That sounds extremely awkward for everyone," she managed to say. It was the most diplomatic way to express her thoughts.

When he smiled, Ava's breath caught at the sheer gloriousness of it. This man could get a modeling contract if he wanted one.

"It's definitely awkward and it's my job to make sure it doesn't turn into something worse." Sam looked around. "Where should I put my things?"

She made a decision. Maybe she was crazy, but she

liked this man, and she hadn't liked the way Chloe had talked to him one bit. She knew she should put the engaged couple—the people sponsoring this vacation—in her best bedroom, but she had a better idea.

"Come on. Hurry." She grabbed Sam's hand and tugged him straight to the staircase. "Move," she hissed when he didn't follow fast enough.

"Yes, ma'am," Sam drawled but continued upstairs at his own pace.

"That way." Ava pointed to the ocean end of the house. When they'd traversed the central hall, far too slowly for her liking, she pulled open the last door on the left and pushed him in. Darting around him, she quickly crossed the room to the bed, tore the comforter back and messed up the sheets, then went into the bathroom, ran water, soaked a washcloth and tossed it with a towel on the floor near the doorway.

"What are you doing?" Sam watched her curiously as she emerged again.

"Trust me." She needed to do one more thing before Chloe discovered where they'd gone. One more thing that required Sam's cooperation.

She crossed the room again to stand in front of him, put both hands on his chest and pushed.

Sam didn't move.

Ava pushed harder. She knew she didn't have much time before Chloe tracked them down. Women like her had a way of sniffing out the best of everything, and this room was by far the best in the house. Chloe didn't deserve it. Sam did.

But he still wouldn't move.

"For god's sake, get on the bed!" she ordered him.

He smiled that incredible smile again, and her insides went molten with the sheer deliciousness of it. "Look, you're pretty, but we just met," he joked.

She stared up at him, hearing his words but not comprehending their meaning, too lost in daydreams of what she could do with a man like this. What was he saying—?

Oh.

Whoops.

"I'm not trying to seduce you. I'm trying to help you. Would you just trust me, big shot?"

He gazed at her impassively, but in the end, he nodded.

She shoved him again, and this time he gave way, stepping backward with each push until the back of his legs met the edge of the bed. She pushed him over on top of it.

"Scramble up there." She pointed to the headboard.

"I don't scramble. And I've got my shoes on."

"All the better. Do it. Now."

With a long-suffering sigh, Sam pushed himself back until he was sitting square on the bed, his back against the headboard, his legs stretched before him. "Are you going to do a lap dance now?"

"No." She couldn't believe him. Did he not understand the genius of her plan?

Probably not, she realized too late. He hadn't traveled around the world with her and didn't know that the quickest way to claim the best spot in a crowded hostel required getting there early and then clearly marking your territory.

Right on cue, Chloe burst in, Ben close behind her. "What are you doing in here, Sam? This is our room!" she exclaimed when she caught sight of the two of them.

"This room has been claimed already, but there's another one down the hall," Ava said steadily when Sam didn't answer quickly enough.

"But—" Chloe began.

"The en suite bathroom is a nightmare in this one," Ava told her. "You don't want to deal with that toilet, believe me. There's a trick to getting it to flush—I already had to help Sam. Come on, I'll show you the room you'll want to take."

"I want this one!" Chloe said, refusing to budge when Ava tried to herd her back into the hall. She pointed to the view. "It's the best one, which means it's mine." She headed for the bathroom to see the problem with the toilet for herself, and Ava had no doubt she'd send Ben for a toolkit if she thought anything needed fixing. She should have known the woman would call her bluff. Before she could think of another excuse, Sam called out, "Woah, Chloe, better hold up. I kinda stunk up the place when I first got here."

Chloe recoiled and quickly retraced her steps to her fiancé's side. Ben took her hand. "Come on, Babe. Let's just grab a different room."

"But this is the best one."

"You should have told me you called dibs," Sam said. He laced his hands behind his neck and moved his feet across the snowy white sheets, his running shoes leaving a streak of dirt on them. Ava winced to think of the work it would take to get them clean again.

Chloe let out a disgusted noise.

"Come on," Ben said again, guiding her toward the door.

Chloe shot Sam a withering look over her shoulder. "We'll talk about this later," she said venomously. When she met Ava's gaze, her smile was insincere. "I guess I should have made it clear I had a plan for who would occupy each room. I would have thought it was obvious the bridal couple should take the best one."

"I think you'll find all the rooms are charming in their own way," Ava assured her.

"There's another door right across the hall, babe," Ben announced. "That room will have ocean views, too."

The couple left, but Ava braced herself, knowing what they'd find. A moment later Chloe exclaimed, "This one has bunk beds! I'm not sleeping in a child's room." She dragged Ben away in search of a better one. As soon as they were gone, Ava realized she'd probably created a mess for herself. If Chloe left scathing reviews of her accommodation, she might lose future business.

She turned to find Sam still on the bed.

Grinning.

"That was worth the price of the flight from Chicago," he told her.

Her sense of humor came rushing back. To hell with Chloe Spencer. "Anything to satisfy a customer." She gave a little curtsy.

Sam raised an eyebrow. "Anything?"

The tendrils of desire that had been sparking to life inside her burst into full-fledged flames. She probably would do just about anything to attract the attention of a man like him, but Samuel Cross was a guest, not a possible partner.

"I'd better go. Here's a key—this room has a lock," she stammered. She pulled the key ring from her pocket, got the one she needed off with some difficulty and placed it on a nearby side table, then escaped into the hall as quickly as she could. Hurrying to avoid crossing paths with Chloe again, who was checking out another bedroom, judging by the open door and voices arguing inside it, she made it to the stairs and down to the first floor. Outside, she hurried to the far side of the house, and clattered up the separate, exterior staircase to her third-story suite. Only when she'd locked her door behind her did she let out a breath and fall onto her own bed.

What was she doing, letting herself be attracted to a man like Samuel Cross? Someone who'd be in and out of her life before she could catch her breath?

She was only going to get hurt again.

LEFT ALONE IN his large guest room, still chuckling at the memory of Ava's shocked—but interested—expression when he'd hinted he might want something more from her, Sam leaned back against the headboard and wondered how he'd gotten into this mess. Why on earth was he on a fourteen-day vacation with two people who'd utterly betrayed him?

It was all Chloe's fault, of course. She was the one who'd led him on a merry chase for two years, upending his life, demanding more and more and more, including a share in his company—until he'd snapped and told her she couldn't have it.

Which meant maybe it was Ben's fault. His best friend was the one who'd recruited Chloe to Scholar Central in the first place. Now Sam wondered if Ben had been after Chloe all along. He hadn't guessed it at the time and one night, working late with her, a couple of kisses had led to a sexual encounter in the break room that had blown his mind. A few weeks and several dates after that, Chloe had suggested she move in with him—then made it clear she wanted him to trade his apartment for a downtown Chicago condo. He'd happily obliged, stretching his finances thin to make it happen but confident the condo would grow in value along with his ability to pay for it. Back then he'd found her exciting. He'd appreciated her drive to climb the economic ladder. Unfortunately, his opinion of her had changed over time.

As soon as they'd moved, she'd declared their furniture needed upgrading to match their new surroundings. Then Sam's wardrobe came in for an overhaul. It wasn't long before Chloe was hinting about a ring.

He'd bought that for her, too.

He wasn't bitter about any of it. Most of the upgrades he'd made for her had benefited him as well. He drew the line at making her a partner in his company, though. Scholar Central was his brainchild, and he'd built it from scratch with Ben. He thrived on calling the shots and he and Ben worked seamlessly together. He'd been willing to cede control of his home and personal style because Chloe was going to be his wife, and women cared about those things more than men did. He wasn't going to cede control of his company and he wasn't going to fool himself by thinking Chloe wanted anything less.

They'd fought about it several times, but after their final argument, when he'd made it crystal clear he wouldn't change his mind, she'd gone away to Cabo for a long weekend to "get some space." When she came back, Ben was with her. All three of them had been very civilized over the next few months as she exchanged Sam's ring for Ben's. After all, Ben was his business partner. Chloe was an employee.

What other choice did he have?

Especially now that Ben and Chloe had bought the condo one floor up from his. They were his neighbors as well as his co-workers, as Chloe liked to remind him, as if that meant he had to behave. Even so, he'd never have come on this vacation if Ben hadn't started hinting that maybe Chloe should take on a bigger role in Scholar Central.

She was making another play for control and Sam would be damned if he let her win.

His phone buzzed, and when he saw it was Chitra calling, he picked it up. Of his three older sisters, she was the one to whom he'd always been closest.

"Are you in California?" she asked when he said hello. "Hold on, I'm connecting everyone." There was a pause and she was back. Sam knew his other sisters would be on the line, too. They always did this.

"I arrived half an hour ago," he told them.

"Did Chloe give you the smallest room?" Chitra asked.

"I'm sure she planned to." He glanced at the key Ava had left him. He'd better lock his door whenever he went out or he'd probably come back to a dead fish in his bed.

"But you outsmarted her?"

"Actually, the landlady did." He told her what happened. "I'm going to have to pay her extra to buy new sheets."

Chitra laughed. "I like the sound of her. What's her name?"

"Ava."

"Is she hot?"

Sam could tell by the way she asked the question she thought she was being funny. No doubt Chitra pictured Ava as a middle-aged married woman.

Was Ava married? He hadn't seen a ring on her finger. She was young, tan, athletic. Her auburn hair had been arranged in a messy bun on top of her head and she wore the kind of clothes that would work as well on a hike through the woods as they did for errands in town. On his way through the house, he'd spotted a bird's nest on one of the console tables and a pile of interesting pebbles on the windowsill of one of the windows. There were nature prints and framed maps everywhere. Ava was outdoorsy. A nature girl.

The exact opposite of Chloe.

"She is kind of hot," he admitted.

"Ooh, this gets better and better. You should ditch the rest of those idiots and spend the next two weeks with her."

If only he could. Sam shifted into a more comfortable position. "I doubt she's lacking for company." Ava had the kind of toned beauty that attracted men like him.

"Don't write her off before you even try. Just because Chloe dumped you doesn't mean you need to stay single forever. Have a little fun and figure out what you're going to do next."

Not this again. "What I'm going to do next is come back to Chicago and keep working on launching Scholar Central. It's almost ready. We just need to find some clients."

"Oh, right. It's very important that you hurry home to work with the two people who stabbed you in the back. Come on, Sam! You've got to leave that startup and go somewhere else."

"Chitra, stop it. Sam, don't listen to her!" Another of his sisters broke in. "You are doing exactly what you should do. Spend two weeks enjoying your vacation with your friends and then come home and work hard. You are on the brink of the payday you've been waiting for. You have a home, your family and your business. That's all anyone needs."

Sam remembered it was Sunday, which meant his sisters had just had dinner at their parents' house and were probably still there, lounging around the living room in a post-meal stupor, each of them on their phone. Priya was the oldest of Sam's siblings. Always a supporter of the status quo, she'd been a tyrant when they were kids—a sterner mother-figure than their real mother.

To read more of Beach House Vacation, visit:
www.coraseton.com/books/beach-house-vacation

About the Author

With over one-and-a-half million books sold, NYT, USA Today and WSJ bestselling author Cora Seton writes contemporary women's fiction and romance. She has thirty-nine novels and novellas currently set in the fictional towns of Seahaven, California and Chance Creek, Montana, with many more in the works. Cora loves the ocean, kayaking, gardening, reading, binge-watching Jane Austen movies, keeping up with the latest technology and indulging in old-fashioned pursuits. She lives on beautiful Vancouver Island with her husband, children and two cats.

Visit **www.coraseton.com** to read about new releases, contests and other cool events!

Printed in the USA
CPSIA information can be obtained
at www.ICGtesting.com
LVHW102122280823
756462LV00007BA/282

9 781988 896465